Connor could hardly believe the infamous Harper Worth sat across from him.

Now he finally had a face to put with the name—a much prettier face than he had imagined. He'd built her up in his mind's eye as the harpy he'd dubbed her, thinking she'd be thin, gaunt, with unnaturally long teeth and beady eyes.

But she was still the woman who'd nearly ruined his career, he reminded himself.

"You don't even know who I am," he said.

Her eyebrows dipped in confusion. "Sorry, should I? Have we met?"

"Connor Callahan?" he repeated his name. "Éire?"

He felt a triumphant satisfaction as he watched the color slowly drain from her face.

"Éire?" she whispered.

"Ah, you remember what the restaurant was called, even if you can't remember the name of the man whose reputation you destroyed."

"Oh. *That* Connor Callahan."

Dear Reader,

Recently, my eight-year-old niece and I were at Disney World, watching the fireworks for the Magic Kingdom's nighttime show, Wishes. As the production began, with beloved characters expressing their hearts' desires, Emily kept tugging my arm, wanting to know when she should make her wish. I reassured her that the opportunity wouldn't pass her by, but she made me promise to let her know when she should cast her wish for the maximum benefit. I waited until the finale, the moment after the Blue Fairy encouraged us to always believe in wishes, before a final cavalcade of fireworks bloomed across the evening sky, and then leaned down to whisper, *"Now."*

Whether they're cast upon a star or held tightly in the palm of your hand, wishes are a powerful thing, made even more complex when they collide. Sometimes, we're forced to sacrifice one wish for another. This is a conflict Harper knows all too well as she grapples to see her wish come true...and risks losing a love she didn't see coming.

Harper's Wish is the first book in my Findlay Roads series, focusing on the residents of a small community beside the waters of the Chesapeake Bay. To learn more about this fictional town and its characters, visit www.cerellasechrist.com.

Cerella Sechrist

HEARTWARMING

Harper's Wish

—

Cerella Sechrist

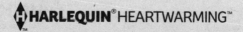

◆ **HARLEQUIN**® HEARTWARMING™

Recycling programs
for this product may
not exist in your area.

ISBN-13: 978-0-373-36741-2

Harper's Wish

Printed in U.S.A.

Cerella Sechrist lives in York, Pennsylvania, with two precocious pugs, Darcy and Charlotte, named after Jane Austen characters. Inspired by her childhood love of stories, she was ten years old when she decided she wanted to become an author. These days, Cerella divides her time between working in the office of her family's construction business and as a barista to support her reading habit and coffee addiction. She's been known to post too many pug photos on both Instagram and Pinterest. You can see for yourself by finding her online at www.cerellasechrist.com.

Books by Cerella Sechrist

Harlequin Heartwarming

Gentle Persuasion
The Paris Connection

Dedicated to my dad, Wayne: for the example of his work ethic and his devotion to what he loves. But mostly, for teaching me how to have faith.

Acknowledgments

Special thanks to my editor, Laura Barth, for hanging in there with me. You have definitely earned the MVP award on this one! And to my Harlequin Heartwarming blog partner and author mentor, Loree Lough, for the phone calls, emails and recipes. You make my writing days brighter, my friend.

CHAPTER ONE

HARPER WORTH STOOD in front of the brick building and stared at the weathered wooden sign. Rusty Anchor. Who in their right mind had thought that was a good name for a restaurant? It had been difficult to find, tucked out of the way along the docks instead of with the other restaurants and shops on the main street of town. It looked a little run-down, although *dive* wasn't exactly the term she'd use. It was clean—the windows were clear of dirt and smudges, and the front stoop was swept spotless. There were several potted plants nestled around the entryway. If it hadn't been for the name and the peeling paint, the restaurant might have been homey.

Beggars can't be choosers, Harper reminded herself. All the other local restaurants were hired up for the season. It was down to the Rusty Anchor or the questionable Crab Shack on the far side of town. That place had received a number of health code violations in recent years, and Harper suspected the only regular customers were salty old fishermen.

"So. The Rusty Anchor it is."

She could hardly believe she'd fallen this far. From lauded restaurant critic to desperate waitress. The fates must really be having a laugh at her expense. Well, no point putting it off any longer.

She went up the front steps, opened the door and was greeted by the not-unpleasant aroma of sautéed onions and the yeasty scent of bread as a brass bell hinged to the door chimed her arrival. Moving past the threshold, she approached a podium she assumed was the hostess station. The wooden pedestal bore several nicks and scuffs, giving it the appearance of weathered driftwood. There was no one there to greet her so Harper waited, taking the opportunity to survey the restaurant's interior.

It was meticulously clean but worn, with several gouges in the walls, battered chairs and tables and outdated light fixtures. But despite its shabby appearance, it had a warm, welcoming air—like stepping into a friend's house rather than the pristine anonymity of the shiny, sleek new restaurants she'd visited earlier in the day. It was the opposite of every establishment she'd ever reviewed, yet somehow she found herself drawn to its quaint atmosphere.

As she waited for the hostess to appear, she began to tap her foot impatiently. Looking around, she noticed less than half a dozen tables had diners. There were several couples, a group of three girls and what appeared to be a family of five at a table in the center of the room. But she didn't see a single server.

She glanced around, searching for any restaurant employee, but there didn't appear to be one anywhere. A quick glance at her cell phone screen confirmed the time, and she wondered why the place wasn't buzzing when the clock was approaching the lunch hour. Perhaps the out-of-the-way location had something to do with it. And where was the staff hiding?

Moving around the podium, Harper scanned the doorway at the back of the dining area and willed someone to appear. Several seconds later, her wish was rewarded as a wiry young man with a black goatee, and a mess of curly hair pulled back into a ponytail, entered from the back of the room. She frowned as he looked around the dining room with a bewildered expression. His eyes widened as he took in the tables.

He began to duck back into the doorway as though trying to escape but then seemed to think better of it. He moved into the dining area and approached the family of five just as the youngest child, who was maybe three years old, began banging on her high chair with a spoon. The sound seemed to startle the young man, and he backed up again.

Harper feared he might make a run for it and decided to take matters into her own hands. Besides, her curiosity was piqued by this odd situation. Before the man could approach the table once more, Harper moved between him and the family.

She searched for a name tag but didn't see one.

"Hi, I was wondering if there was someone I could speak to about applying for a server's position?"

"Wh-what?"

He looked positively befuddled. *Curiouser and curiouser.*

"I just arrived in the area, and I'm looking for a job as a server. Maybe I could speak to the manager?"

"Uh…" He tossed a glance over his shoulder.

What in the world was up with this place?

"We're pretty busy," he claimed.

Harper thought this was a ridiculous statement if not a bald-faced lie. Five tables did not
constitute a lunch rush.

"Oh. Is there anyone else I could speak to?
Or maybe I could fill out an application and
leave my contact information? I have experience," she tossed out, hoping that might in-
crease her odds of employment.

A spark of interest lit the young man's eyes.

"You have experience? As a server?"

"Yes. I worked as a server during high
school and all through college."

To her stupefaction, he grinned.

"Follow me."

Before she could protest, he grabbed her
arm and tugged her after him.

"Excuse me. Sir? We're still waiting to
order."

Harper caught the irritated expression of
the father at the table of five as the unknown
man pulled her toward the back of the room.

"No worries, buddy, we'll be right with
you!" the young man called out.

At this point, Harper wasn't even sure she
wanted to apply for a job here. Something
about this place wasn't quite right.

"You know what? I think I changed my

mind." She tried to tug her hand free but he held on tightly.

"No way. We need you." He tugged her onward, through the back doors and down a short hallway. "I'm Rafael, by the way."

"Harper," she automatically replied.

"I'm the dishwasher and busboy around here. And occasional janitor."

Harper opened her mouth and then closed it, not even knowing what questions to ask.

"Here ya go." He pushed open a set of swinging doors and pulled her through behind him and into the back rooms. She immediately noted the chaos of a kitchen humming with activity and felt a spike in her adrenaline just being in the crackling atmosphere.

"Hey, Bossman?"

"Bossman" must have been the one in the middle of the storm, surrounded by steam and wiping his face with the back of his sleeve every few seconds. His black hair clung to his temples and forehead, and he didn't even glance up at Rafael's questioning tone. A pot began to boil over, and he reached for it, sliding it off the burner. He then shifted to another pan and quickly flipped what looked to be chicken before moving on to begin plating another dish. Harper was impressed with his movements. Though he was tall with broad shoulders and strong arms, he shifted gracefully through the steps of preparing multiple dishes at once.

"Connor?" Rafael tried again to get his attention.

"I told you, Rafael," the chef snapped, "I know you've never done the serving before, but you have to do this. Just hand them the menus, write down whatever they want and bring the orders to me. I'll handle it from there, yeah?"

It took Harper a second to sort through the Irish accent rounding each word. Before Rafael could reply to his boss, Harper laid a hand on his arm.

"Where's everybody else?"

Rafael made a face. "Nobody else, chica. Just us."

"What?"

"And push the soup, okay?" Connor barked without looking up. "I've got plenty of that, and it's already made."

Both Harper and Rafael shifted their attention back to the frazzled chef.

"Boss, there's a lady here, and she's looking for a job."

"I don't have time for job applicants right

now. She should have applied six weeks ago before the tourist season got under way. Tell her to come back tomorrow. Or next week. Or never. Does it look like we can take on any additional staff?"

"Not to state the obvious but…what staff? It doesn't even look like you have a server out there, just the busboy." Harper spoke the words loud enough to be heard above the chef's frantic movements.

Her words got the attention she'd wanted, and the chef, Connor, stopped for a full five seconds as his gaze zeroed in on Harper. His eyes were green, she noted. A deep, mossy color that seemed fitting for his Irish brogue. His dark hair was long enough to fall across his forehead, wild and unruly as he swept his forearm across his brow to brush it from his eyes. There was a smattering of stubble across his jaw, lending him a slightly rugged look that was enhanced by his broad chest and shoulders. It was clear that he was irritated by the intrusion.

"Who are you and what are you doing in my kitchen?"

Harper knew she'd better talk quickly. Connor obviously didn't have time to waste.

"I stopped by to apply for a job. I have experience. I don't know what's going on, but I can help get you through this." She spoke with a confidence she didn't entirely feel. It had been several years since she'd done any serving, but she had to be better than the overwhelmed Rafael.

Connor made a sound of exasperation as he turned his attention back to the cooking.

"My scheduled server was a no-call no-show, and my sous chef had to step out due to a family situation. I tried calling in my part-time server, but I couldn't reach her. We're not normally very busy over the lunch hour, but we got a call for a party of fifteen who couldn't get a reservation at any of the other restaurants. We need the business, so it's up to Rafael to fill in as a server."

"Which I've never done," Rafael said. "I might occasionally help out on the line, but I've never done the serving."

Connor slid several finished plates up onto the hand-off pass. "Order up. Get these dishes out."

"Boss," Rafael pleaded, clearly out of his depth. "Give her a shot, okay? I have no idea what I'm doing out there."

To Harper's surprise, Connor paused and eyed her through a cloud of steam.

"You said you have experience?"

Harper nodded vigorously. "About seven years' worth, between high school and college."

Connor arched an eyebrow. "How long ago was that?"

She placed a hand on her hip, annoyed at how he was trying to deduce her age. "It's been a few years." More like ten. "But it's the same as riding a bike, isn't it? It comes back to you as soon as you touch your feet to the pedals." And that was how she felt, already craving the familiar adrenaline of working through a lunch rush as if she was still a server.

"You're a feisty one. What's your name?"

"Harper."

He frowned briefly. "Well, Harper, you'd better get these dishes out or you'll be fired before I even hire you."

Harper turned to a relieved-looking Rafael. "Get me an apron. And an order pad."

The younger man didn't ask questions. He grinned as he moved to do her bidding.

"What's the soup of the day?" she asked.

"Sweet corn and crab chowder."

"Anything else I should know?"

This question drew Connor's full attention once more. "I need this afternoon to go well.

Help me pull that off, and we'll talk about getting you a permanent position."

Harper nodded in understanding and then turned, catching Rafael's eye.

"You're a lifesaver, chica."

Two minutes later, Harper emerged from the kitchen wearing a hunter green apron over her sundress and carrying an order pad. She drew a breath and moved into the dining area, hoping she'd have enough time to take all the current orders before the fifteen-person reservation arrived.

"Hi, welcome to, um…" She faltered for a minute as she tried to remember the restaurant's name. "The Rusty Anchor." Her smile widened. "Sorry about your wait. Can I start you off with something to drink?"

TWO-AND-A-HALF hours later, Harper stretched as the last of the party of fifteen walked out the door. She placed her hands around her hips and dug her thumbs into her aching back. She'd forgotten how exhausting serving could be when you were on your feet for hours on end. And she'd barely spent a full afternoon at it.

"Need me to finish clearing your tables?" Rafael asked as he stepped up beside her.

"Yeah, it looks like things are going to quiet down for a while."

"You showed up at a good time. I was really starting to freak out at the thought of doing all that serving. Hope it means the boss will give you a shot here."

Harper followed Rafael to the last couple of tables that needed cleaning up.

"Connor's the boss, I take it?"

"Yep. Owner and chef. Inherited the restaurant from his old man."

"It's normally pretty slow around here?"

"Oh, yeah." Rafael nodded. "The place is usually dead, especially through the week like this. It used to be a favorite of the locals, but when Connor's old man passed on, they stopped coming. And now, with all these fancy newer restaurants in the area, the tourists are more interested in hitting those than seeking out a local treasure."

Harper didn't say anything, but she couldn't help wondering how much money she'd be able to make serving at a place like the Rusty Anchor. For now, though, any income was better than nothing.

"Is Connor a nice boss?"

Rafael began loading water glasses into a

plastic bin. Harper helped by gathering up stray silverware.

"Yeah, he's a good guy. A little uptight at times, but he's got a lot on his plate, running this place and raising his daughter."

"He has a daughter?"

"Yeah, Molly. She's six. Keeps us all on our toes but especially Bossman."

Harper digested this information as she reached for a fork.

"Rafael?"

The sound of the Connor's voice startled Harper, and she dropped a handful of silverware. It clattered to the table.

"Mind if I borrow our new friend?"

Harper began scooping up the forks and spoons once more, the back of her neck tingling as she felt Connor's eyes on her.

"Sure thing, boss."

Rafael took the utensils from her hand.

"Go on," he urged.

And before she got out of earshot, she heard him whisper, "And good luck."

CONNOR ESCORTED HARPER through the doors at the back but instead of heading right, toward the kitchen, he moved left in the direction of his office. He entered the room and frowned at the disarray of papers scattered across his desk, files piled on the floor, broken restaurant equipment stashed in the corner and various cookbooks and periodicals stored haphazardly on a sagging bookshelf. There was also a plastic crate filled with Molly's toys and coloring books, which she used to entertain herself when she was forced to wait around in his office.

He was about to gesture for Harper to sit when he noticed the only other chair in the room, besides his own, was stacked with inventory paperwork. He quickly moved to gather up the clipboard and sheets and then nodded for Harper to take a seat. She still had to nudge a box out of the way to sit down.

"Rafael doesn't tidy up the office as part of his janitorial duties, I take it?"

He didn't know if she was trying to be funny or criticizing his lack of organization.

"I don't let the staff mess around in here."

"I'm kidding. It was a joke. Sort of."

He ignored her and took his own seat on the other side of the desk, suddenly embarrassed at the peeling upholstery with tufts of gray padding poking through.

"You seemed to handle yourself pretty well out there this afternoon," he remarked, trying to get them back on track and forget about the state of his office.

"Thanks. Like I said, it's no different than riding a bike. It all comes back pretty quickly."

Connor leaned back in his chair and took a moment to study the woman across from him. She had caramel-tinted brown eyes and a cute, upturned nose. Her lips were bow-shaped, and there was just the slightest dimple in her chin. Her blond hair was still swept up in the ponytail she'd made before jumping into the role of server, but now several wisps had come free to softly frame her face. The sundress she wore looked to be of the designer variety, but her manner was warm, even down-to-earth.

"You're new to town?" he questioned as he began riffling through papers on his desk in search of a clean notepad.

"I am," Harper confirmed. "My sisters and I used to spend summers here when my grandmother was still alive. She owned the white cottage out on Bellamy Drive. Now that she's passed, my younger sister, Tessa, lives there. I've always thought Findlay Roads is a sweet little town."

He grunted. "Not so little as it once was," he remarked. "We were named one of the top five Chesapeake Bay towns to visit in a national magazine a few years ago. Since then, we've seen an influx of celebrities and political figures looking to try the latest resort destination."

He couldn't find a notebook, but his fingers finally landed on a piece of paper with a half-formed recipe scribbled on the back. He flipped it over to use the clean side and scratched out a few highlights.

New to town. Sisters. Tessa. Cottage on Bellamy Drive.

"I take it you're not here on vacation, so what brings you to town?"

She seemed to hesitate at this question but then began to explain.

"I lost my job in Washington, DC. I needed a break from the city after that, so I decided to come stay with my sister for a bit, until I get back on my feet."

"Uh-huh." He made another note.

"And what did you do in the city?"

She visibly swallowed. "I, um…worked in the food industry."

He raised his head. "You said you were a server in high school and college."

"I was."

"And you're still in the food industry?"

"Kind of. I review restaurants for a living. Or rather, I did."

He tensed, as he always did, at the mention of critics.

"A restaurant critic." His tone came out flat.

"Yes."

He dropped the pen he'd been holding, his gaze narrowing.

"Harper."

"Hmm?"

"What was the name of your critique column?"

"*Worth It?* I reviewed restaurants and determined whether they were worth spending money on. It's a play on my name—"

"You're Harper Worth."

She flushed but still managed a smile. "Guilty as charged."

"Get out."

He'd obviously stunned her because she sat there blinking for several long seconds.

"Excuse me?"

"I said…*get…out.*"

Harper Worth. In his restaurant, his *second* restaurant, after all this time. And not as a critic but looking for work. He wasn't sure whether to feel outraged or vindicated.

"My name is Connor...*Callahan*," he stated, the words clipped.

Her expression didn't budge, not a glimmer of recognition there.

He'd never seen a proper photo of her. Restaurant critics often concealed their identities so they wouldn't be recognized when visiting establishments. And with Harper's vitriolic reputation, he assumed she'd made every effort to keep her image from being exposed when dining out.

Now he finally had a face to put with the name—a much prettier face than he had imagined. He had built her up in his mind's eye as the harpy he'd dubbed her, thinking she'd be thin, gaunt, with unnaturally long teeth and beady eyes.

She was nothing of the sort. But she was still the woman who'd nearly ruined his career, he reminded himself.

"You don't even know who I am," he said.

Her eyebrows dipped in confusion. "Sorry, should I? Have we met?"

He couldn't help it. He cursed.

"Connor Callahan?" he repeated his name. "Éire?"

Satisfaction flooded through him as he watched the color slowly drain from her face.

"Éire?" she whispered.

"Ah, you remember what the restaurant was called, even if you can't remember the name of the man whose reputation you ruined."

"I—" But she stopped there, seemingly at a loss for words.

"Let me see if this rings any bells." He cleared his throat before he began the recitation of her review from memory.

"Though barely competent, Éire's executive chef tries too hard with the menu, putting on airs with mediocre aptitude."

Her face whitened further, her expression becoming pinched as he continued.

"The filet mignon, though a fine cut of meat, is decimated by the lack of skill in preparing it. It will never measure up to the succulent cuts to be had at nearby restaurants in the district, and if ingredients as pure as this can be prepared with such average talent, then imagine the rest of the dishes."

"Oh. *That* Connor Callahan." She attempted nonchalance, but by the pink rising in her cheeks, he knew he had her right where he wanted.

"Can I tell you my favorite line? The one my investors quoted when they pulled out on me?"

She shifted in her seat. He injected a full Irish brogue into his voice and spread his arms to accommodate the full theater of the words.

"Éire is owned by Institute of Culinary Distinction–trained Irishman, Connor Callahan, who clearly believes his own blarney when he claims his restaurant is a dining experience to delight the senses. Perhaps he could use a taste of humble pie since I remain unimpressed and dub his establishment *not...worth...it*."

The silence that followed these words was thick. He watched the fine cords in her neck flex as she swallowed. Her cheeks were stained crimson with what he hoped was embarrassment and shame, the very same emotions he'd felt when he'd read her defamatory review.

"Well. Clearly, it all worked out for the best." Her gaze skittered around the office's interior, came back to his face, and then quickly looked away again.

He ground his teeth together. Hadn't she been paying attention? Could she really be so self-focused?

"Perhaps it's *best* you leave now." He didn't think he could control his temper much longer if she stayed.

To his aggravation, though, stay is exactly what she did.

"I, um… I admit that review was perhaps a bit…harsh."

"A bit?" He tightened the arms crossing his chest, trying to hold the worst of his anger inside. "When my customer counts dropped, I lost my investors, all my backing, and after that, I didn't stand a chance. You ruined me."

He didn't dare mention how Chloe had left him and Molly shortly before Éire's failure. While he knew he couldn't place the blame for that directly at Harper's feet, the memory of that time, with all its bitterness and disappointment, still chafed.

Harper looked into his face, and he suspected that took some courage on her part. Her eyes sparked. "You can't blame your restaurant's failure entirely on me. My reviews are just words. People can decide for themselves."

"Sure, if they would have given me a

chance. But scarcely a single patron darkened my door after that review."

"That's not my fault."

"Isn't it?"

She hesitated again.

"Maybe you're right. I should go," she suggested at last.

"Yes, I think you'd better," he tossed back.

She took one last glance around, almost as if she wished she could stay. The very idea threw him and deflated some of his ire.

"Well, I appreciate your taking the time to speak with me, Connor Callahan."

She backed up without taking her eyes off him, as though she was wary of letting down her guard. He felt a twinge of guilt at that. Had he really come off so fearsome? Wounded was more like it. This woman had callously ruined his reputation in an industry where reviews like hers could make all the difference.

"I wish you the best this time around," she offered before finally turning and exiting his office.

When she was gone, he experienced another ripple of irritation.

She *had* ruined him. His first restaurant had struggled a bit at first, but his father's faith in him had carried him through the rocky beginning. Yet when Éire had been awarded the "not worth it" rating, the clientele he'd been building suddenly dispersed into the dining rooms of trendier, more popular establishments. He knew it hadn't all come down to Harper's review, but her critique certainly hadn't helped. And it wasn't just the criticism. It was one thing if she didn't like his food, but her words had been outright cruel, disdainful and full of snobbery. After that review…everything had begun to fall apart.

But here she was, the woman who had been the catalyst to his first restaurant's failure, obviously as down on her luck as he had been three years ago. There was a certain poetic justice in that, and he couldn't help feeling a deep sense of satisfaction. It wasn't that he wished anything truly horrible on her. After all, she had just gotten him out of a tight spot. But he had to admit, there was something satisfying about learning she'd fallen from grace. It made him wonder if the old adage was true—what goes around comes around.

CHAPTER TWO

"IT WAS HUMILIATING," Harper pronounced as her sister loaded another helping of summer squash salad onto her plate. "He was about to offer me the job, and then as soon as he found out who I was, he kicked me out of the restaurant."

Tessa froze. "Seriously? He didn't physically remove you or anything, did he?"

"No, nothing like that," Harper hastened to reassure her. "He just made it clear I wasn't welcome on the premises."

Tessa clicked her tongue in disapproval, and while Harper appreciated her sister's support, she knew she couldn't entirely blame Connor for his reaction.

"I kind of deserved it," she admitted. "It was a pretty mean review. In fact, it was the one that jump-started my column, gained me all sorts of attention."

"You should apologize. Then maybe he'll hire you."

Harper didn't know whether to laugh at her sister's naïveté or cringe at the suggestion of facing Connor Callahan once more.

"I don't think it's that simple, Tess. He's obviously not the kind of guy to forgive and forget. I think it's best if I give him and his restaurant a pretty wide berth." She paused, surprised at how disappointed she felt following this observation. It shouldn't have mattered any more than the other restaurant owners who had turned her away. But she couldn't help wishing she'd have a chance to see Connor Callahan again. "Have you ever been to his restaurant?"

Tessa shook her head as she forked into the quiche Harper had made for dinner. "No, it's kind of out of the way."

"True." She stabbed a piece of squash and nibbled it in contemplation.

"Have you told Mom and Dad?" her sister asked after swallowing a bite of the quiche.

"About losing my job?" Harper cringed. "Not yet. But I'll email them in another day or two."

The thought stole what little appetite Harper had, and she put down her fork.

"You should at least tell Paige," Tessa said. "Maybe she can help you out, pull some strings to get you another job in the city. Not that I don't want you here," Tessa quickly assured. "In fact, you're welcome to stay at the cottage as long as you like."

Harper gave Tessa a grateful smile, trying to mask her discomfort at the thought of telling her older sister how she'd been fired from her job. Paige was the golden girl of the family—graduating with top honors from college and going on to attain her master's in risk management analysis before she'd been hired on at their father's investment firm. Paige had climbed the ladder with her usual dexterity and efficiency, and while Harper loved her, she always felt inferior around her older sister. The last thing she wanted was to ring her up and ask for job help.

"I can't wait that long," Harper said. "I need a job *now*. And I appreciate your offer to stay here for as long as it takes, but I refuse to live here without contributing to the household expenses."

Tessa opened her mouth to protest, but Harper held up a hand.

"I mean it, Tess. I'm not going to sponge off my baby sister. I want to pull my own weight."

"Harper, this cottage is as much yours as mine—"

Harper held up a hand to forestall this thought. "No, Tessa. This is your home. I appreciate your letting me stay here until I get back on my feet, but the cottage belongs to you and you alone."

After all, Tessa had been the one who had moved in here when their grandmother was dying. She had nursed Nana in the last days of her life. It was a role she was already qualified for as a pediatric nurse, but that hadn't made the task any easier. Because her baby sister had been there for their grandmother on a daily basis, and because Tessa loved this town, Nana had left the cottage to her. Nana had made sure Paige and Harper received bequests of equal value upon her passing, but since Findlay Roads had become a resort destination, the burgeoning real-estate market had tripled the value of the cottage.

But Harper didn't begrudge her. No, the cottage was Tessa's and for good reason. And Harper had no intention of living there as if the place were her own.

She pushed her plate aside and suppressed a sigh. Of all the people in the world, why did it have to be Connor Callahan who owned the Rusty Anchor? She drummed her fingers on the tabletop, lamenting every harsh review she'd ever written and letting a sigh escape.

"How about if we do lunch tomorrow? I could take the afternoon off. We'll go shopping in that new boutique on Second Street. My treat."

Harper shook her head. "Thanks, but I think I'll hit the pavement again and see if I can find any other job openings." There had to be something available, even with most establishments already hired up for the season.

Tessa stood to clear the dinner dishes. "Try not to stress yourself out about it. Things will look up soon. I'm sure of it."

She touched a reassuring hand to Harper's shoulder, and Harper nodded. But as soon as Tessa turned around, she rested her cheek in her palm and frowned.

"Wake up, my lazy bones."

Connor nudged his daughter's sleeping form and grinned at the way she burrowed her head beneath her pillow with a tiny groan.

"Dad!" He heard a muffled cry of indignation.

"It's too beautiful a day to stay in bed." He tugged the coverlet down and laughed as she squirmed. Seating himself on the edge of the mattress, he gently pulled aside the pillow. Molly blinked owlishly at him and then gave a yawn.

"I told you not to stay up so late, didn't I?"

She huffed in annoyance.

"I'm dropping you off at the Evanses' for the day. What do you want for breakfast?"

She stretched out her arms and legs and curled her toes as she sighed. "Pop-Tarts."

He clicked his tongue. "No, Molly, a *proper* breakfast."

She twisted around and rolled herself into his lap. "Pop-Tarts are a proper breakfast. They're made with whole grains. It says so on the box."

He smothered a laugh at this logic. "How about blueberry pancakes?"

Her eyes lit up. "With whipped cream?"

He eyed her.

"And extra blueberries?" she pressed.

"You drive a hard bargain. That's not much better than Pop-Tarts."

But she grinned, knowing she'd already won. As a single father, he found it difficult to deny her some days. As if his acquiescence could make up for the way her mother had walked out on them.

"Extra blueberries it is."

She gave a tiny squeal of joy, smacked a kiss on his cheek and then hopped out of bed before padding in the direction of the bathroom. He rose and headed for their apartment kitchen above the restaurant.

Forty minutes later, Connor finished cleaning the remains of the whipped cream off Molly's face.

"How are you enjoying your summer so far?" he asked as he tossed the paper towel into the waste bin. "Do you miss the first grade?"

"Nope," Molly replied. "Summer is my favorite time of year because it means no more school."

Connor pretended to be shocked. "But Molly...what about Christmas? I thought that was your favorite time of year."

Molly sighed as if exasperated by her father's lack of understanding. "That's only 'cause there's presents at Christmas."

Connor laughed as he cleared the table of the remains of the breakfast. Molly helped bring over her plate and fork. Before she could scamper away, he knelt down so he was eye level with her.

"Now, listen, Molly, I want you to be on your best behavior at the Evanses' today, yeah? No more pranks like you pulled at the Marshalls' last week."

She nodded, but he knew better. Molly seemed to find mischief no matter how many times she promised not to.

"That means no taking Piper's mom's makeup and using it to paint the baby."

Molly frowned. "Piper's mom doesn't have a baby."

"Right." That had been the Browns. "Well. No trying to shave the dog, either."

Molly rolled her eyes. "Piper has cats, not a dog."

Connor sighed. "Okay. My point is…no getting into trouble, right?"

She nodded, her expression all innocence. "Yes, Daddy. But can't I just stay with you today?"

Connor tugged on one of the braids he'd made in her hair. He noted they were already coming loose with stray wisps of his daughter's brown hair fluttering around her face. He'd never been that good at doing her hair.

"I thought you liked spending time at Piper's house," Connor replied.

Molly shook her head. "Piper's house is too clean," she pronounced. "And Mrs. Evans makes us pick up all the toys before we can do anything else. I'd like it better if Piper came here instead. Can she, Daddy? Please?"

Connor felt a guilty tug. Molly didn't get to have friends over that often. It was hard enough to keep an eye on his daughter while running the restaurant; he could never manage two children while working. And what little free time he did have, he liked to keep for just the two of them. He worried that he didn't spend enough time with her as it was.

"Ah, not today, love. But maybe on Monday, when the restaurant's closed. You can show off the place, yeah? Don't forget, you have a job here, too, after all."

This reminder elicited a grin, and Connor noted the tiny gap where one of her baby teeth had come out last week. His little girl was growing up.

"Official taste tester," she proudly proclaimed.

"That's right."

Molly beamed, and Connor leaned forward to press a kiss on her forehead. "Now, go on and get your backpack while I finish clearing the table."

Connor stood, watching his daughter skip from the room and feeling his chest tighten at the sight. She was growing up so fast. In a few more years, he feared he'd be completely out of his depth with her. He and his sister, Rory, had been close growing up, especially after their father had moved them from Ireland to the States. His own mother had died in his birth country, and the lack of a maternal influence in his life left him feeling extremely unqualified to raise a little girl on his own.

Just then, his cell phone vibrated, and he tugged it from his pocket to check the caller ID. He frowned at the number that appeared on the screen and then answered, trying to curb some of his irritation.

"I wondered if you ever planned to call me back."

HARPER ROLLED OUT of bed in time to say goodbye before Tessa headed off to work and then poured a large mug of coffee as she heard her sister pulling out of the drive. She dosed her java with creamer and took a sip to fortify herself for the day ahead. She'd been up late the night before, searching the local classifieds for job openings. The listings were slim, but she'd found an ad for a pet-store clerk and another for a cashier at the local supermarket. She planned to shower and dress and then head out to drop off some résumés.

She sat at the kitchen table and scrolled through the emails on her phone, deleting the junk mail and archiving the personal ones for later. She was halfway through her mug of coffee and her in-box when the doorbell rang.

Straightening, she felt a wave of annoyance. Who could that be first thing in the morning? Surely all of Tessa's acquaintances were at work or knew she was. And Harper had only been in town forty-eight hours—she couldn't imagine anyone would be coming to see her. She ran a hand through her hair, knowing it must be standing on end. She hadn't even bothered to look in the mirror yet this morning.

She was debating whether to run to the bathroom to at least pull a brush through her tangles when an impatient knock sounded on the door. She grumbled "where's the fire?" beneath her breath and then tugged at her nightshirt and sleep shorts, wishing she'd brought a robe downstairs with her.

She opened the door and almost shut it again.

Connor Callahan was standing on the cottage doorstep.

CONNOR BLINKED AT the sight of Harper, hair mussed from sleep and dressed in a modest

T-shirt and pajama shorts, as she stared at him from inside the cottage doorway.

He experienced a mixture of relief and embarrassment. "Oh, good, it's the right house. You didn't leave an address, so I had to go off your description from our conversation yesterday."

Harper was still staring. "It's you," she stated.

"Aye." He fidgeted uncomfortably. "It's me."

He was somewhat prepared to have the door slammed in his face, after the way they'd parted the day before. But to Harper's credit, she seemed more baffled than angry.

"What are you doing here?" she asked.

"I wondered if we could...talk."

"Talk?" She shook her head. "Look, if you came here to chew me out again about that review, I'd really rather skip it. I'm still looking for work, and I'd rather not start my day with a reprimand about how I ruined you."

He cleared his throat. "Actually, I came to offer you a job."

It was gratifying to see how her mouth sagged open. Seconds later, her eyes narrowed to suspicious slits.

"Are you messing with me? Because if so, I swear—"

He rolled his eyes. "I'm not messing with you. I'm serious. Look, can we talk or are you not interested? Because if you're not, I don't have any time to waste. I need to find another server."

This statement made her reconsider. "Well… if you're serious…then why don't you come inside?"

She stepped out of the way and gestured for him to enter the cottage. He moved inside, and she shut the door behind him.

She seemed to recall her manners. "There's coffee brewed. Would you like a cup?"

He nodded, and she led the way into the kitchen, pulling a mug from the cupboard and setting it on the counter.

"There's creamer in the fridge and sugar on the table. I'm just going to head upstairs for a minute and change. Help yourself."

"Thanks."

While Harper disappeared to make herself more presentable, Connor poured a mug of coffee and added a pinch of sugar. He didn't want to be nosy and roam around the house so he sat down at the kitchen table and nursed the hot brew as he waited for Harper to return. He let his eyes travel over the tidy room with its weathered white cabinets and pale blue doors. A driftwood rack hung on the wall from sturdy hooks and held various copper pans and utensils, along with ceramic mugs and jars with bold navy-and-white stripes. The room was a cozy blend of vintage and modern. It left him curious, not only about Harper but about the sister she'd mentioned and the grandmother who had owned this place before passing on.

He was admiring the butcher-block counter on the kitchen island when Harper finally re-entered the kitchen, dressed in capris and a short-sleeved shirt with her hair neatly brushed and pinned behind her head. She looked much more poised and confident, but he found he rather missed the adorably disheveled woman who had answered the door.

"It's a nice morning," she remarked as he rose to his feet at her entrance. "Why don't we talk out on the back porch?"

She grabbed her coffee mug off the table, leading the way through the hall and out the patio door. Connor followed. She gestured toward the porch swing, which looked to be the only seat available. He settled himself on it, holding his mug in one hand and stretching his legs out before him.

Harper eyed the remaining space on the

swing and must have decided it was too close. She leaned against the nearby porch railing instead, and he felt a ripple of amusement and a strange disappointment at the distance she placed between them.

"Contrary to the impression our conversation yesterday likely created, I don't really bite, you know," he remarked.

She appeared flustered by this and placed her coffee mug on the porch rail before crossing her arms over her midsection. She cleared her throat.

"Does that mean you came to apologize?"

"Apologize?" He straightened abruptly, and a few droplets of coffee sloshed onto his hand. He placed the mug on the porch floor and wiped his hand across his pants. "Why should I apologize?"

Her lips tightened into a thin line, and he couldn't help thinking how cute her mouth would be, full and kissable, if she stopped grimacing like that.

"Because you practically kicked me out of your restaurant yesterday," she protested.

"And you deserved it," he shot back.

She spluttered. "Deserved it? I helped you through that lunch rush, free of charge—"

He held up a hand. "All right, all right. You

have a point," he grudgingly conceded. Besides, arguing with her wasn't going to benefit either of them at the moment.

He stood and she backed up slightly. The sight made him frown. "Look, I'm sorry. You did me a good turn yesterday, and I appreciate it." Saying the words aloud choked him a bit. It was difficult to humble himself where Harper Worth was concerned.

But the apology had its intended effect. Harper relaxed.

"Thank you. I appreciate your saying so."

"Good. So, now that that's out of the way…"

Her lips turned down at this.

"…let's get down to business. I've come here to offer you that server's position you wanted."

She eyed him studiously, as though trying to determine his motivations. "Why?" she asked.

He took a few steps across the porch, uncomfortable with having to admit the tight spot he was in.

"Because my server who didn't show up? Apparently, she broke her leg in a motorcycle accident yesterday morning. She was in the ER and was understandably too distracted to phone in that she'd be missing her shift. I just heard from her a bit ago. And of course now she's out of commission for the rest of the summer." He drew a breath. "The Anchor may not be the busiest restaurant in the area, but I still can't manage with only a part-time teenage server and my sous chef filling in occasionally. I need another person."

He didn't add that he was hoping business would pick up soon, and if it did—*when* it did—he'd need a decent server on board. And with the summer season under way and everyone hired on at other restaurants, finding good staff right now was nearly impossible.

"Why me?" Harper asked, as if sensing his reluctance to elaborate on the matter. "I thought we were sworn enemies."

He ran a hand through his hair. "Well, even enemies can get along if they're both in a tight spot, right? I need a competent server, and you've proved you can keep your cool under pressure. And you need a job. Surely we can work together for a few months?"

She seemed to be considering. "Are you sure you're not doing this for some sort of revenge? Hire me on and then fire me in another week or something?"

He placed a hand across his heart. "Your distrust wounds me. Besides, you're giving yourself too much credit. I'm trying to run a restaurant—I don't have time to be playing petty games of revenge."

She blushed at this.

"But I will confess that I wouldn't mind seeing the great Harper Worth scrubbing toilets at the end of the night." He went on to explain. "You should know that we're operating with a skeleton crew, and each member of staff is expected to pitch in with various chores on their shift."

"What sort of chores?" she questioned.

"Why? Are you too proud to do a little cleaning?"

She ground her teeth together, and he felt a happy satisfaction at the sound. He was getting under her skin, and he had to admit—he liked it.

Keeping up the momentum, he asked, "I wondered—what happened that cost you your job as reigning queen of restaurant reviews?"

She winced at the title, and he wondered if he'd pushed her too far. But after a pause, she answered, "I made the mistake of reviewing my boss's goddaughter's restaurant…only, I didn't know their connection at the time."

"Ah. I take it you were your usual, barb-tongued self?"

She sighed and lowered her voice. "Yes. It's

what I'm known for. Harper Worth, the snide, snarky critic."

"Don't forget snobby."

She glared at him. "Now you sound like my readers."

He arched an eyebrow. "I thought your adoring fans lapped up your condescension."

"They used to. But now...they're saying I'm too harsh, that I never have anything nice to say, there's no pleasing me." She made a face. "An audience's affections are a fickle thing."

He watched as she moved to the swing and sat down.

"I know what they call me," she went on. "The harpy. But I'm not a total shrew. I did offer up some nice reviews, after all. What I learned about those nice reviews?" She sat down on the edge of the swing. "Nobody read them. I think the public just enjoys watching others get cut down. Flip through the television channels, and you'll see plenty of reality TV shows with people spouting opinions even harsher than mine."

Connor moved closer and leaned one shoulder against the porch post.

"You'll forgive me if I can't offer much sympathy for your predicament."

She shrugged. "I'm sure this feels like justice for a lot of people."

He didn't reply. Justice? She'd lost her job. He'd lost his as well, along with a restaurant and all his savings. He didn't really think it was the same thing. But he couldn't afford to argue that point right now.

"Well, then, what do you say? Do you want the job or not?"

She looked up at him. "You really drove over here just to offer me a job? With no ulterior motives?"

"Strange as it may seem... I did." After all, it wasn't as if they were becoming friends. She was just coming to work for him. He still held the upper hand—as her boss, he'd be calling the shots.

"All right," she finally agreed. "When can I start?"

She didn't say so, but he sensed the same desperation in her that he'd been feeling. She needed this job as much as he needed her to start immediately.

"Can you come in this morning, say around ten?"

He noted a flicker of relief in her eyes before she blinked.

"That should be fine."

"Great. Then, if you'll excuse me, I really need to be getting back."

She stood to show him out and they walked back through the cottage to the front door.

She opened the door, and he stepped through.

"Connor?" she said, her voice soft.

He paused.

"I guess I should say...thanks."

He inclined his head ever so slightly at this and then walked toward his truck.

HARPER FELT A ripple of nerves as she stepped up to the Rusty Anchor's door for her first day on the job. The restaurant wasn't open yet, and the door was locked, so she rapped soundly on the glass and waited. She scanned the docks fronting the building, impressed with the glossy serenity of the bay in the midmorning sunlight. The Anchor might be a bit out of the way, but the view of the water was worth it.

She was watching a pair of ducks floating near the shore when the sound of the door opening jerked her attention back to the restaurant.

"We're not open for business yet."

Harper looked into the assessing hazel eyes

of a woman about her own age. "Oh, I know. I'm Harper. Connor hired me as a server."

The other woman's frown deepened. Not a reassuring sight.

"You're younger than I thought you'd be."

Harper didn't know what to make of this. "Um…thanks?"

The woman's mouth twitched, ever so slightly. "I mean, I always thought the *Worth It?* column was written by some older, soured socialite."

"Oh." Harper's reputation as a critic had clearly preceded her. What had Connor told his other employees?

"Never mind. Come on inside. I'm Erin, Connor's sous chef, part-time manager and occasional server."

Though Connor had said his sous chef also worked as a server, she blinked at the multiple roles the other woman juggled. Erin shrugged. "Times are tough around here, so we all take on additional duties to help out. At least it keeps us from getting too bored. Come on into the back, and I'll introduce you to Leah. She just got here."

Erin led the way through the main dining area and toward the back of the room. "Tomorrow, you can enter by the back doors off the alley. Connor unlocks those every morning."

They emerged from the hallway and into the kitchen. A slim, long-legged teen with hair so black it had a blue sheen stood to the far right, pouring herself a cup of coffee. Erin ignored her and showed Harper the rooms behind the kitchen area. There was a stockroom, a walk-in refrigerator and a laundry area to wash the restaurant linens.

"We use those lockers to store our personal belongings while we're here." She gestured to a row of much-abused gray lockers with peeling paint.

Harper followed Erin back into the kitchen. "Leah?"

The dark-haired woman looked up.

"This is Harper, the new server I was telling you about."

Leah cocked her head. "I thought you said she was older."

Erin cleared her throat. "I was wrong—that was just my assumption."

Harper decided to make the best of this awkward introduction and stepped forward to extend a hand.

"I'm thirty years old," she offered.

Leah's face melted into a grin. "Sorry. I

didn't mean that like it sounded." She stuck her hand in Harper's. "Is it true you used to be a big-city restaurant critic?"

Harper felt a stab of pain at this reminder. Is this how she was forever to be introduced? *Harper Worth, once a well-known restaurant critic of the DC area...now a modest server.* But Leah's smile was warm and friendly so Harper offered one in return.

"Yes. I'm known for the *Worth It?* column."

Leah's eyes widened. "Oh, I think I've heard of that. You're always cutting on restaurants, right?" She went on in a single breath, "It must be so great to live in the city and dine at all the exclusive places."

Harper winced at Leah's description of her column. It was sadly accurate. Fortunately, Erin cleared her throat before Harper could respond.

"Leah, I'll get Harper started off today, but you might have to show her some of the ropes later on."

"Sweet. Maybe you could tell me what it's like, living in a big city?"

Harper nodded, and Leah beamed at her. Well, at least it looked as if she might have one friend around here. She hoped Rafael would show up soon, and then she might feel reasonably welcome at her new job. Of course, there was still… She looked around.

"Where's Connor?"

Before Erin could respond, Connor stepped through the kitchen's doorway. A shiver ran through her at the sight of him, whether from nerves or something else, she couldn't be certain. He looked rather dashing in his chef's uniform, the crisp, white fabric hugging his broad shoulders. His eyes fell on Harper.

"Ah, I see my newest employee has arrived."

He clapped his hands together and gave Harper the once over. She tensed at the sound.

"Let's get you started, shall we?"

HARPER STARED AS Connor held out the handle of a mop in her direction.

"What's that?" she asked with some trepidation.

"What's it look like?" Connor turned the question around.

He shook the handle to get her to take it, and she gripped it in her hands as he released it to her.

"What am I supposed to do with it?"

"The bathrooms need a thorough going-over. You can start by mopping, and then I'll show you where the rest of the cleaning supplies are kept so you can do the toilets, sink and the like."

Harper stiffened. Connor had warned her there'd be chores, but she hadn't expected she'd start her first shift cleaning the restrooms. "Shouldn't I be learning the menu first?"

Connor clicked his tongue at her. "Tsk, tsk, Ms. Worth. Are you so high and mighty that you won't lower yourself to scrub a few floors?"

Harper bit the inside of her cheek to keep from snapping back an undignified reply. Had this been Connor's motivation when he offered her a job—saddling her with the most demeaning duties in the restaurant?

"I did tell you that you'd have to pitch in with the cleaning tasks," he reminded.

"You did," she conceded, "but you seem kind of smug about it."

"Smug?" He scowled. "Might I remind you that you're speaking to your new boss?"

She cringed. What had she gotten herself into?

"Don't tell me you're thinking of quitting before you've even begun," he goaded.

Of course. He'd enjoy that—for her to admit defeat. Was that what he'd wanted all along?

Or did he really need a server? Well, it didn't matter. She needed this job, and she was not the stuck-up snob he implied. She had no problem cleaning toilets—her father had instilled a driving work ethic in her from the time she was small. But her pride prickled at the way Connor had presented the job.

She raised her head and looked Connor in the eye. "You'd better show me where the mop bucket is kept."

Satisfaction rippled through her as surprise flitted across her boss's features. Her gratification was short-lived, however, as he gestured for her to follow him to the back room where a rack of cleaning supplies and a mop bucket were stored.

Once she was outfitted with the mop, bucket and a pair of gloves, Connor led her to the restrooms and propped open the ladies' room door. "Make sure you get in all the nooks and crannies," he reminded her, "and when you're done with the floors, start on the commodes."

He lingered, arms crossed over his chest as he surveyed her standing in the middle of the restroom. She had a feeling he was taking a mental snapshot to replay whenever he remembered the sting of her review.

She sloshed the mop into the water and then

used the bucket's lever to press the excess liquid from its strands before she got to work. She did her best to ignore Connor's presence, and after a couple of minutes, she looked over her shoulder to realize he'd gone. She straightened and surveyed the wet floor before catching her own reflection in the restroom mirrors. Her blond hair was pulled back into a ponytail, but already the efforts of cleaning the restroom had caused a few strands to come loose around her face. The yellow rubber gloves she wore contrasted with the white button-down shirt and khakis that were a server's standard uniform at the Anchor. If she'd known she'd be working as a cleaning lady, she'd have shown up in a grubby T-shirt and jeans. She blew the hair out of her eyes and looked away from her reflection.

How far she had fallen. From famed restaurant critic to humble janitor. She was glad her father couldn't see her now. It had been hard enough for him to accept her choice not to come work for him after college as her older sister, Paige, had done years before. Seeing her reduced to cleaning bathrooms would only deepen his disappointment.

Putting aside those musings, Harper turned her attention back to mopping. When the floors in both bathrooms were spotless, she set to work on the sinks, mirrors and toilets.

Connor popped back in to check on her as she was finishing the men's room commodes. She sensed him before she saw him, turning to find his lips twitching with amusement at the sight of her hunched over the toilet bowl. She ground her teeth together and swiped at a drip of perspiration along her temple, careful to use her upper arm so she didn't brush against the rubber gloves she wore. It grated that Connor appeared so unfazed, leaning against the bathroom doorway as she struggled with her task. And what right did he have to look so ridiculously handsome while she was a sweaty mess?

"You missed the base," he cheerily pointed out, directing her attention to the bottom of the toilet.

She took the opportunity to glare at him before attacking the area he'd indicated. He stepped into the room as she scrubbed at the last of the porcelain surface, and when she stole a glance upward, she saw him surveying her work.

"Not bad," he finally admitted as she stood and stripped off the rubber gloves.

"Not bad?" she repeated in disbelief. "These

restrooms are so clean, you could set up tables in here and serve dinner."

He affected an expression of horror. "But, Harper, what would a restaurant critic say if they should happen to see something like that?"

She squeezed the rubber gloves in her fist and refused to rise to the bait.

"Well, then," he said when he saw she wasn't going to reply. "On to the next order of business."

Connor looked so eager that she felt a twinge of dismay at what he had planned for her.

The grease trap.

She should have guessed. Cleaning it was one of the worst jobs in a restaurant, and one that was often contracted out to a service company. But with the Rusty Anchor's tight finances, Connor had decided to keep the task in-house. As frustrating as bathroom duty was, Harper knew it was a plush job compared to cleaning the grease trap. All the oily sludge and congealed chunks of fat from cooking were routed into the trap in order to save the pipes. Even Rafael, whose task it normally was to clean it, eyed her with pity when Connor gave her the instructions. When she first pried off the lid, the sulfuric smells nearly made her gag. She turned her head and saw Connor standing several feet away, watching her with suppressed enjoyment.

With a grimace, she took a deep breath and went back at it, determined not to reveal any more of the disgust she was feeling.

By the time she finished, her stomach was twisted with nausea from the smell, and her arms were covered in black streaks of slick, stinky grease. Her once-pristine white shirt was soaked with sweat, and there were permanent smudges covering the front. But she was secretly pleased. She doubted the grease trap had looked this clean since the day it was installed. Her pride in the achievement was short-lived, though—Connor came over, inspected her work and shrugged.

"I suppose it'll have to do."

She gritted her teeth and forced back a growl.

"Since you're finished with that, why don't you scour the grills next?"

Connor knew he shouldn't be enjoying himself this much. But there was something so… *satisfying* about seeing the haughty Harper

Worth at manual labor. It almost made up for that crummy review she'd given him.

Almost. But not quite.

He had to give it to her, though. He'd thought she'd quit on the spot when he handed her that mop bucket. And after the thorough cleanings she'd given the restrooms, he was sure the grease trap would finish her off. Not that he wanted to see her quit, exactly. He hadn't been lying when he told her he needed a server. Leah was just a high school kid, after all, working part-time over the summer. And Erin couldn't keep juggling so many responsibilities in the restaurant. But he didn't see why he should make things easy on Harper just because he was in need of another server.

"Make sure you put some elbow grease into that," he said as he walked by the grill on his way to the stockroom.

He just caught the face she made before he turned his back and disappeared into the stock area, humming a tune beneath his breath. He had to admit, having Harper around had certainly put him in good spirits.

By the time he emerged from the stockroom, she'd finished scouring the grill top and was at the wash sink, lathering up her hands with soap. He felt just the faintest twinge of shame at the sight of her. She had streaks of black grease smudged not only on her pants and the hem of her nice white shirt but also tattooed across the back of her arms. When she turned around, drying her hands on a towel, he noted her outfit was ruined from the cleaning tasks he'd assigned. Her blond hair had come loose from its ponytail and fell in thick strands across her cheeks. She looked in need of a hot shower and large glass of wine. And he thought, just for the length of a breath, about placing his palms on her shoulders and massaging away the tension riding the ridge of her back.

He frowned at the idea and determined not to let guilt get the better of him. This was the harpy, after all. She deserved none of his sympathy. He told himself he was doing this for every restaurateur who had suffered an unjust review from some ego-inflated critic.

Still, the way Harper's shoulders sagged when she caught sight of him tugged at his conscience. He decided to ease up, but only a little.

"If you're finished here, why don't you iron the linen napkins?" he suggested. "The laundry is back that way—" he pointed behind him " and there's an ironing board and iron in there, as well."

She gave a curt nod and tossed aside the towel before heading toward the back room.

Rafael had carried in a bin of dishes just in time to witness Connor's instructions. He placed the plastic tub beside the sink and frowned in his boss's direction. "She hasn't complained once, boss. Not even while cleaning the grease trap. Don't you think you're coming down a little hard on her?"

Connor shrugged. "What's that saying? If you can't stand the heat, get out of the kitchen?"

"But shouldn't you be preparing her to start serving? Erin may have picked up the slack this week but what about next week? You need to put Harper out on the floor."

"In time," Connor replied. "But I think it's best to find out if she's committed first, don't you?"

Rafael didn't meet Connor's eyes. "Whatever you say. You're the boss."

Connor sensed Rafael's disapproval and felt another pinch of shame. But Rafael only knew the recently humbled Harper. He was unfamiliar with the self-important critic who'd destroyed Connor's business.

"I wouldn't worry about her if I were you, Rafael. She's the type of woman who doesn't stay down for long."

When Rafael didn't reply, Connor felt a ripple of irritation. Was he the only one who knew Harper for what she really was?

CHAPTER THREE

DURING HER FIRST week at the Rusty Anchor, Harper learned to bite her tongue each time Connor asked her to do something. She became adept at offering him a forced grin and going about the most odious chores he assigned, determined that he would have nothing to complain about regarding her work. If he was looking for a reason to fire her as payback for that long-ago review, she'd give him none. And if he thought piling on the cleaning duties would cause her to give up, he clearly didn't know her that well.

She did everything he required to the best of her ability.

The bathrooms sparkled. The floors were soon spotless. The stainless-steel counters and sink in the kitchen positively gleamed. She dusted, she scrubbed, she polished. She did the laundry and even ironed the linen napkins without being asked. And eventually, at the end of that first week, Connor ran out of chores.

"Have you cleaned the bathrooms?"

"Done."

"Disinfected the waste bins?"

"Finished."

"There were some dishes—"

"Scrubbed, dried and put away."

He finally looked up from where he'd been studying an order form on his desk.

"The flatware?"

"Polished and the place settings laid."

He opened his mouth, but she continued before he could speak.

"The napkins are ironed, the glasses are shining, the trash cans are empty, the floors are mopped, the salt and pepper shakers are filled, everything is stocked and I disinfected all the menus. Rafael and I finished cleaning the oven hood, and we organized the storage room like you wanted. I even helped Erin prep ingredients for the dinner crowd."

Connor closed his mouth, and she felt a surge of triumph.

"Will there be anything else?" She knew her voice was a touch too syrupy by the way Connor's eyes narrowed.

"All right, then," he said grudgingly. "I suppose it's time to teach you the menu."

THE FOLLOWING DAY, Harper surveyed the multitude of dishes spread across the stainless-steel counter in the Rusty Anchor's kitchen. Connor stood on the counter's opposite side, sporting his chef whites with his arms crossed over his chest in what Harper could only label a defensive posture. She was more nervous than she'd thought she'd be, now that she was faced with learning the restaurant's menu.

"So, we're just tasting the dishes?"

Connor's expression remained flat. "I'll explain a dish, then you'll taste it so you can make the appropriate recommendations to customers."

She swallowed. "Okay. Where should we start?"

He pointed at the plate nearest to her. "Let's begin with the fish. Pecan-crusted seared salmon with wilted greens and a maple balsamic glaze. Sides are either the wild-rice pilaf or sweet-potato pancakes, which is what I've plated here."

Harper used her fork to flake into the fish. The salmon's color was beautiful with a pale pink center. She scooped up a bite and popped into her mouth, all too aware of Connor's eyes on her. The fish was cooked well, and the pecans lent a nice crunch. She wasn't impressed by the maple glaze, which was a bit too sugary for her palate. She chewed and swallowed, trying to avoid Connor's gaze as she twirled one of the wilted greens around her fork tines. Clearing her throat, she reached for a glass of water to wash down the flavors before cutting into the sweet-potato pancake. Still not looking toward Connor, she popped it into her mouth and was pleased with the crispy exterior followed by a meltingly creamy interior studded with bits of pancetta and the faint flavors of herbs. While she'd expected more of the sweetness she'd encountered in the rest of the dish, the pancakes were perfectly balanced with savory ingredients against the sweeter vegetable.

She swallowed and kept her expression neutral as she finally looked at Connor. She found him watching her expectantly.

"Okay, now what?"

He made a face. "Describe it to me. As if I were a customer."

She narrowed her eyes. "Really?"

"Really. And don't forget, in the kitchen, the proper way to address me is *Chef.*"

Harper felt a flicker of annoyance. "Fine, *Chef.*" She cleared her throat a second time. "Pecan-crusted seared salmon, cooked to perfection but a touch heavy on the maple glaze. The nuts add a nice crunch but would be better if they had been toasted longer before being ground for the crust, in order to balance out the sweetness. I can't recommend the wilted greens, given their soggy, overly saccharine taste, but the sweet-potato pancakes are deliciously crisp with a satisfying marriage of salty pancetta and the licorice touch of fennel."

"Soggy? Overly saccharine?"

"It was like eating moss drizzled with honey."

His jaw clenched, unclenched and clenched again. "I didn't hire you to critique my food. I hired you to serve it. Serving it means you have to sell it. And if that's your best sales technique, then I'm not sure you're capable of doing this job."

His words pricked her ego. "I am more than capable of doing this," she informed him, trying to measure her tone.

"Then forget that you used to be a restaurant critic. There is no place for it in your position unless you can find only good things to say."

"You want me to lie to your customers?"

He threw up his hands. "You don't need to lie. If you don't like the wilted greens, recommend they trade them out for a side salad. Or maybe the squash medallions."

"With that salmon?" She wrinkled her nose. "I'm not sure that's the best pairing."

"Harper." His voice had taken on a decidedly warning tone.

"Let's move on to the next dish," she suggested, by way of a truce.

He eyed her suspiciously and then gave a short nod. She picked up her fork and moved on to another plate. Reaching for a nearby knife, she sliced into the pork chop and piled some of the mango chutney onto the bite before lifting it toward her mouth.

Not bad, but again, the topping was sweeter than she liked. The au gratin potatoes were good enough, though, and the red pepper slaw added a nice spot of color and crunch to the dish.

"Grilled pork chop topped with a mango-pineapple chutney. The au gratin potatoes are layered with four different kinds of cheese including Gruyère, Jarlsberg, Parmesan and fontina, lending a nutty, almost caramel flavor that pairs nicely with the faint sweetness of the Yukon gold potatoes. The plate is rounded out by a red pepper and onion slaw, seasoned with spicy ginger and peppery cilantro."

When she looked back at Connor, his shoulders had relaxed, and his expression lacked its previous tension. It occurred to her that perhaps he'd been nervous about what she'd say. After all, the last time she'd commented on his food, it hadn't been a favorable experience for him. She suddenly felt bad for thinking only of herself in this tasting.

"How was that, Chef?"

"Better." He released a sigh that sounded like relief. "Much better. There might be hope for you yet."

And though a chef's opinion had never mattered to her before, she couldn't help feeling a tingle of pleasure at his words.

"You have to admit, she's not doing bad."

Connor chopped through a row of carrots with unnecessary force in response to Erin's words.

"I have to hand it to her, I thought she'd be out of here after you made her clean that grease trap." Erin shuddered. "The girl's tenacious. I admire that."

"Whose side are you on?" Connor demanded as he scooped the carrots onto the edge of his knife and into a bowl.

"Don't be such a grouch. I'm on your side,

you know that. I'm just saying that she's not what I expected her to be."

"And what did you expect?"

"I don't know, a simpering prima donna who refused to get her hands dirty? But she works really hard. Harder than Leah or Rafael or even me. These past two weeks she's worked almost as hard as you do."

He pierced Erin with a look, and she held up her hands in defense. "I said *almost*. But she puts in more hours than the rest of us, coming in early to help get ready for the day, and Rafael says she's still here when he leaves at night. And somehow, I doubt she's actually handing in a time card with all those hours."

Connor stopped to consider this. He'd never thought about comparing Harper's presence to the actual amount of hours on her time sheet. "I didn't ask her to work without pay," he protested. "I wouldn't demand that of any of you, not even her."

Erin's voice softened. "I know that, Connor. You're a good boss. But you're riding her a little relentlessly, don't you think?"

He turned back to his prep work. "We all share the chores around here. You know that."

"I know, but I think you're giving her just a *little* bit more than her fair share."

He didn't respond.

"Look, I get it, Connor. I do. I guess it just bothers me because she's not the harpy I thought she'd be. And you…" She touched him lightly on the shoulder and then dropped her arm to her side. "You're not the sort of man who takes revenge. What would your dad say?"

Of all the things Erin might have said to get him to ease up on his newest employee, she had to have known that this was the one he'd take to heart.

HARPER POURED THE last of the dirty water down the drain and righted the mop bucket. She released a sigh of relief that the day's chores were finished and moved toward the sink to wash her hands. As she lathered soap in her palms, she thought back on her shift. She'd had a handful of customers in the early evening, but the later hours had shown a noticeable decline in clientele. While on her break, Harper had walked from the docks by the Anchor on up to the main thoroughfare and noted that the other downtown restaurants were packed.

She had watched as several well-dressed couples waited outside one of the busier restaurants. Their designer clothes matched the building's ultra-modern appearance. Was that part of the problem? Did the Anchor's humble exterior prevent people from taking a closer look?

She'd mused on this as she headed back in the Rusty Anchor's direction, and her curiosity had remained in the background of her thoughts as she finished up her shift. Now, with the tables cleared and the dishes put away, she had nothing left to do but head out for the night. But to her surprise, she found she wasn't interested in leaving just yet.

Tossing the last of the cleaning towels into the washing machine in the back, she walked toward Connor's office and found her boss totaling the day's receipts.

"Hey," she ventured and waited until he looked up. His eyes were bloodshot. His black hair was mussed and standing slightly on end. She had the overwhelming urge to run her fingers through it, to smooth it into place. This swell of tenderness surprised her, and she wondered if she felt a little bit responsible for Connor's current predicament. It couldn't be an easy thing, to bounce back from the sort of review she'd given him.

"I'm all finished."

He gave a curt nod and looked back down. She felt the sting of dismissal.

"Is there anything else I can do?" she offered.

He looked back up.

"Anything else?" he repeated.

"Yes, I mean..." She shifted awkwardly. "...do you need anything before I go?"

"Oh. No, thank you." He returned his attention to the receipts in front of him. She waited, but he gave no indication he intended to speak further. Dissatisfied with this, she moved from the doorway and farther into his tiny office, taking the seat on the other side of his desk.

"I just wanted to ask..." She took a breath. "Why did you give me this job?"

He didn't say anything, nor did he look up.

She crossed her arms at his seeming indifference. She hated to admit it, but she felt a sense of obligation toward Connor. Though she didn't feel it was fair for him to blame his first restaurant's failure on her review, she also recognized she had done him no favors with that critique. He, on the other hand, had done her one when he agreed to give her this job. She'd never admit it to him, or anyone else, but she felt just a little bit indebted to him. And she didn't like owing anyone anything, especially not this irritable Irishman.

"You gave me a job when no one else would. I know you needed a server," she clarified, "but all the same, I want you to know…" She swallowed, struggling to force out the words. "I…well, I appreciate it."

There. She'd said it.

He eyed her. She couldn't guess at what he was thinking. He might have been touched by her gratitude…or more likely, annoyed by the distraction when he was trying to work. At her prolonged study of him, he dropped his eyes.

"I wouldn't be giving me too much credit. I'm not sure my motivations were entirely… honorable."

She frowned, suspicion surfacing. "Did you really need another server? Or were you just looking for a cleaning lady?"

His gaze shot to hers, his brow wrinkling with aggravation. He seemed about to fire back some insult, but then, unexpectedly, he dipped his head.

"I told you the truth when I hired you—that my previous server was out of commission, and I needed a replacement. But you're right that my treatment of you the past two weeks may have been less than fair."

"Less than fair? That's one way of putting it." She knew the admission shouldn't have rankled her so much. He'd still given her the job, hadn't he?

He sighed. "All right, I admit it. I loaded you up with chores. And I apologize for it."

This unanticipated apology caused her to falter, and she floundered, trying to regain her feelings of injustice.

"Yes, well. It was pretty underhanded, if you want to know the truth—hiring me on with the pretense of serving and then making me your janitor," she primly informed.

"I agree."

He did look truly penitent, but she wasn't quite ready to let him off the hook just yet.

"And so was making me clean out that grease trap."

His face remained completely serious. "But you did a great job on it. It's never been cleaner."

She narrowed her eyes. "You've enjoyed this just a little too much, haven't you?"

"I can't remember the last time I've had so much fun."

His smirk was endearing, as much as it was aggravating. She didn't know whether to be charmed or frustrated. "Does that mean we're even now? For the review?"

His brows lowered, all humor evaporating. "I hardly think a bit of mild hazing makes up for the damage your words caused me years ago."

"Mild hazing? Is that what you'd call it?"

"Well, what would you call it?"

"Juvenile. And petty."

The darkening of his eyes warned her she'd gone too far. "Petty, is it? Do you have any idea what your review cost me? Do you even care?"

She shifted uncomfortably. "It was *one* review."

"No, it was the only review that mattered. I was an up-and-coming chef. I had backing and positive buzz. And your criticism tainted all that."

"You can't expect to open a restaurant and not receive a little harmless negative feedback?"

"Harmless?" Connor rose, knuckles planted on his desk as he leaned forward. "Do you even know the circumstances of the night you visited? Did you even bother to come back a second time to make sure we weren't having an off night? I wasn't even there when you ate at Éire. Do you know where I was?"

She knew better than to respond.

"I was *here*, in Findlay Roads. My father had a heart attack, and I rushed home to be with him. My sister, Rory, was across the country on a music gig, and she couldn't get back right away. But I dropped everything and came because that's what mattered. And because I wasn't there at my restaurant, things weren't running as smoothly as they should have been. My sous chef was filling in, and it was the first time he'd had to run the kitchen without me. It was a rough night."

He eased back, seeming embarrassed by this outburst. The anger dissipated, and he dropped back into his chair, running a hand over his face. Harper heard the stubble of his jaw rasping against his palm, and she wondered what it would be like to feel the rough grain of his cheek against her fingers. Her palm itched at the thought, and she squeezed her hand into a fist to refocus.

He made a good point. She should have paid more than one visit to Éire, but she'd been under a deadline and only interested in her own career, not some unknown restaurant owner's reputation.

"I didn't know," she murmured. "I'm sorry."

He didn't say anything at first.

"I apologize for piling so many chores on you since you started here, but you'll still have to do your fair share. With business so slow, everyone pitches in where necessary."

Harper felt a twinge of embarrassment at this. It was true, she'd only been doing the tasks that someone else had done before her.

"If that's going to be a problem—"

"It isn't," she assured him.

She wanted this job. It represented independence, her ability to take care of herself even when the worst had happened. She may have lost her critic's job, but she could still find work.

And it wasn't just that. Something about this restaurant reassured her, made her feel as though she belonged here. Connor still held her at arm's length, but the rest of her coworkers had embraced her, even Erin, and made her feel they were friends.

"Then…truce?"

She released a breath she hadn't known she'd been holding.

"Truce," she agreed.

But as she gathered her things, she wondered if she and Connor would ever really be able to find a state of peace between them.

TRY AS HE MIGHT, Connor wasn't able to get his conversation with Harper out of his mind. Days after their chat in his office, he was still conflicted about his newest employee. It seemed unbelievable that the woman he'd blamed for destroying his first restaurant was now working for him.

And even more unbelievable was how well she was doing at the job. Since he'd apologized, she'd accepted each task he'd given her with an air of agreeability. He'd eased up a bit, spreading the chores out among all of them, himself included, and she'd pitched in, continuing to pull her weight and seamlessly becoming one of the team. It grated on him a little, he realized, how his crew had accepted her. Even Erin, who had initially been uncertain about taking on the infamous restaurant critic, now greeted her pleasantly each day. Rafael had taken to teasing her with the occasional flirtatious overtones he was known for and Leah, at a mere seventeen years of age, looked to Harper with something akin to hero worship. She was forever asking Harper about life in the city and her time working at the newspaper. Thankfully, Harper always steered the conversation away from her career, at least when Connor was nearby.

He was still musing on Harper as he tossed a handful of sliced shallots into a pan and swirled them around as they hissed after making contact with the oil. A fragrant cloud of steam surrounded him as the shallots caramelized, and he lifted the towel draped over his left shoulder to wipe at the sweat dotting his forehead.

"You know, every time I smell onions, I think of Gavin," Erin remarked as she worked at the prep counter, peeling potatoes.

Connor grunted with amusement as he added a pinch of salt to the sauté pan.

"That's not something you often hear a woman say about her husband."

Erin laughed. "It was, like, our fourth or fifth date, and I decided to cook for him. I settled on making steak with a balsamic reduction. But I was so nervous about what he'd think of the dinner that when I picked up the onions at the market, I got really strong, yellow onions. When Gavin showed up at my door, I was just streaming tears from chopping them up, and he thought I was getting ready to break up with him."

Connor chuckled. "Poor bloke. What else was he to think?"

"I know, but then a couple years later, when I was pregnant with Kitt, Gavin was determined to pamper me, so he decided to make me dinner one night. He was going to make spaghetti, and he started frying up the onions, and the smell made me really, really sick. I walked into the kitchen and threw up all over the counter."

Connor laughed loudly as Erin grimaced.

"That was the first and last time he ever tried to make me dinner."

Connor shook his head and added the prepped carrots he had resting in a bowl nearby.

"How is Gavin, by the way?"

"Pretty good," she answered, dropping a handful of peeled potatoes into a bowl of ice water. "He's still stationed in Afghanistan, working on one of the army's water sanitation projects. He's enjoying it, but he misses home."

Connor slid a glance her way and caught the frown tugging at Erin's mouth. He hadn't meant to make her melancholy.

"It's no easy feat, being an army wife. Especially not with a son to raise."

"You're telling me," she replied, and then she paused. "Kitt misses him. A lot." She sighed and seemed to rally herself. "But it's only for a few more years, and then we can be a family again."

Connor felt a tug of both sympathy and envy for his friend. He knew it was rough on her, having her family separated. Gavin had moved his family into his great-aunt's bed-and-breakfast shortly before his most recent deployment, and Connor knew how much Erin wanted them to be reunited under one roof. On the other hand, he felt the familiar pang of his own regret. Though he did his best to juggle the role of both mother and father to Molly, he sometimes felt as though part of their family dynamic was incomplete, as well.

Uncomfortable with this line of thought, he ladled some chicken stock into the sauté pan and watched as it hissed once more.

"Do you think you could get started on the corn fritters, after you've finished those po-tatoes?"

"Sure thing, Chef."

And just like that, he and Erin resumed their roles of chef and sous chef. Sometimes he thought the titles sounded a little fancy for the restaurant his father had first started, but

Connor had trained at one of the most prestigious culinary schools in the country. Erin's skills were more of the trade-school variety, but they both observed the proper appellations in the kitchen.

He and Erin worked a familiar dance around each other, reaching for a pan or grasping a slotted spoon. They'd worked together at the Rusty Anchor for over three years now, even before his dad had passed on. It was long enough that they'd become comfortable with each other's routines. And when Connor had taken over the restaurant following his father's death, Erin's loyalty had eased his transition to boss and owner.

Connor finished cracking half a dozen eggs into a stainless-steel bowl and began to whisk vigorously, the rhythmic motion requiring little thought and allowing his mind to wander. It was hard to believe Patrick Callahan had been gone for two years. Just the other day, he'd caught Molly squinting at the last photo he'd taken of his dad—he kept it on the apartment fridge. When he'd asked her what she was doing, she'd replied, "Trying to remember what Grandpa looked like."

He'd experienced a swell of melancholy at this admission. In two years, Patrick Callahan's image had already begun to fade from Molly's memory. In another two, would she even be able to remember him at all without the aid of photographs? He missed his da, especially during the mornings when he first entered the restaurant. How many times had he stepped into this very kitchen and caught his father humming under his breath, singing snatches of Irish folk songs, as he began to prep ingredients for the day?

"Connor."

He stopped whisking at the sound of Erin's voice and realized the eggs were beginning to form peaks. He'd been agitating them for too long.

"Connor, the phone."

He heard it then, the insistent chirp of the kitchen's wall phone. Dropping the whisk and bowl onto the counter, he headed toward it.

"Let's hope it's a dinner reservation for twenty people."

Erin snorted. "That's about as likely as the Irish prime minister calling to schedule an afternoon tea."

"Hey, a man can dream, can't he? And you never know about the prime minister."

Erin rolled her eyes, and he grinned as he grabbed the phone off its hook.

"Rusty Anchor," he answered.

"Mr. Callahan? Connor?" the woman on the other end responded.

His lips slipped downward at her sharp tone. "This is he."

"This is Geena Evans."

Connor's heart sped up. "Molly? Is she all right?"

The lingering silence on the other end of the line caused his chest to tighten further.

"Is my daughter all right?" he repeated and was vaguely aware that Erin had come to stand beside him, her face pale with concern.

"She's all right. However, I think it would be best if you came to pick her up. Now."

The tension in his chest eased but was soon replaced by a prickling uneasiness.

"What did she do?"

"I'm not comfortable discussing it on the phone."

Connor expelled a long sigh. "The lunch hour is about to start. Might there be a chance I could pick her up after it's over?"

This time, the silence was loaded with irritation. He could sense it crackling across the line.

"I would really prefer if you would come get your daughter *now*, Mr. Callahan."

He blinked. Whatever Molly had done during her playdate with Piper Evans, it must have been quite serious.

"I understand. I'm on my way."

Geena hung up without replying. Connor stared at the receiver for the space of another heartbeat and then slid the phone into its cradle.

"That was Geena Evans. She's insisting I go pick Molly up immediately."

Erin's forehead creased with concern. "Is she all right?"

"It seems so. Only she must have gotten into some mischief."

The lines above Erin's eyebrows deepened. "Geena Evans is an overprotective mother."

"Mmm." Connor didn't know how to comment. Overprotective though she might be, Molly was a handful, even for him. "Do you think you can manage without me for a bit? I shouldn't be gone more than a half hour."

Erin waved a hand, unconcerned. "I'll be fine."

Connor hesitated. "Are you sure?"

"Yeah, no problem. Besides, Harper should be arriving any minute now for her shift."

The reminder of Harper put his thoughts

squarely back where they'd been only moments ago.

"Go get that mischief-making daughter of yours."

"Right. Call my cell if you need me. I'll be back in a half hour."

He began removing his chef's jacket and braced himself to confront whatever sort of trouble Molly had gotten into this time.

CONNOR HELD HIS tongue as Molly swung her foot up and down, beating it against the glove compartment until he shot her a warning look. She dropped her leg with a sigh and looked out the window instead. It was a typically busy summer day on the main street of town, with plenty of people strolling the sidewalks and shopping in the many posh boutiques that had appeared in recent years. He noticed Molly cycing a woman walking a pair of dogs, and she pressed her nose to the passenger window as he drove by. She turned forward and noticed the sign for the ice cream shop up ahead.

"Can we stop for ice cream?"

Connor looked at her but didn't reply. As much as he wanted to give in, he knew he had to stand his ground. He couldn't take her out for ice cream right after he'd had to pick her up for misbehaving at her playmate's house.

"Pretty please?" she added, softening her voice to the tone that always turned him to putty.

He brought his attention resolutely back toward the road.

"Molly, this isn't a Sunday drive. Mrs. Evans was very cross with you."

Molly huffed and slouched in the seat, folding her arms over her stomach.

"It's not *my* fault. Piper *asked* me to do it."

He cast her a calculating glance, wanting to believe her but knowing her excuse was unlikely. Molly had a way of finding trouble, and no matter how much of that innocent charm she mustered, he'd learned to see through her words.

"I swear, Daddy! It wasn't my idea!"

He turned his head briefly, caught her eye, then looked back at the road. He wasn't buying it.

"Well, it wasn't just my idea," she amended. "Piper said she wanted me to do it."

"Molly."

She kicked the glove compartment again.

"Molly."

"It's not fair! I always get blamed."

He sighed. "You cut off all of your friend's hair," he pointed out.

"But we were just playing! It will grow back."

"Mrs. Evans liked Piper's hair long. She was planning to enter her in a beauty pageant this spring. Piper has never had her hair cut. Ever. What made you think you should cut it all off?"

"I didn't know about the beauty pageant," Molly murmured, and he felt a twinge of uncertainty about his daughter's intentions. "It's not fair, though. Piper has hair just like Aurora's in *Sleeping Beauty*." Molly tugged at a piece of her own brown locks. The braids he'd made that morning had mostly come unraveled, and the strands were knotted into frizzy tangles.

"We thought if we cut it off, she'd look like Tinkerbell."

"If you thought no one would be upset, why did you flush her hair down the toilet? Why didn't you just throw it in the trash after you chopped it off?"

Molly lifted one tiny shoulder in a shrug and turned wide eyes on him. "I don't know. I just did."

Connor groaned. "You clogged their toilet, Molly. I couldn't fix it, and Heaven knows I tried. Mrs. Evans is going to have to call a plumber, and I promised I'd pay for it. We don't have the money—"

He stopped talking then. He didn't like mentioning money in front of her. There was no need to burden his young daughter with his concerns about the restaurant and its finances.

"I'm sorry, Daddy," she ventured, and he sensed she knew more about things than she let on. He felt a swell of weariness. The last thing he wanted was for Molly to be worried about the future.

"It's okay, Moll. You apologized to Mrs. Evans, and that was the right thing to do."

"Mrs. Evans is mean," Molly announced. "She called me a terror."

Connor's hands tightened on the steering wheel.

"Did she at that?" His Irish accent grew more pronounced, as it always did when he became angry.

"She said I'm a bad in-flu-scents." Molly paused. "I don't know what that means," she confessed.

"In-flu-scents?"

"That's what she said. After Piper told her I was the one who said we should cut her hair."

"Do you mean she said you were a bad *influence*?"

"Yeah. That's what she said."

Connor prickled at Geena Evans's careless tongue.

"Maybe it's best if you don't spend any more time with Piper. Or at least not at Mrs. Evans's house. And I may have a word with her when I drop off the check for the plumber." He grunted. "Bad influence. Just because she plans to make her daughter a beauty queen doesn't mean Piper Evans is the perfect child."

A few seconds later, they pulled into the back of the restaurant.

"Am I going to be punished?" Molly asked.

Connor reached over to undo the seat belt for her.

"No. But you'll have to stay in my office while I'm working and behave for the rest of the day, all right?"

Molly made a face, and he anticipated an argument.

"But I hate being stuck in your office! It's *boring*."

"Molly." He employed his best "don't question me because I'm the dad" voice.

"Fine," she muttered and then brightened. "But can I have ice cream later?"

"Don't push your luck, Moll."

CONNOR DIDN'T BOTHER to check the time as he lifted Molly from the truck, but he knew he'd been gone a lot longer than the thirty minutes he promised Erin. The situation at the Evanses' had been more dramatic then he'd anticipated. Not only had he endured a fifteen-minute lecture on his own faults in raising his daughter, but he'd spent an additional twenty-five minutes snaking the toilet and trying to fix the clog that had been caused by the excessive amount of hair Molly had flushed down the commode. He secretly wondered if the cute but enterprising Piper had already been flushing items down in a sort of secret rebellion.

Though the girl seemed outwardly sweet, he sensed a dissenting spirit behind that adorable facade. At one point during Mrs. Evans's lecture to him, he'd looked over and caught Piper smiling as she happily patted her head. That child was not innocent, despite what her mother thought.

Though granted, Molly shouldn't have chopped all the girl's hair off, no matter whose idea it was. For all his faults as a father, at least he didn't excuse Molly's behavior. He wasn't blind to his daughter's mischief, as Geena Evans seemed to be where Piper was concerned.

It didn't matter, though. He'd made his apologies, and he would pay the plumber's bill to keep the peace. Mrs. Evans wasn't the first parent to call him up and complain about Molly's antics. He couldn't afford to be making enemies of them all. In fact, better to try to make friends who might turn into customers. Heaven knew he could use the business.

He tugged open the back door to the restaurant and stepped inside, breathing in the familiar scents of the nearby kitchen along with the smell of disinfectant and laundry detergent from the stockroom and washing machine to his left. He closed the door behind him as Molly scampered down the hall that opened into the kitchen. He followed, wondering how Erin and Harper had fared through the lunch hour. As he entered the kitchen, Molly was already reaching for a bag of cookies while Erin was just hanging up the phone. She turned toward him with a frown.

"That was the bank calling. Were you supposed to have a meeting this morning with the loan officer?"

Connor groaned and raked a hand through his hair. "I completely forgot." In truth, he'd been too wrapped up in thoughts of Harper this morning and his mixed feelings about his newest employee.

"They can see you right now, if you want to head over there."

He hesitated, his eyes darting to Molly as she rifled through the cookies Erin kept around just for her.

"There's no one to watch Molly."

Erin's eyes slid in the little girl's direction and then looked at him questioningly.

He sighed. "It's a long story."

Erin nodded, a fellow parent's signal of understanding.

"I can keep an eye on her."

"Not if we get any customers, you can't. You'll be working the kitchen."

"Between Harper and me, we can handle it."

He hated to ask it of them, especially Harper, who hadn't spent that much time around Molly. As if his thoughts had summoned her, his newest employee entered the kitchen.

"Oh, hey, I thought I heard Erin talking to

someone." Her gaze landed on his daughter. "Hi, Molly."

Molly ignored her as she fished another cookie from the bag.

"Molly," he chastised, embarrassed by his daughter's lack of social graces. "Put the cookies down and say hello."

Molly huffed in annoyance and crumpled the cookie bag before licking her fingers clean. He grimaced at her behavior.

"Hi," she greeted, obviously nonplussed.

"Hey, kiddo," Erin said. "How would you feel about spending the afternoon with Harper and me while your dad takes care of some things at the bank?"

Molly shrugged. Connor's eyes landed on Harper, who shifted her weight from foot to foot. Was she uncomfortable with the idea of watching Molly? He hated to ask his staff to play babysitter in addition to their other tasks It didn't seem fair.

"Have you had lunch? I can make you a sandwich," Erin suggested.

Molly made a face. "I'd rather have ice cream."

"Molly," Connor used his best "don't go there" voice. His daughter sighed dramatically.

"No, thank you."

"Are you sure you know what you're getting into?" He spoke the words to Erin, but his attention lingered on Harper.

"Please, I have a four-year-old son. I can handle Molly."

Harper didn't look so sure.

"It's only for an hour." He spoke the words in Harper's direction and then moved to Molly's side, kneeling down and turning her to face him.

"I'll be gone for a bit, but while I'm away, you listen to Miss Erin and Miss Harper, okay?"

"Yes, Daddy." The word came out by recitation rather than sincerity.

"I mean it, Moll. You do as they say. No mischief."

"When you get back, can I have ice cream?"

"We'll see."

She turned to skip away, but he grabbed her hand and drew her back. "Hey, are you trying to break my heart here?"

She grinned saucily, knowing full well that she had him wrapped around her little finger.

"Right here." He tapped his cheek, and she shook her head.

"Then how about here?" He touched his other cheek, but she placed her little hands on each of his cheeks and smacked a kiss directly onto his lips. Then she turned and slipped out of his embrace, somehow managing to grab the bag of cookies and take them with her as she brushed by Harper and escaped the room.

He stood.

"Call my cell if you need me."

Erin nodded, her expression more concerned than he would have liked. "Good luck at the bank."

"Thanks."

He feared he would need it.

CHAPTER FOUR

HARPER WATCHED CONNOR leave and then looked over her shoulder, wondering where Molly had disappeared to so quickly. She was slightly uneasy with his request to watch the little girl. She'd never been very good with kids, and though she didn't know Molly well at all, she'd gotten the impression that Connor's daughter was a bit wild. Remarks from Rafael had confirmed this notion, and when she'd finally worked up the nerve to ask what had happened to Molly's mother, Rafael gave her a condensed version of the story, admitting he didn't know many details. Apparently, Connor's ex-wife had walked out on them when Molly was still a toddler, not long before his first restaurant had folded. This stirred Harper's sympathies, and she wished she might befriend Molly in some way, but she didn't know where to begin. Bonding with kids had always been Tessa's talent, not hers.

"Well, I guess I'll get started on prepping

for the dinner crowd," Erin broke into her thoughts with this announcement.

"Okay. Anything in particular you need me to do?"

"Just keep an eye on front of house in case anyone wanders in. And would you mind checking where Molly went?"

Harper hesitated. "Um…sure."

"Great. Thanks."

Erin moved back to the counter, and Harper left the kitchen to track down Connor's daughter.

IT TOOK HARPER nearly fifteen minutes to find Molly. She knew the little girl wasn't in the kitchen, stockroom or utility area because she'd watched her leave through the kitchen door. She checked in Connor's office first, but his daughter wasn't there. Carefully closing the door behind her, she made a sweep of the hall and even wandered up the stairs to the apartment on the first floor to make sure Molly hadn't headed that way. The door was locked, however, and Harper doubted that Connor had given his daughter a key. Heading back downstairs, she searched behind the bar and around the hostess station, and even walked out onto the restaurant deck overlooking the water. While on the deck, she scanned the docks, fearing Molly had dared to wander down the pier. But if she had, she'd made a quick getaway since there was no sign of her in either direction.

Coming back inside, Harper was beginning to fear she'd have to file a missing persons report when she heard what sounded suspiciously like the crinkling of a cookie bag. She followed the sound to a table near the front of the dining area and caught a glimpse of a tiny sneaker sticking out beneath the tablecloth. She lifted the fabric and finally found Molly, with cookie crumbs scattered in her hair and clothes. How had she managed to get cookie in her braids? There was also a heavy smattering of crumbs all over the floor beneath her.

She tried coaxing her out from under the table, but Molly refused to budge.

"No! I like it here." And then she stuffed another cookie into her mouth.

After several minutes of pleading, Harper finally had to grab her by the foot and tug her free, an action that only angered the little scamp. Once she was standing upright, she stomped her foot and scurried off in the direction of the back hall. Harper followed just closely enough to see her sneak into Connor's office and slam the door.

Assured that she now knew Molly's whereabouts, she located the vacuum and sucked up the cookie crumbs beneath the table. By the time she finished, it felt as though the entire restaurant was just a little too quiet. She slipped down the back hall and pressed her ear to Connor's office door. All was ominously silent within. She held her breath and tried the door handle.

Locked. Drat.

She knocked.

No answer.

"Molly?" She tried to affect a sweet and soothing voice. "Molly, honey, are you in there?"

"Don't call me honey!" came the muffled cry of indignation from beyond the door.

Harper cleared her throat and tried again. "Molly, can you open the door please?"

No response.

"Molly. Please let me inside."

Nothing.

"Molly. Unlock this door. *Now.*"

Her temper began to fray as the little girl refused to respond. What could she be doing in there? Harper began to have all sorts of visions of the trouble Molly could be getting into in Connor's office. He didn't encourage his employees to be in there without him present but what about his daughter? He had to have precious information stored inside. Records. Financials. Inventories. Her stomach twisted into a knot.

"Please, Molly," she pleaded. "Please open the door."

"What's going on?" She jumped as Erin appeared at her side.

"Molly's in there. The door's locked, and she won't open it."

Erin shook her head in dismay and rapped insistently on the door.

"Molly, it's Erin. I need you to open the door."

"No," she called back. "Not until the harpy goes away."

Harper gasped. *Harpy?* "How did she learn that word?" she demanded of Erin.

Her coworker grimaced. "Little pitchers have big ears. She probably overheard…" She trailed off, and Harper frowned.

Was that what they all called her when she wasn't around? Granted, it was a nickname she'd earned during her time as a critic. But she thought she fit in at the restaurant. The idea of her new friends referring to her by that name stung. Of course, maybe it was only Connor who called her that. That would be the most logical explanation of how Molly had heard it, wouldn't it?

"Molly Caitlin Callahan. You open this door *immediately*."

Things fell quiet as they waited.

"I'm counting to five, young lady," Erin warned. Harper was impressed. Erin had the mommy thing down pat.

"One...two...three..."

Erin shook her head. "Four...fi—"

They heard a fumbling with the lock, and then the door inched open. Molly peered out at them, defiance written clearly on her features. Erin nudged the door open the rest of the way.

"You owe Harper an apology."

Molly pursed her lips. Erin knelt down on her level. "We don't use names like that, okay? Remember when you got mad at the boy in your class who called you Hot TaMolly?"

Molly's lips scrunched together even more.

"You didn't like it, right? It hurt your feelings."

She un-pursed her lips to agree. "It was mean."

"Well, calling Harper a harpy is mean, too. So I think you should apologize."

Molly obviously wasn't too keen on the idea. "She made me come out from underneath the table."

"What table?"

"She hid herself beneath a table in the dining area," Harper explained. "I couldn't get her to come out so I had to pull her out."

Erin shook her head in disbelief. "You can't play in the dining room, Molly. I know your dad has talked to you about that."

"But he's not here!" she protested.

"Just because your dad isn't around right now doesn't mean you can do whatever you want. Do you think he'd like it if you were playing in the dining room?"

She lowered her head and kicked at the door frame. "No," she muttered.

"And you can't blame Harper for asking you to stop. She's only doing what your dad would want her to."

Harper knew Erin was trying to help, but the glare Molly cast her way just then made her wonder if her coworker had only made things worse.

"Now, I know your dad said it was okay for

you to play in his office, but you have to leave the door open so we can check on you, okay?"

Molly looked down and dug the tip of her sneaker into the carpet.

"Molly?" Erin prompted.

"Okay," she mumbled beneath her breath.

Erin rose. "All right then. I'm going to be in the kitchen, but Harper will be peeking in once in a while."

Molly didn't respond to this, but as soon as Erin was out of earshot, she turned her defiant green eyes on Harper.

"Tattletale," she whispered. And then stubbornly nudged the door nearly closed.

HARPER CONTINUED TO periodically check on Molly, but every time she inched the door open to peer into the office, the little girl would defiantly turn her back. It was ridiculous to feel offended at being snubbed by a six-year-old, but Harper couldn't help wondering what she'd done to earn such dislike.

She tried not to dwell on it as she went about her chores at the restaurant, but the lack of customers and the monotony of washing windows and wiping down tables for the fourth time was an open invitation for her mind to wander. She thought again about Molly's mother. Was her absence part of the reason the little girl behaved so mischievously? Connor seemed like a good dad. She recalled the way he'd coaxed a kiss from Molly before he'd left for his appointment. The sight of it had moved her. He obviously treasured his daughter. So how come Molly had such a terrible attitude at times?

Maybe she'd have to ask Tessa about it. As a pediatric nurse, her sister was around kids every day. Maybe she'd have some insight into the little girl's motivations. Pushing these thoughts from her brain, she reminded herself it was really none of her business and went to check on her charge once more.

This time, she found the office door wide-open with Molly missing. She nearly groaned aloud.

Not again.

She moved toward the kitchen to see if Molly might have joined Erin there. She seemed to like Erin well enough, or at least she listened to her better than she did to Harper. As she stepped inside the room, she froze.

Molly balanced precariously on a stool, reaching across a set of burners for a pot that Harper could see boiling. The little girl grasped the pot's handle and attempted to lift it from the stove, but the stool beneath her began to wobble.

"Molly!"

Harper raced from the doorway to the stove, grabbing Molly in her arms as her foot slipped from the stool and it toppled over. Her tiny hands released the bubbling pot of liquid, and it sloshed over the stove top, some of the hot liquid splashing up and onto Harper's arm. She turned, whisking Molly out of harm's way and wincing as her skin stung in protest.

Seconds later, Erin rushed into the kitchen from the direction of the stockroom.

"What's going on?"

Her eyes were wide as she took in the steaming stove top, the water hissing loudly as it evaporated against the heat. Molly struggled in Harper's arms, kicking her feet against Harper's shins.

"Put me down!"

Harper gently placed Molly on the floor, and the girl immediately pushed away from her. Harper grabbed a towel and dabbed it against her arm. The flesh had already turned a bright pink.

"I'm gonna tell my daddy on you," she declared.

Both Erin and Harper ignored this statement as Erin came over and removed the pot from the stove with one hand while turning off the burner with the other.

"What happened?" She directed the question to Harper.

"I don't know what she was trying to do. She wasn't in the office when I went to check on her, and when I came in the room, she was standing on that stool while reaching for the pot. The stool was teetering—"

"Was not!" Molly interjected.

"I ran over to help," Harper continued, "and grabbed her as the stool gave way."

Erin checked Harper's arm and then grabbed a towel, dropping it onto the floor to soak up the water that had overflowed from the stove top and onto the tile.

"Molly, what were you doing? I said I'd be right back. You were being so good, settled there on the stool." Erin was more distraught than Harper expected her to be. She turned with a worried expression. "She was just sitting there. I was only going to the walk-in for some cream."

"I wanted my macaroni and cheese," Molly said.

"I told you I was making it. Why did you try to take the pot off the stove?"

"I thought maybe it was ready," Molly whined.

"Molly, that wasn't very safe. You should never try to take things off the stove by yourself." Harper tried to touch her shoulder as she said these words, but Molly pulled away.

"You can't tell me what to do!"

"Hey. What's going on in here?"

All three of them turned at the sound of Connor's voice, but it was Molly who summed up Harper's reaction.

"Uh-oh."

"WELL?" CONNOR PROMPTED the trio of startled females. "I asked what's going on in here?"

"Nothing, Daddy," Molly immediately sang out.

"No, it's not nothing," Harper said. He could see she was distressed by the way she bit the corner of her lip. He found the sight oddly distracting, causing him to focus overlong on her mouth, even as she continued speaking. "Molly tried to take a boiling pot off the stove when Erin stepped out of the room. She could have been seriously injured."

Connor's focus on Harper's lips shifted as he considered what might have happened to his daughter.

"Erin said she'd make me macaroni and cheese!" Molly protested.

Connor looked from his daughter's defiant expression to Harper's concerned one. He turned to Erin.

"I started boiling the water for the pasta but left the room to get some cream for the roux. I didn't see what happened, but it seems…" She slid a glance at Harper. "It seems like Molly was trying to take the pot off the stove by herself."

"Molly," Connor looked to his daughter. "Is that true?"

Molly's jaw was working hard, as if she were trying to hold back her answer. She looked at Harper, and he followed her gaze, noting the streak of red running along Harper's arm. He could only assume it was from whatever had been happening in the kitchen before he arrived.

"Molly, I want you to go to the apartment door and wait for me on the stairs."

Molly opened her mouth to protest, but he cut her off. "*Now*, Molly."

She clamped down on whatever she'd been about to say and stormed from the room, stomping her feet with each step.

His eyes slid closed, and he raked a hand

through his hair. What was he going to do with her? She became more of a troublemaker by the day.

He opened his eyes and felt a twinge of embarrassment to see both of his employees eyeing him with what appeared to be pity. "I'll speak to her in a second. For now, let's get this mess cleaned up. Erin, would you mind finishing up the macaroni and cheese while I see to Harper's burn?"

He caught a flash of Harper's brows furrowing but didn't pause to consider the meaning behind her reaction. Instead, he went for the nearby first-aid kit and rummaged inside until he found a packet of cooling burn gel. He carried it to Harper.

"Let me take a look at that arm."

She drew back. "It's fine. Don't worry about it."

"Don't be daft. It looks like it hurts."

She appeared wary. "Maybe a little."

He opened the gel packet and squeezed a bit onto his fingertips. Holding Harper's wrist with his free hand, he used the other to dab some gel gently onto her skin. Her wrist was soft beneath his touch, and he could feel her pulse pounding erratically beneath his fingers. His head was bent near hers, but he kept his attention solely on the angry red streaks, clicking his tongue at the sight.

"It may yet blister," he remarked, but Harper didn't respond.

He was careful to cover the entire area and couldn't help noticing how the hairs along her arm raised with gooseflesh as he spread the gel across her forearm. As he finished, he shifted his head, ever so slightly, to look at her face. Only then did he realize how close they were standing, how he could feel her breath against his jaw. His face was startlingly near hers, and he couldn't be certain if the fast, shallow breaths she was taking were due to the pain…or something else.

"Does that help?" he asked, embarrassed to realize his voice was low and rough.

She nodded and released a soft sigh. He found himself staring at her once more and then blinked, forcing himself to look away. But he was still aware of her proximity. He'd never been this close to her, had never been able to smell the citrus scent of her skin. He swallowed and stepped back, taking a deep breath to clear his head.

Harper took a step back as well, as though she, too, needed the space. He heard Erin working at the stove behind him but didn't turn. His eyes were caught on Harper's face.

"Well." He coughed. "I'd best see to Molly."

He was nearly out the door when Erin called after him.

"How did it go at the bank?"

He pretended he hadn't heard the question and kept on walking.

CONNOR SAT IN his office, staring at the photo of his dad that he kept on the desk. After a stern conversation with his daughter, he'd left her sulking in her bedroom upstairs. Now his mind wandered back to his afternoon and everything that had occurred before his return to the restaurant.

The meeting with the loan officer hadn't gone in his favor. He'd been counting on the restaurant's years in the community to purchase himself a little goodwill in refinancing the terms of the mortgage. Even he had to admit, however, that the summer season was well upon them, and the Rusty Anchor hadn't picked up business as he'd hoped. The winter and spring seasons were always the most challenging in a town like Findlay Roads, where tourism had become a staple of the residents' income. He kept telling himself it was only a

matter of time until his restaurant was redis-
covered as a small-town jewel amid the newer,
trendier establishments that had flooded the
area in recent years. But nearly a third of the
way into the summer, the Anchor wasn't that
much busier than it had been in the spring.

And since he'd fallen further and further
behind on his mortgage payments, the bank
had issued a final offer. Unless he could amass
ten thousand dollars by summer's end to put
toward the loan, they'd be forced to foreclose
on the property.

This ultimatum had been like a punch to the
gut. Ten thousand might as well be a million.
He had no savings left to float the payments.
If only his dad hadn't mortgaged the place in
order to pay for Connor's culinary training.
After all, it hadn't done them much good. Connor possessed a fancy degree and the skills for
haute cuisine, but neither had helped him suc-
ceed as a restaurateur.

Connor flicked a glance upward. "If you're
listening, Dad, a little miracle wouldn't go
amiss." He paused and closed his eyes. He
wished his father were still here. There were
times, like these, that Connor felt completely
out of his depth and longed to talk to him once
more. But on the other hand, he was grateful

Patrick Callahan hadn't lived to see the gradual demise of the restaurant he'd loved.

Connor's eyes were still closed when a soft knock sounded on the door. He paused before responding, opening his eyes to the photo as he traced the threads of silver in his dad's hair, the lines of his face and the twinkle that the camera had managed to capture. What would he have said to his father if he were still here? What would he think of the state Connor found himself in, his second restaurant on the cusp of failure? His dad had held so many dreams for his son, believed his culinary talents would lead him to great things.

It hurt to think his father's faith in him had been misplaced. Not only had he lost Éire but now he was set to lose this second restaurant, the one his father had started on his own when he emigrated from Ireland.

He noticed his office door creaking open and stifled a sigh at this gesture of impatience. But before he could respond to the intrusion, Molly peeked around the crack in the door, revealing one eye and half of her frowning mouth.

"Daddy?" she spoke, her voice faint. "Can I come in?"

He melted at the timidity in his daughter's tone. "Of course, love. Come in."

Molly slipped inside and rushed to him, and he caught her in his arms, pulling her onto his lap. She buried her face against his chest, and he stroked the tangled strands of her braids.

"Hey now. What's all this about?"

She sniffled. "I'm sorry."

"Ah. And what are you sorry for, then?"

Molly pulled her legs up and curled into a tight little ball against him. "I'm sorry for cutting Piper's hair," she murmured.

"Mmm-hmm. Is that all?"

She seemed to be struggling with herself. "And for putting it in the toilet?"

He cleared his throat and waited, still stroking her hair. She picked at a stray thread on his shirt.

"Do you want to talk about what happened in the kitchen?"

He felt her body go rigid with tension. "It was the harpy's fault," she muttered.

"Molly." He sat up straighter in the chair, shifting his daughter on his lap so he could look at her face. "Where did you hear that word?"

She dropped her eyes. "I heard you say it before. You called Harper a harpy."

He frowned, ashamed that his daughter had heard him criticizing an employee—or anyone—in such a way. "Do you know what that means?"

Molly considered. "Does she play the harp?"

He felt a tickle of amusement and coughed to cover it. "No, she doesn't play the harp. At least, I don't think she does."

"Then why do we call her that?"

"We *don't* call her that."

"Yes, we do. *You* do. I heard you."

He shook his head. "Ah, you'd make a fine lawyer one day for how you love to argue."

"I'm not arguing. It's the truth," she calmly informed him.

He scratched the back of his head. She had a point.

"Well, what does it mean then?" she pressed. "What's a harpy?"

"It's not very nice," he admitted.

"You mean like the time I called Billy Stevens four-eyes?"

"Aye. Just like that."

"But you made me apologize when I did that."

He didn't reply.

"Does that mean you're going to apologize to Harper?" she asked.

He swallowed at her irrefutable logic. "I… suppose so."

She nestled against him once more. "I didn't think daddies ever had to apologize for things."

His hand automatically went to smooth her braids again. "We all have to apologize on occasion."

She sighed. "And I had an extra lot today."

He dropped a kiss on the top of her head. "But I'm proud of you for doing the right thing and saying you're sorry."

He felt her relax following this reassurance. And for just a few minutes, holding his daughter in his arms, he was able to forget that there were some mistakes no apologies could fix.

WHEN CONNOR ASKED to talk to her in his office, Harper couldn't help feeling a rush of uncertainty. After her experience watching Molly the day before, she wasn't entirely sure what to expect. She took the seat Connor pointed to and rubbed her palms across her khaki pants as she waited for him to speak.

"It's been brought to my attention that I owe you an apology."

She blinked.

"What?"

He folded his hands on the desk.

"There was a time or two in the past when I—" he licked his lips "—called you a harpy." He winced. "Apparently, my daughter overheard me. We had a discussion yesterday, and she pointed out to me that I should make amends for calling you names. It was not only unprofessional of me, as your boss, but perhaps…maybe…" He looked extremely uncomfortable as he avoided her gaze. "It might have been undeserved."

She placed a hand on her hip. "Do you think you could repeat that last part? Just in case I misunderstood?"

He rolled his eyes before letting them rest on her.

"This doesn't mean I've forgotten that review."

"Of course not. I'm sure you can hold a grudge as long as anyone. Maybe longer."

"I'm wondering if you're purposely trying to get beneath my skin or if annoyance is just a natural reaction for me where you're concerned."

She smiled at him. "I think I may have that effect on a lot of people."

"I wouldn't be surprised," he said drily.

"So…does this mean I'm forgiven, even if the sin is not forgotten?"

He studied her for so long that she felt herself begin to flush beneath his stare.

"You're forgiven."

She felt a swell of relief, as though a burden had been lifted from her shoulders. She hadn't realized until now just how badly she'd needed to hear him say these words.

"And your apology is accepted."

He nodded, but she sensed he had more to say.

"I also need to…thank you."

Her eyes widened. "Careful. I don't know how much of this Irish charm I can take."

Rather than respond to this banter, he cleared his throat and became serious.

"I appreciate your watching out for Molly yesterday. I know she's not always the easiest child to handle."

Harper softened at this. "I'm sure it's hard on her without her mother around."

"She's a tough kid," he said, seeming to measure the words carefully.

"I don't doubt it. Pretty spunky, too. I'm guessing she gets that from you."

He snorted. "More than likely. Her mom—" He stopped. She had never heard him mention Molly's mother before this. She thought he might not continue but after a pause, he did. "Chloe left us when Molly was just a tiny thing. I was working all the time, trying to keep Éire going, and Chloe resented that. She hated my long hours, hated not seeing me as often as she'd like. And she decided if that's what motherhood and being married to a chef meant, then it wasn't for her."

He looked down after sharing this, and sympathy tugged Harper's heart. How hard it must have been for him, to watch his marriage disintegrate and then his restaurant, too. All while trying to be a father to little Molly. She admired him the more for raising his daughter on his own.

"Being married to a chef is difficult," he went on, his eyes still lowered. "The restaurant always comes first. There aren't too many people who can live with it. And Chloe couldn't."

Harper's voice was quiet, out of respect for the difficulty of the topic. "Why didn't she want Molly?"

He was quiet for a long time. She sensed this was something he never talked about, a taboo subject he didn't share with others. She didn't really expect him to answer, especially as the minutes dragged on. But then he lifted his eyes to Harper's.

"I don't think she ever wanted her. She just thought that if we had a child, I'd spend less time at the restaurant and more time with her."

"Oh, Connor," Harper breathed in sadness. "Does she ever visit Molly? Or ask to see her?"

He shook his head. "She sends a card on occasion, for holidays and once for Molly's fifth birthday. And she called me one time, from Greece, where she's been living the past few years. She asked about Molly, but when I offered to put her on the phone, she said it wasn't necessary."

Harper felt Connor's pain as if it were her own. No child deserved to be so summarily dismissed.

"I can't tell you how much that weighs on me," he admitted. "I feel personally responsible for my daughter's lack of a mother. If I'd only been able to balance things more. If I'd given up the restaurant. If I'd begged her to go to counseling or… I don't know. Something. Anything to keep her from leaving me and abandoning Molly."

The angst in his expression made her want to reach out and wrap her fingers around his.

She gripped them tightly in her lap to keep from touching him.

"If Chloe could so easily leave her child then I'm not sure how much you could have done to make her stay."

He looked at her then, as though startled.

"Do you think so?" he asked, his Irish accent making him sound even more vulnerable.

"I do. I'm sure you both made mistakes. But Molly is as much Chloe's responsibility as yours, and I don't think you can blame yourself for her leaving your daughter behind."

He gave a thoughtful nod, and Harper noted that some of the tension seemed to leak out of his shoulders. She experienced a strange satisfaction at the sight. Somehow, the thought of easing just a little of Connor's burden made her glad.

After another minute, Connor cleared his throat.

"Ah, well…thanks for that."

She nodded, and though she knew she should make some excuse about getting back to work, she found she didn't want to leave him. There was something warm and comforting about the two of them in the tiny office, talking so intimately.

But she soon realized that Connor likely had better things to do than sit and chat with her.

"I guess I better let you get back to work," she said, standing.

To her surprise, he stood as well, and shifted his weight from one leg to another.

"Um… Harper, if you don't mind… I'd prefer it if you kept this conversation to yourself."

She found his sudden nervousness touching.

"It's just that I don't share much about my ex-wife. It's hard enough on Molly without…" he trailed off, at a loss.

"Without the possibility of other people saying something she might overhear. I understand."

He appeared relieved. "Thank you."

She turned to go but paused with her hand on the door. "But, Connor, you should know… I think Molly is still one lucky little girl."

His eyebrows furrowed in question.

"Because she has you for a dad."

Unexpectedly embarrassed at speaking this thought aloud, she slipped out of the office before he could reply.

CHAPTER FIVE

THE REST OF the week dragged by with fewer and fewer customers trickling through the Rusty Anchor's door. After the conversation between Connor and Harper in his office, things became easier between them. She still experienced a bit of uncertainty in their encounters but the tension that had radiated between them had been replaced by friendly banter.

She knew that Connor was a good man. He was certainly an attentive father and a fair employer, but even outside those roles, she sensed he was someone she would like to know better. If things had been different between them, if their situation wasn't so complicated, then maybe...

She quashed the idea before it could fully develop. She wasn't looking for romance right now. She'd been in her share of serious relationships, including one that had nearly blossomed into a proposal. But as soon as she'd seen the signs, she'd broken things off. She'd cared about the guy but had known she didn't love him enough to marry him. He'd been the sort of man Paige would have chosen—a bright and successful lawyer who was poised to be the youngest attorney ever to make partner at his firm. But that wasn't what Harper wanted.

She wanted someone who would be there for the day-to-day—for movie nights and lazy Sundays at home. She wanted someone who wished for simple things, like she did. And while she sensed Connor might be the type to appreciate the everyday connections, he had a restaurant to save and a child to raise. She couldn't imagine him making time for romance. And, she reminded herself, she had to keep her focus elsewhere and decide what she was going to do with the rest of her life.

She finished wiping down the tables in the dining area for the third time and then placed her hands on her hips, surveying the room. She'd already cleaned everything twice over, swept the front walk outside and scrubbed the windows and door. She'd had a handful of customers around lunchtime, but things had been quiet for the past hour. One thing she'd noticed during her time at the Rusty Anchor was that she grew bored after she ran out of cleaning tasks. There weren't enough patrons to fill the hours of her shift, and she often found herself asking Connor for extra chores rather than standing around with nothing to do.

Today was even slower than most, however, and she decided to step outside and take a quick walk up to Main Street, which sported most of the shops and restaurants. She told Rafael where she was headed and promised she wouldn't be long. Then, untying her apron, she walked out the door.

She passed by the docks and up a side alley to emerge on Main Street. Even after the peak lunch hour, the other eateries were busy with late-afternoon shoppers and vacationers. She stepped aside as a pair of women brushed by, laughing and toting a carryout bag from Celadon, the trendy restaurant several doors up, operated by a celebrity chef Harper recognized as already owning several popular establishments.

Was that part of the problem? Was Connor not famous enough to make a go of it in his hometown turned resort destination? The Anchor's menu wasn't phenomenal but neither was it horrible. Average would have been Harper's honest description of it. So what did the other restaurants have that Connor's didn't?

Disheartened by this question, she watched the tourists for a few minutes before resignedly heading back to the Anchor. Once there, she tied her apron back on and picked up the nearby broom. She stepped into the back hall and noticed Molly rustling around in the closet where she'd intended to place the broom. The little girl was muttering beneath her breath as Harper approached.

"Did you lose something, Molly?"

She jumped at the sound of Harper's voice, whirling around to squint warily upward. Her braids bobbed at the movement, several frizzy strands standing out wildly around her head like an electrostatic halo. She eyed Harper suspiciously.

Harper held up the broom. "I was just going to put this back," she explained.

Molly peered into the gloom of the closet once more.

"Can I help you find something?" she offered.

Molly seemed to weigh this offer, and Harper wondered if the little girl would ever trust her. "Daddy said I could have the old restaurant menu folders that belonged to Grandpa. But they're not here."

"Your dad said they were in the closet?"

Molly nodded up at her.

"What were you going to do with them?" Harper couldn't help asking.

Molly hesitated for only a few seconds. "Daddy said I could set up a pretend restaurant in his office, and I need menus."

Harper felt a tiny thrill of understanding. "Oh, I used to do that all the time when I was your age."

Molly appeared skeptical. "Really? You did?"

The child's face was an exact mirror of her father's, her green eyes slightly narrowed in suspicion as though she wasn't sure if Harper was having one over on her.

"Oh, yeah." Harper nodded enthusiastically and then crouched down so she was eye level with Molly. "Can I tell you a secret?"

Molly may not have been entirely ready to trust her yet, but what little girl could resist a secret? Her eyes widened slightly as she nodded.

"The first time I played restaurant, I decided I needed pictures of the food to serve since I didn't have *real* food. I planned to place the pictures on plates so they looked like real restaurant dishes. So I took a couple of my grandma's cookbooks, and I cut out all the pictures of the things I wanted to serve at my restaurant. Nana wasn't very happy with me when she found out what I'd done."

Harper knew that Molly had gotten into her fair share of antics, but Harper's own bit of mischief had clearly stunned her. Her eyes widened farther.

"You cut up her cookbooks? Daddy doesn't even like me to look through his cookbooks."

Harper felt a growing connection with the child.

"I bet they're really important to your dad since he's a chef."

Molly nodded in agreement.

"My grandma loved cookbooks, too. She wasn't a chef, but she was a great cook. And she didn't like me cutting up her collection."

"Did you get in a lot of trouble?"

"A bit," Harper admitted. "My grandma explained that I should have asked her for help instead of just taking the cookbooks that belonged to her. She was right. Because you know what she did after that?"

"What?" Molly asked.

"She gave me a whole big box of cooking

magazines and let me cut them all up to use in my play restaurant. She trimmed the pictures I wanted into circles, like plates, and then we made up menus, and she helped me come up with a name for the restaurant."

Harper's gaze drifted as she sank deeper into the memory. She had nearly forgotten how much she'd enjoyed that playtime. As a child, she'd wanted to be a chef when she grew up. She remembered the summers spent with her grandmother in Findlay Roads, long afternoons in the sweltering kitchen as she mixed flour and eggs for bread and helped stir batter for cookies. The cottage hadn't had air-conditioning when she was young (Tessa had it installed after she inherited the place), and her grandmother used to have a fan constantly stirring the steamy air. Harper hadn't minded the heat. Her skin had prickled with sweat, and Nana's forehead had beaded with perspiration, but they'd kept at it, cooking all sorts of goodies to be munched on throughout the week.

"She helped me set up tables on the back porch—they were made out of old stuff in the garage. One was a rusty birdcage she took the top off and turned upside down. Another was just an old drywall bucket that she flipped over. And another was the big box she'd been storing the magazines in. We used step stools and my grandpa's toolbox for seats. And then my sisters pretended to be customers while Nana took their orders, and I played chef."

She had forgotten that. She wondered if Tess and Paige remembered.

"What did you call it?"

"Hmm?" Harper blinked, coming out of her reverie.

"You said your grandma helped you name the restaurant. What was it called?"

Harper searched her memory. "I don't remember. But I do know my grandma glued pieces of construction paper to the cardboard of a picture frame, and she traced the letters so I could color them in. I think the sign was yellow with red letters. We had so much fun making it."

Things fell silent as Harper experienced a swell of nostalgia. She missed her grandmother. Maybe that's what she liked about the Rusty Anchor. Something about it felt familiar. Perhaps it reminded her of those summers spent at her grandmother's, before her priorities had shifted.

Before she'd become someone she hadn't really wanted to be.

Molly's soft voice drew her back when she

asked, "Do you think you could help me name my restaurant?"

Harper focused on the little girl, her expression both wistful and unsure. She felt a rush of tenderness and reached out to smooth some of the flyaway strands on the girl's head.

"I'd like that, Molly. I'd like that a lot."

MOLLY HAD SPREAD out her entire stock of colored pencils, crayons and even a few permanent markers she'd found in Connor's desk drawer. Harper had traced the lettering for Molly's pretend restaurant onto several pages of copier paper they'd taped together. Now she was trying to assemble some pieces of cardboard into a standing sign, using a roll of thick tape and the office stapler.

They'd found a sleeve of white paper cups in the corner of the office, and Molly was busy decorating them with the words *Shamrock Café*.

Harper finished piecing together the sign and stood it up for Molly's inspection.

"There. What do you think?"

Molly didn't look up immediately, and Harper willed herself to be patient. The little girl had warmed to her a bit over the past thirty minutes as they'd collaborated on her restaurant project, but she was still wary. After another beat, she looked up and inspected the sign. Her critical inspection put Harper in mind of her father, and she bit back a smile at the similarities she saw between them. They both wore the same thoughtful expression when asked for their opinion.

Molly gave a nod, looking quite serious. "It looks good," she affirmed, and then she went back to her lettering.

Harper felt a touch of pleasure at the little girl's approval.

"Maybe we should cover it with wrapping paper or something to give it more color."

Molly looked back up. "Can we do that?" she asked, obviously liking the idea.

"Sure. I can bring some wrapping paper from the house. And if you don't like any of it, maybe we can run out and buy some together."

Harper's insides warmed at Molly's smile, seeing a little gap where she'd obviously lost one of her baby teeth not too long ago.

"How are the cups coming?" she asked.

Molly surveyed her work. The letters ran off-kilter around the circumference of several cups, evidence of a child's hand. But the sight of the squiggly, imperfect letters filled Harper with affection.

"I think they're looking pretty good," Harper announced.

Molly looked up. "Really?"

"Yeah, I like how you're doing the letters in different shades of green. It's pretty."

Molly beamed at this.

"Maybe we can find some shamrock stickers to add to them when you're finished."

"Oh! Daddy already has some!"

"He does?" she asked, amused by the child's enthusiasm.

"He keeps them in his drawer." She pointed at the desk. "Sometimes he puts them on my homework papers."

This small, fatherly touch made Harper smile.

"He's a good dad, isn't he?"

Molly nodded. "I don't have a mommy. Daddy is all I have. And Aunt Rory, but she doesn't live here."

These matter-of-fact statements caused Harper to speak carefully.

"You're really special to have such a great daddy. He loves you very much. I can tell."

Molly didn't seem to doubt this. She continued writing.

Harper gathered up a few markers and returned them to the box.

"If you want," she said, "when I get home tonight, I can make up some menus for you on the computer. If we can find those old menu folders of your grandpa's, we can put them in there. And if we can't, we can still decorate them with the shamrock stickers."

Molly looked up. "Can we print them green?"

"Sure," Harper agreed. "You'll just have to tell me what dishes you're going to serve in the restaurant, and then I'll type them up for you."

"Ice cream," Molly said. "In twenty different flavors."

Harper laughed. "Whoa, maybe you should be opening an ice cream parlor and not a restaurant."

Molly's eyes widened at this thought, and Harper held up a hand.

"Let's stick with the restaurant for now, okay? If it's a success, you can expand your empire."

"But can we still have ice cream on the menu?"

"Of course. But maybe not twenty flavors just yet. Let's add some other desserts in, too."

This seemed an agreeable suggestion to

Molly. "Okay, then I want vanilla, chocolate, strawberry and blueberry."

"Blueberry?"

"I love blueberries," she solemnly announced.

"Then blueberry it is. And you'll have to decide on more dishes than just the dessert ones. We'll need appetizers, entrées and side dishes, too."

"Hamburgers and fries," Molly immediately supplied. "And chicken nuggets. And Grandpa's shepherd's pie. That's my favorite."

"You have a wide range of tastes," Harper said approvingly. "I'd better start writing these down."

She shuffled through the scraps of paper littering the floor but couldn't find any to suit her purpose. She stood and moved to Connor's desk instead, grabbing a few sheets from the printer. As she was looking down, a flash of metallic green caught her eye, nestled in a partially open desk drawer.

"Oh, I found the shamrock stickers," she announced and opened the drawer to pull them out. She froze, her fingers hovering over the little booklet with the shamrocks, their shiny leaves winking in the fluorescent light. She barely noticed the glossy shimmer. Her eyes had caught on something far more interesting: a letter from the bank, lying open with Connor's name and address at the top. She had no intention of reading it; it would be an invasion of privacy. But she didn't have to. Several words stood out so starkly that they told her everything she needed to know at a glance.

Impending foreclosure. Ten thousand dollars. And a date. August 31.

She grabbed the stickers and slammed the desk drawer closed so hard that Molly looked up. She smiled at the little girl, hoping she wouldn't pick up on the strain Harper felt. She wished she could rewind time, just for two minutes. Just enough that she could nudge that drawer closed as she approached the desk and keep from seeing that letter. She didn't want that burden, didn't wish to know just how precarious Connor's situation was. It was difficult enough that she was growing to like him… perhaps even fighting something more. She didn't want to feel sorry for him on top of that.

"Harper? Are you going to write down the menu?" Molly pressed.

Harper swallowed. "Yes. Um… I just need a pen." She scanned the desktop quickly, landed on a pen and grabbed it, willing her eyes not to encounter anything else she wasn't meant to see. She remembered the first time she'd stood in Connor's office, how he'd told her he didn't like his staff messing around in there. She'd never paused to consider that, by helping Molly, she'd gone against his wishes.

Carrying the paper and pen back to their spot on the floor, she tried to erase the letter's words from her mind. But no matter how hard she tried to forget, the reality of it settled on her consciousness with a weight.

At the end of the summer, the Anchor would be finished.

ON THE DRIVE home from work, Harper's mind was full with the knowledge of what she'd uncovered. She couldn't help thinking of Connor and Molly wondering what they'd do when the bank took back the Anchor. Not only was it Connor's livelihood, but it was their home. Where would they go? What would they do? And was there another option?

She considered the walk she'd taken earlier in the afternoon to observe the other restaurants in the area. She felt a growing certainty that the Rusty Anchor had great potential, but some changes would be required if it were to stay afloat. There was nothing special about the restaurant, no reason for people to seek it out over the establishments along Main. But with Connor's stubbornness, she doubted he'd be willing to reinvent things. The idea chafed at her, though. If he didn't do something drastic, it was obvious the Anchor couldn't hold on much longer. Was he really so intractable that he'd risk losing the restaurant rather than changing things up?

And if the Anchor closed, what would Connor do? Would he stay in Findlay Roads or would he move on? The idea of this town without him left a strange sort of hollow feeling in the pit of her stomach. She was becoming far too attached to Connor and his daughter.

Then there was the restaurant itself. Harper had to admit she loved the place. She looked forward to stepping through its doors each day. She liked the worn touches that spoke of a long history. Its cozy warmth reminded her of the summer days she'd spent in this town, cooking with her grandmother and dipping her toes in the bay. It seemed a shame to think of the Anchor passing into another owner's hands, or worse, being destroyed to expand the docks or put in a line of shops. What would someone else do with the place? If the other restaurants in town were any indication, it would likely be gutted and remodeled to a new and shining establishment, losing its sense of character.

She sighed as she turned onto Bellamy Drive. If she had a restaurant like the Anchor, she'd do whatever she could to hold on to it.

These thoughts were cut short as she approached the cottage driveway. A sinking feeling settled in her stomach like a rock tossed into the tide. She recognized the Lexus dominating the space in front of the house. It belonged to her father.

It seemed Allan Worth had decided to pay his two youngest daughters a visit.

"I TRIED CALLING to give you a heads-up," Tessa whispered as she met Harper at the front door seconds after she'd stepped inside. "But you didn't answer your phone."

Harper distractedly fished her phone from her purse and noted several missed calls and voice mails.

"I was distracted. I didn't check my phone when I got off work. Did Mom come, too?"

Tessa nodded as Harper hung up her purse. "Yeah, they're both here. We didn't have dinner. He wanted to wait for you."

"Tessa, is that your sister?"

Harper felt a flutter of nerves at the sound

of her dad's voice. She took a deep breath, composing herself and smoothing the white button-down shirt and khakis she wore, her standard server's outfit. She wished she had time to sneak upstairs and change, but she decided not to keep her parents waiting any longer. Tessa nodded encouragingly and led the way into the living room, where their mom and dad were settled on the love seat.

"Mom, Dad, I didn't know you were coming." She moved forward and accepted an embrace from her mother before turning to drop a kiss on her father's cheek.

"We wanted to surprise you and Tessa," Vivienne said. "I wish Paige could have come, but she and Weston already had plans for the weekend."

"That's all right," Harper reassured. She wouldn't have minded seeing her older sister, but she was relieved she didn't have to contend with her and their father at the same time.

"I'll go get dinner on the table," Tessa announced. "It should only be a few minutes." She disappeared before Harper could offer to help. Not that it mattered. She knew she couldn't escape the conversation that was coming.

"It's nice to see you, Harper," her father

said "I was beginning to think you were avoiding your mother and me."

She shook her head. "Of course not. Things have just been crazy since—" she steeled herself "—since losing my job at the paper."

"But you're working again? At a restaurant, you mentioned in an email?"

Was that a hint of disapproval in his tone? She couldn't imagine he was happy that one of his daughters was working as a lowly waitress. His standards had always been much higher. It was the very reason she'd taken the coward's way out and left a voice mail on his office line to tell him about losing her critic's job. Since then, she'd managed to conveniently dodge phone calls from him and her mother, responding by email instead and keeping the details of her new life here vague.

"Yes, at the Rusty Anchor down by the waterfront."

"The Rusty Anchor?" He frowned at the name.

"How is it?" her mother quickly cut in. "Do you like it there?"

"I do. It's good," she offered as she settled into a chair across from the love seat.

"That's all? Just *good*?"

"Isn't that enough?" Harper replied, struggling to keep her tone even. It pained her to think that in just another couple of months, the restaurant might be gone.

"Allan," her mother cautioned, her voice soft.

"Well, I'm curious," he insisted. "I receive a cryptic voice mail that she's lost her job and then I find out she's moved in here with Tessa and is working as a *waitress*. So?"

"So," Harper echoed. "What do you want to know?"

"Well, I suppose I'm wondering if you have a plan."

"A plan?"

He waited, as if this were an entirely legitimate question. Maybe it was, but she didn't feel like discussing it.

"Are you going to look for another job as a critic? Do some other sort of journalism? Or do you plan to remain a waitress for the foreseeable future?"

She worked to remain calm. "I'm finished with the critic thing." She considered. "And I don't think I'm interested in being a journalist just now."

He seemed to approve of this answer. "Well, I'm honestly glad to hear it."

She wasn't sure what this meant.

"Because I've been talking things over with your sister."

Harper's eyes shifted to her mother, whose head was bowed. She looked back to her dad.

"With Tessa?" she asked in confusion.

"No, of course not Tessa. With Paige."

Harper felt her stomach twist in discomfort. "You and Paige have been talking about... me?"

The discomfort turned to anger. How dare they? This was her life. It hardly called for a family summit.

"Well, she *is* the head of my risk management and analysis department."

"And?" She recognized her petulant tone even if her father didn't. It was the same attitude she'd affected in her youth when she'd often been compared to Paige.

"If you're going to come work at the company, Paige will need to give approval. You'd be directly reporting to her."

"What?"

From the corner of her eye, she was aware of her mother raising her head.

"I never said I wanted to come work for you," Harper pointed out.

Silence settled over the room, and seconds

later, Tessa reentered. She seemed to sense the tension and didn't speak.

"Listen, Dad, I appreciate the offer," Harper said. "But I think I need to figure this out on my own."

"And how exactly do you plan to do that? You're working as a waitress, Harper. I raised you to do more than wait on tables for the rest of your life."

The words stung, causing her cheeks to flame.

"Dad, come on…" Tessa tried to halt the discussion, but her quiet protest was ignored.

"I'd think you'd be glad I'm doing something with this time rather than sitting at home feeling sorry for myself," Harper said.

"I don't see how working as a waitress is much different. Why didn't you stay in the city instead of running off with your tail tucked between your legs? You'd have had a lot more opportunities there, between your connections and mine."

She began to tremble and clenched her fist to keep her frustration in check. "I didn't want to be in the city anymore. I was tired of it, and deep down, I was sick of the job, too. That isn't what I wanted to do with my life. I didn't enjoy it anymore. And if I'm honest, I'm not sure I ever did."

"Don't be absurd. You're becoming overly emotional about this. You always were melodramatic when things went wrong. Put this in perspective, Harper. If you're not planning to remain a restaurant critic, then it's time for you to choose a new career path. You can always pursue other journalistic options. Or you can come work for me. If you perform well, apply yourself like I know you can, you'll advance quickly."

Harper gripped the arms of her chair and raised her chin. "I said I don't want to be a critic anymore. But I never said I don't have a plan."

Her father's eyebrows rose, but he didn't speak, obviously waiting for her to reveal her intentions. She felt a flutter of nerves at his expectant face.

"I have dreams of my own, and I don't intend to return to DC. I'm staying right here."

"Please tell me you've got grander ambitions than waiting tables. Because I refuse to see a daughter of mine settling for less than she's worth."

"It's not settling if you're doing what makes

you happy. There's more to life than ambition, Dad. I wish you could understand that."

"I understand that you're being stubborn."

"No, actually. I'm not. I'm just…waking up, is all."

"And what is this newfound enlightenment? What do you plan to do with your life in the long term?"

It came to her instantly without any deliberation or hesitation. Whether it was the memories she'd shared with Molly about her own pretend restaurant in childhood or the thought of the Anchor passing into a stranger's hands, she knew her answer as soon as her father asked the question.

"I'm going to open a restaurant."

Once she'd voiced the idea aloud, she realized it was what she wanted. It was all she'd ever wanted—to be in a restaurant, her restaurant, not as a critic but as an owner. She wanted a place to call her own, that she could pour herself into and reap the rewards of her labors.

The silence in the room following this statement was profound. She held her father's eyes for a minute and then looked at Tessa. Her sister's eyes were wide, but when Harper caught her stare, she snapped to attention and smiled. The sight propelled Harper onward.

"Maybe I'll buy the restaurant I'm working at now," she mused. Though saddened at the thought of the Anchor closing, she experienced a swell of excitement at the same time. Maybe this was the way to save the place. "It has all this potential and loads of charm. It was once a local favorite—"

"Wait a minute," her father interrupted. "Is the restaurant where you're working *for sale*?"

She flinched, realizing she'd revealed more than she should have.

"Well...not exactly." She didn't like to share what she'd learned about the foreclosure. She knew Connor wouldn't want her to know that, and he certainly wouldn't want it revealed to others.

Her dad was shaking his head. "Harper, I appreciate that you're passionate about restaurants, and I've tried to support your choices. But don't you think it's time to look elsewhere, to position yourself for greater things?"

She felt the sting of rebuke but refused to be cowed.

"Success is relative, Dad. I can't measure it in terms of portfolios and stocks. Maybe it's

just about finding something I love to do…
and doing it."

He seemed to consider this argument. "And
this is what you want? To own a restaurant,
with the long hours and the headaches?"

"When I was a little girl, it was all I dreamed
of doing. I want to recapture that dream and
turn it into a reality."

"And you think you can make a success of
it?"

She inhaled a deep breath and felt suddenly
imbued with confidence. "I do."

She expected him to argue further, but to
her surprise, he looked contemplative. She
waited for his response, but her mother spoke
first.

"Harper, that's wonderful."

Though grateful for this promising reaction,
she still tensed for her father's reply.

"But this restaurant isn't for sale?"

"It's complicated," she replied. "But it may
be on the market later this year. I'd like to purchase it then."

"How do you plan to fund this venture?"
he asked.

"I've become acquainted with several restaurant investors through my time as a critic.

I'm confident I could use those contacts to help me finance it."

"And deny your old man the opportunity?"

She stared at him. "You mean...you'd be interested in investing with me?"

"You're my daughter, aren't you? And I am a financial adviser, after all. Do you have a business proposal prepared?"

"I..." She didn't want to tell him how recently this idea had come to her. "No. Not yet."

"Well, pull one together, and I'll review it. If it's up to snuff, I'll shop it around for you."

"That would be...wonderful."

She felt floored by her father's unexpected faith in the idea...and in her.

He beamed at her, and the sight buoyed her further. For the first time in Harper's life, she had the sense that her father approved of her plans.

In the back of her mind, there was a looming cloud of doubt, however. She didn't want to see Connor lose his restaurant. And yet she wanted the Anchor for her own.

She knew she couldn't have both.

HARPER'S PARENTS HAD to head back to the city first thing in the morning, so after an early breakfast, she and Tessa saw them out the door. As soon as they were gone, Tessa pulled her back into the kitchen.

"Why didn't you tell me you were planning to buy the Anchor?" she demanded.

Harper avoided her sister's gaze. "Because I only just realized it's what I want."

Tessa was quiet for so long that Harper couldn't bear it any longer. She looked at her sister.

"Is your boss planning to sell it to you?"

Harper tried not to flinch. "I don't think so."

Tessa waited. Harper sighed. If there was anyone in this world that she could trust with what she'd seen, it was Tessa. She knew her sister wouldn't tell another soul if she confided in her.

"He's on the brink of foreclosure, Tessa, okay? I saw a letter from the bank in his office."

"You were snooping in his office?" Her sister's tone was decidedly disapproving.

"No! Not exactly. I saw it by accident."

Tessa sat down at the kitchen table. "You better start at the beginning."

So Harper did. She grabbed another cup of coffee and sat down across from Tessa, revealing everything from her curiosity about the Anchor's slow business to her time with

Molly to how she'd stumbled across the letter in Connor's desk drawer.

"And it just occurred to me, when Dad was pressing about what I want to do with the rest of my life that this is it. Remember that play restaurant I had when I was little, the one that Nana helped me with?"

Tessa chuckled at the memory. "Yeah, when you cut up her cookbooks? We had so much fun on those afternoons."

"We did, didn't we?"

Tessa cleared her throat. "But, Harper, running a real restaurant is not the same as the games we played as kids."

"I know that. I'm not entirely naive. But I want this."

"Are you going to tell Connor about seeing that letter?"

Harper shifted uncomfortably in the chair. "I don't see what good can come of it. He'll just accuse me of snooping, which I wasn't. We've finally found our footing, and I think he's forgiven me for the review. But he hasn't forgotten. If I tell him about seeing that letter, it might unravel everything. Besides, it's not like I'm going behind his back in any way. I just want to be prepared when—if—the time comes. If the worst happens, and the bank forecloses, I want to be ready to purchase the restaurant before someone else gets it and guts the place. And if I end up as owner, I'd also like to offer Connor a job."

Tessa's eyebrows arched. "You think he'd come work for you after that?"

She didn't like the skepticism in her sister's tone. "I'm hoping he'll be happy if the restaurant goes to someone who knows its history and cares about the place."

The doubt written on Tessa's features caused her to look away.

"Why not see if Dad can find someone to invest in the Anchor while Connor's still owner?" Tessa suggested. "Wouldn't that help bail him out?"

"I thought of that," Harper admitted. "But Dad won't consider the Anchor a stable investment with the way things are going. He'd never be willing to pitch it to any of his clients."

"Then maybe you should consider another restaurant?" Tessa suggested.

Harper shook her head. "You know what a challenge that would be. Real-estate pricing in this town is through the roof since the tourist boom. And I'm sure just putting in a bid would be highly competitive. But with the Anchor,

I sort of have the inside track. As soon as it goes into foreclosure, I can make an offer to the bank. That is, if I have the investors already lined up. Besides... I don't want just any restaurant. I want that one. It's special. Maybe it's the history of it, how Connor's dad opened it after they moved from Ireland or the fact that it sits along the water, but there's just something about it."

"Okay," Tessa said. "You know I'm behind you, whatever you want to do. But I think you should consider telling Connor your plans."

"I can't, Tessa. Not now. Maybe as the time draws closer but not yet."

"It's your call," Tessa said. But Harper could tell her sister didn't agree with her.

Tessa didn't understand, though. Harper was relieved that Connor had forgiven her for that review, and she didn't want to jeopardize things with him all over again. She only hoped that by the time the foreclosure happened, if it happened at all, Connor would understand why she'd kept her plans from him.

SINCE HARPER HAD the day off on Sunday and the restaurant was closed on Mondays, she decided to drop off the menus she'd printed for Molly on Sunday night. She'd also picked up several rolls of wrapping paper to decorate the standing sign she'd made along with a pack of striped green paper plates she thought Molly might like to use in her pretend restaurant.

As she approached the Anchor, she noted the dining room lights were dimmed, and the place appeared to be closed. Parking her car, she headed around back and tried the kitchen entrance. It was unlocked, so she slipped inside, calling out a greeting as she did. She smelled something savory cooking, and her mouth began to water. She'd spent the entire day formulating a business proposal to give her father and belatedly realized she hadn't eaten anything since breakfast. She was starving and whatever dish Connor was preparing, it smelled heavenly.

She emerged from the back hall and into the kitchen to find her boss with his shirtsleeves rolled up, steam billowing upward from a sauté pan. As she drew closer, she couldn't help admiring the cords of muscle flexing in his forearms as he worked the pan, jerking it occasionally to stir the contents. He looked up as she approached, and for a moment his unguarded expression revealed such warmth that she felt herself tingle with pleasure.

"Hey, what are you doing here?" he greeted

before dropping his gaze, as though realizing how tenderly he'd spoken the words.

Her heart seemed to beat a little faster, and she found it difficult to look away. She held up the bag she'd brought, even though he wasn't looking.

"I promised Molly I'd print some menus for her play restaurant, and I brought her a few other things."

His eyes found her again, his expression softening with that same affection she'd just witnessed. It left her slightly dizzy.

"You made a special trip just to drop them off?"

She shrugged. "I promised her I would."

"That was kind of you. Thank you."

His Irish inflection made the words even sweeter, and she moved closer to him.

"The dining room's closed up," she observed as he took a pinch of salt from a nearby container and seasoned the food in the pan.

"It's been dead for hours. I figured I might as well shut the place up early and call it a day."

"What are you making then?"

"Shepherd's pie. It's my dad's recipe and Molly's favorite."

"She told me that yesterday. It smells fantastic."

As if on cue, Molly wandered into the kitchen holding a stack of construction paper and crayons. She froze at the sight of Harper.

"Hey, Molly." She held up the paper bag. "I brought the menus and some wrapping paper for the sign. And I found some cool paper plates I thought you might like for the restaurant. Plus a few stickers and things, for decorating the cups and menus."

Molly grinned at this and rushed forward, reaching for the bag.

"Let me see!"

"Molly," Connor chastised. "Don't you think you should thank Harper first?"

"Thanks," Molly automatically offered, and Harper surrendered the sack of goodies into her hand. She dropped the paper and crayons she'd been holding as she began to rifle through the bag. She gasped with delight as she pulled each item out.

"I think that's a hit," Connor remarked as Harper looked down at the little girl.

"I hear your dad's making your favorite for dinner," she said.

"Grandpa's shepherd's pie!" Molly looked

up from where she'd unloaded the bag on the floor. "How soon, Daddy? I'm starving."

Harper watched as Connor grinned at his daughter. "I've only just begun, love. You'll have to be patient."

Molly pouted. "Can I have some cookies?"

"Only one."

Molly went for the cookie bag that Erin had replenished. She pulled out two cookies, and before her dad could chastise her, she handed one to Harper. Harper took it from her fingers with a soft "thanks."

"Are you going to stay and eat shepherd's pie with us?" Molly asked before stuffing the cookie into her mouth.

The question startled Harper. She automatically looked to Connor, but his head was lowered in concentration, and she couldn't read his expression.

"Oh, I don't know, Molly," she said. "I'm sure you and your dad want to spend some time together."

"But you can stay and finish making the sign," she protested around a mouthful of cookie.

"Molly," Connor said. "Harper has been very generous helping you with your restaurant. This is her day off, and we'd best let her have the evening to herself. She likely has plans."

"Oh, I don't have anything planned." Harper said the words before she considered how it might sound. She wasn't begging an invitation, after all. Though she was a bit curious to taste this famed shepherd's pie. Her stomach gurgled softly, and she hoped Connor couldn't hear it.

It was as if Molly had read her mind. "And I bet she wants to try Grandpa's shepherd's pie, too," the little girl said.

Connor paused and looked straight at Harper, his eyes searching her face. He must have been satisfied with whatever he read in her expression because the next words out of his mouth were, "All right then. Harper, would you like to join us for dinner?"

"I don't want to impose."

She felt a little better when Connor declared, "You're not imposing at all. It would be our pleasure."

CHAPTER SIX

MOLLY INSISTED HARPER join her in the office so they could finish the signs and menus while Connor worked on the shepherd's pie. By the time Connor called them for dinner, Harper was ravenous, the cookie having done nothing to ease the growling in her stomach. Connor suggested they eat on the restaurant deck over-looking the bay, so they loaded up their arms with plates, utensils and glasses and headed to one of the outdoor tables. The early-evening light glowed with the nearly tropical hue of warm orange and pale lavender. The waves on the bay lapped gently against the docks, and several ducks quacked as they floated on the water. It was an idyllic setting for dinner, in Harper's opinion.

They settled into chairs at the table clos-est to the deck's railing and spread out their plates. Connor offered a short blessing, and then they each turned to their food. Harper forked into the steaming, savory meat and potatoes. She brought the bite to her lips and blew to cool it, then tasted it.

She paused, marveling at the perfect layering of flavors in what she had always thought of as a simple, even rustic, dish. The cheese topping was faintly nutty, and the potatoes were buttery rich, studded with chives and melting like little clouds of cream on her tongue. The lamb was infused with the malt flavor of Guinness stout, and the vegetables were crisp but tender, well seasoned with garlic, thyme, basil and rosemary.

In all her years of eating, in some of the best restaurants in the world, this meal ranked easily within her top ten most memorable. She was so busy devouring her own portion that it took her several long minutes before she realized the rest of the table had fallen as silent as she had. She looked over and saw Molly concentrating on her own food. Then her eyes shifted to Connor and found he was focused entirely on her. She swallowed and reached for her water glass.

"Connor, this is…amazing."

"Meets your approval, does it?"

She finished another bite. "It more than meets it. If I had eaten this in a restaurant, I'd have given it four stars."

He snorted.

Harper put down her fork. "No, I'm serious. This is absolutely perfect. Everything about it—texture, taste…it's wonderful. It's one of the best things I've ever eaten."

To prove her point, she raised her fork once more and inserted another mouthful.

"Daddy makes it special, just for me," Molly informed her, but Connor remained silent.

"I had no idea you could cook like this. Everything else you've made is so…" She cast about for a word that would describe how she'd felt about Connor's skills without causing offense. "Just so…typical of a classically trained chef. But this…this is something else entirely."

"Thanks. I think."

She lowered her head, realizing what she'd said.

"Why don't you cook like this all the time?" She slid another bite into her mouth.

He took a sip from his water glass. "I didn't realize I was cooking so differently."

"Of course you are. In the restaurant, everything is about haute cuisine. It's fine dining. This is comfort food. But it's better than any gourmet dish you've ever made."

"Harper, I'm not quite sure whether to be offended or flattered."

"Flattered," she shot back around a mouthful of pie. "Definitely flattered."

"It was my dad's specialty. He made it for every special occasion—holidays, birthdays, you name it."

The silence that fell over the table felt strained. Harper swallowed a bite, the food sticking in her throat. She drank some water and coughed. Connor didn't speak much about his father. She didn't know how to respond. Thankfully, Molly spared her.

"It's my favorite." She used her finger to nudge some wayward potatoes onto the tines of her fork.

"Molly," Connor said. "Use your knife."

Molly licked her finger clean and then reached for her knife, struggling to scrape the rest of the food onto the fork.

"It might just be my new favorite, too," Harper declared. She turned to Connor. "You have to serve this in the restaurant. It'll be the most popular dish on the menu."

"No."

His flat refusal stunned her.

"No? Why in the world not?"

"It doesn't fit in with the rest of the cuisine. It would be out of place."

"Who cares? It'll get people's attention."

She ran her fork around the plate, almost wishing she could use her finger to scoop up the potatoes, as Molly had done.

"It's not what I do."

"Well, it should be."

She hadn't meant the words to sound so snide, but as soon as she'd voiced them, she realized how they must have seemed. She put her fork aside.

"I'm sorry. I didn't mean to imply I know better than you do what's best for your restaurant."

But her instinct, her critic's voice, still cried out that this dish was something special. Connor had taken the plain and simple and made it extraordinary.

"Dad didn't want me to cook that kind of food."

"What? Why not?"

Connor pushed his own portion of shepherd's pie around on his plate. "He thought I could do better. He mortgaged this place to send me to one of the most prestigious culinary schools in the country. And he made me promise that when I took over, I'd stay true to his belief in me and try to make the Anchor into something finer."

Harper took another bite of her meal and chewed thoughtfully.

"Don't you think he'd reconsider, if he could see things as they are now?"

"Harper." Connor's voice had taken on a warning quality. She met his eyes, and he subtly tilted his head in Molly's direction. She felt a rush of embarrassment. Of course, he wouldn't want to discuss this sort of thing in front of his daughter.

"Oh." She cast about for a way to change the subject, but Connor did it for her.

"Why don't you two tell me more about this pretend restaurant? What sort of dishes are you planning on serving, Molly?"

Molly's eyes lit up at this question, and she rushed into an explanation of the menu she and Harper had created.

But even as Harper tuned one ear to the conversation and responded appropriately, a part of her continued to wonder just what might happen to the Anchor if Connor would change his mind…and the menu.

CONNOR WAS GRATEFUL that Harper had taken his cue to drop the subject of the restaurant during dinner. But afterward, her words lingered. He'd clung to his promise to make the

Anchor into something more, a way to honor his father's wishes after he'd passed on. But somewhere along the way, things had gone amiss. And Harper's question echoed in his head—what would his father think if he could see what had become of his request?

This unanswered query rattled around in his brain as he and Harper cleared the table. He sent Molly upstairs to watch cartoons and found he was unexpectedly pleased when Harper insisted on staying to help do the washing up.

She scraped and rinsed plates, and he scrubbed them clean in the restaurant's kitchen sink before stacking them on the drying rack. They worked in silence, side by side, for several minutes. He tried to stifle his awareness of her, but each time their hands brushed when passing a plate or some silverware, he felt the hairs on his arm stand on end. Beneath the scent of dish suds and the lingering aroma of shepherd's pie, he could just make out the fragrant notes of her shampoo—orange and lemon with a hint of something sweeter. He found himself leaning nearer to capture whatever the elusive scent was. She turned her head and caught him standing closer than he should have been. Her eyes widened as he stared. He liked the perfect almond shape of them, the brown of her irises deep and intent. Her inky black lashes. A strand of her hair had fallen across her cheek and caught on her mouth. His fingers itched to touch her skin and brush it free, run his thumb across the full curve of her lower lip.

He cleared his throat and turned back to scrubbing the sauté pan, trying to ignore his attraction to her. He finished cleaning the last dish and placed it on the rack. They stepped back from the wash sink at the same time. Harper cleared her throat.

"Thanks for dinner. It was amazing." She touched a hand to her stomach and gave a soft laugh. "I think ate way too much."

He stepped over to the coffeepot and began to brew up some decaf. "It's good to know you're a woman with a fair appetite," he remarked.

"Oh, I can eat, don't you worry. I always did have a better appetite than my sisters."

He measured several scoops of grounds into the filter. "You don't talk much about your sisters."

Harper shrugged. "I'm a middle child. I have an older sister who lives in DC, and of course Tessa makes her home here, in the cottage that used to belong to our grandmother."

"Tessa's not a city girl then?"

Harper shook her head as he added some more water to the reservoir and slid the pot in place.

"No, she likes the small-town feel."

"So then…how about you? Do you plan to stick around or will it be back to the city for you eventually?"

Despite his intentions to remain detached where Harper was concerned, he found himself anxiously waiting to hear her response. But she took her time in replying, as though weighing her words carefully.

"I think… I'd like to stay here for a while, maybe see what opportunities come my way," she offered cryptically.

He felt an overwhelming relief, as well as a surge of hopefulness.

Careful, mate…

They stood in contemplative silence for a couple of minutes until the coffeepot gurgled, signaling the end of the brew cycle. Connor busied himself pouring them each a cup. He dosed Harper's mug with a healthy splash of creamer from the mini fridge and added a few sugars to his own.

"How about you?" she asked, as he handed her the coffee. "Was it difficult to move back here after…after your restaurant in the city closed?"

"Not as difficult as I might have thought. I missed this town. And especially after my dad's first heart attack, I realized that I wanted to be closer to him. I've never been sorry that I came back when I did. It gave me a couple of years, working alongside him, before he passed on. It was hard, to see my first restaurant close. But maybe… I guess it was a blessing in disguise. It allowed Molly the chance to know her granddad for a time. And I was able to take this place over when we…we lost him." His voice dipped low on the final words.

He watched Harper from beneath lowered lids as she nibbled at her lip.

"Are you close to your own dad?" he asked.

A flicker of some emotion crossed her face, there and gone before Connor could determine what it was.

"My relationship with my dad is complicated."

"How so?" His curiosity was piqued, but he tried to keep his tone conversational.

"He has very specific ideas about how things should be."

"Meaning?"

"It's difficult to get him to see my point of view. He usually thinks he knows best where his daughters are concerned."

"Ah." Just these few words revealed more about Harper's family than he anticipated.

She took another sip of her coffee and then placed it down on a nearby counter.

"I should go and let you spend some time with Molly."

"It's early," he protested, surprised as the words escaped his mouth. "You should stay for a bit," he softly continued.

She blinked several times at this, almost as though she couldn't quite process what he'd said. He set his own coffee aside and moved closer so they were standing mere inches apart. Her eyes widened, and, hard as he tried, he couldn't resist reaching out and resting his palm against her jaw. As she tilted her face into his hand, he closed the tiny space that remained between them and gave in to the temptation to run his thumb along her lip. It was smooth, and she exhaled a tiny breath at his touch, warming his knuckle.

He leaned forward, a thousand thoughts colliding in his brain—how this was *Harper Worth*, the one woman he thought he'd hate forever and how she was nothing at all like how he'd always assumed. She was kind and sweet and confident and beautiful. And even though he knew he shouldn't kiss her, especially as her boss, he couldn't will himself to stop.

He brushed his lips lightly against hers, half expecting her to pull back or push him away, but when their mouths parted after that one, featherlight embrace, she tilted her head in for a second, tentative sweep.

Then there was no more hesitation as he wrapped his arms around her waist, pulled her tightly against him, and she ran her fingers through his hair. He tasted the coffee on her tongue, and he smelled the lemon-sweet scent of her shampoo. She was soft and fit easily in his arms, filling in all the gaps of longing he'd been trying to smother these past few weeks. He ran his hand from her waist up her spine and felt her shiver against him. The feel of her fingers in his hair awakened long-forgotten sensations. He hadn't kissed a woman in years. Not since Chloe had left him…

The reminder of his ex-wife doused his desire like baking soda on a grease fire. He stopped kissing Harper and pulled away.

What was he doing?

Pursuing a romance with Harper was out of the question. With the restaurant on the brink of foreclosure and Molly to look after, he didn't have time for a relationship no matter how much he liked Harper. Plus, what did he really have to offer her? In a few months he'd lose his home and his business, and thanks to him she'd be out of a job, too. Besides, she was his employee. This had been entirely inappropriate.

"Sorry," he murmured, taking a step back. The closer he stood to her, the more tempted he was to pull her right back into his arms.

She was looking at him with a mixture of longing and confusion.

"I shouldn't have done that," he admitted.

She opened her mouth to speak, but he didn't give her the chance. He feared what she would say—that perhaps she'd enjoyed that kiss as much as he had, and then where would he be?

"That was unprofessional of me."

Her brow furrowed, and he felt a twinge of remorse. He had lied, after all. He wasn't sorry, and he didn't care how unprofessional it might be. He wanted to kiss her again.

But this was a path he absolutely could not

travel down. It would only lead to heartache for both of them.

Still, he didn't want Harper to think she was to blame in any way.

"I hope you won't think any less of me for behaving so…irresponsibly."

She swallowed, and the action drew his eyes to the length of her neck. The pulse at the base of her throat was ticking erratically.

"Forgive me?" he asked.

He saw how she struggled to find the words to speak before managing a weak "Of course. No harm done."

The heat that had simmered between them had fizzled to something cold and awkward.

"I guess I'd better get home," she announced though she made no move to leave.

"I'll walk you out," he offered, though every muscle in his body protested at the idea of escorting her to the door. He'd rather keep her with him for as long as possible.

"No, that's not necessary," she said. "I'm fine on my own."

"Please. I insist. It's past dark."

He thought she'd argue with him, but she only gave a short nod. She picked up her keys on the way out, and he followed. He held the door open as they stepped outside. The evening air was deliciously warm with a slight breeze from the bay providing cool relief. He stepped ahead to open her door as she unlocked her car with the keyless remote. She paused beside the vehicle.

"Thanks again for dinner. It was delicious."

"My pleasure," he replied.

He found himself eyeing the curve of her jaw, captured by the way she raised a hand to tuck her hair behind her ear.

"I guess I'll see you on Tuesday," she murmured.

"Tuesday. Right."

She slipped inside the car, and he gently closed the door for her. He lingered as she started the vehicle and watched as she backed out of the space, driving down the alley and out of sight. He stood outside for a long time, gathering his emotions and trying to tamp them down deep. But try as he might, he couldn't erase the feel of her in his arms... nor the memory of her lips on his.

HARPER QUIETLY LET herself into the cottage and hoped Tessa was already in bed for the night. Her mind was so full with everything that had occurred that evening, and she wanted nothing more than to be left alone with her weighty thoughts and ravaged emotions. Her hopes diminished as she heard the soft buzz of the television coming from the living area. Tessa was still up. She thought about slipping upstairs before her sister realized she was home but no such luck.

"I made popcorn," Tessa called.

Harper smelled the lingering aroma of butter. She hesitated and then stepped toward the living room.

"Hey," Tessa greeted from her position on the couch. "I wasn't sure if you ate dinner. You were gone quite a while. There are leftovers in the fridge, if you want."

Harper shook her head and resigned herself to a bit of conversation. "I ate at the restaurant."

"Oh." Tessa studied her, head cocked as Harper curled up on the other end of the couch. She muted the television and placed the bowl of popcorn on the coffee table. "You look—" she fished for a word as Harper shot her a warning glance "—pensive," Tessa finally decided. "Is everything all right?"

"Fine," Harper airily declared as she reached for the popcorn. She pulled it onto her lap and began to pick through the bowl while pretending to be focused on the television, even though there was no sound and whatever Tessa was watching had gone to commercial break. A talking amphibian dominated the screen.

Connor had kissed her. She felt herself shiver at the memory. He had kissed her...and it had been amazing. He'd held her so gently, as though she were something precious, and when he'd run his thumb along her lips, she'd felt an ache she'd never known existed suddenly become soothed.

"Harper? Are you okay?"

She jerked at this question, her eyes darting to Tessa's.

"Wh-what? Yeah," she replied and looked away. "I'm fine. Just tired."

But then he'd released her, backed away and apologized. He'd acted as if the whole thing was a mistake, even asking her forgiveness. And she'd granted it, saying there was no harm done.

But that was a lie. Because there was no going back from a kiss like that. She'd been struggling with her own feelings for Connor, making every effort to deny the growing attraction she felt toward him. And with that one kiss, he'd wrecked her resolve. She couldn't deny it anymore. She was falling for Connor Callahan, and that simply would not do. Things were far too complex with the restaurant and her plans to purchase it after the foreclosure. She felt guilty enough for wanting to buy the Anchor, even though she knew that logically, when the bank foreclosed, *someone* would step in and buy it. Why not her? But as much as she tried to remain optimistic, she didn't think Connor would embrace the idea of her as the new owner of his family's restaurant. She hoped that in time, he'd come around, and even work with her. But she also knew he was far too proud to welcome the change.

Layering on feelings for him would only make the situation more difficult. Besides, he'd apologized so aggressively that she wondered if he actually did regret kissing her. Maybe he'd simply been caught up in the heat of the moment, grateful for what she'd said about his cooking, and had reacted out of that rather than any real attraction to her. How much more of a fool could she be to think that Connor, who had expressed his dislike of her so loudly at first, might now have feelings for her?

She shook her head and realized Tessa had been stealing glances at her out of the corner of her eye.

"Harper? Are you sure you're okay?"

She suddenly felt tears pricking her eyelids and avoided meeting her sister's eyes. She lifted the bowl of popcorn from her lap and placed it back on the coffee table, belatedly realizing she'd only picked at the kernels without tasting one.

"I think I just need to get some rest."

"Okay," Tessa said, obviously not buying it. "At least the restaurant's closed tomorrow so you have the day off."

Though Tessa had meant it to be reassuring, the reminder only heightened Harper's melancholy. With the restaurant closed for the day, she had no reason to see Connor. The thought nearly made her wince. She had it bad if she couldn't even contemplate twenty-four hours away from him.

"Try to sleep in tomorrow," Tessa called as she exited the room.

"Thanks. Night, Tess."

Harper didn't say so, but she had a feeling she wouldn't be getting too much rest tonight.

CONNOR AWOKE FROM a night of tossing and turning, his thoughts filled with the lingering memory of a hazy dream. He must have finally fallen into a deeper sleep near dawn, though. Images of Harper—the feel of her jaw as he'd cupped it in his palm, the soft tenderness of her lips and then, the disappointed light in her eyes as they'd pulled apart still lingered. It seemed that even in his dreams he couldn't forget how wrong it was to kiss her.

His mind skipped ahead, trying to think when he'd see her today, but then he realized it was Monday and the restaurant was closed for the day. With business dragging, he'd made the decision last year to save money by shutting down on the slowest day of the week. He wouldn't see Harper again until tomorrow. And what did it matter? It wasn't as if anything would have changed by then. He'd still have the restaurant and the matter of the impending foreclosure, along with a six-year-old daughter to raise.

He'd do well to put Harper firmly out of his mind. If only that were as easy as it sounded.

As he made the effort to think about something other than Harper's caramel-tinted eyes, he became aware of voices in the kitchen. He jumped out of bed and headed for the hall, pausing only to check Molly's bedroom. The covers on her bed were rumpled and unmade, but there was no sign of his daughter. He rushed toward the kitchen, aware of soft, feminine voices and Molly's giggle. For one, fleeting instant he thought of Harper, his pulse surging at the idea she might have stopped by and Molly had let her in. He couldn't think of anything that would make him happier than for her to be in his kitchen, right this second. But then he emerged from the hall to find his sister, Rory, sharing a pint of ice cream with her niece. His hopeful anticipation fizzled.

"Rory," he said, reluctantly releasing the daydream. He was stunned to see his sister at his kitchen table. "You can't eat ice cream for breakfast."

Molly shoveled in another spoonful, as if she knew the treat would be taken away any minute now.

"It's about time you're up," Rory said as she snuck her own spoon into the ice cream container.

He crossed his arms over his T-shirt. "When did you arrive?"

"Early this morning. I used my key to let myself in, but I woke up Molly in the process."

Molly was making inroads into the ice cream as fast as she could. Connor stepped forward and plucked the container out of her hands. She groaned in defeat.

"Ice cream is *not* a proper breakfast," he insisted.

"We're bonding," Rory announced. "And it's nice to see you, too."

He softened and moved around the table to drop a kiss on his sister's cheek. "Of course it's good to see you. You just took me by surprise is all."

He placed the lid back on the ice cream and stuck it in the fridge, licking a sticky spot from his knuckle. Mint chocolate chip.

He grabbed a paper towel and dampened it at the faucet before he advanced on Molly, who patiently submitted to his ministrations of cleaning up her ice-cream smeared mouth.

"You can't just give a six-year-old ice cream for breakfast," he lightly chastised his sister.

Rory shrugged. "If her aunt can't spoil her, then who can?"

Molly beamed at Rory, and Connor decided not to object anymore. He was pleased to see his sister, even if she had just dosed his daughter with far more sugar than she should have.

"How about I start some coffee?" Rory suggested as she got to her feet. "And then maybe I can convince you to cook me up a full Irish breakfast, just like Dad used to make us on the weekends."

He experienced a flicker of nostalgia at the memory. "With blood sausage and all?"

"The works," she agreed. "All the grease will help the sugar from the ice cream digest, right, Molly?"

Molly was too busy licking a lingering spot of ice cream off her spoon to comment. Rory emitted a soft laugh at the sight and began to pour water into the coffeepot. Connor paused to take a good look at her and noticed a few things he'd missed at first glance. Her dark hair was tangled and thrown up into a messy ponytail. Her eyes were somewhat blood-shot, and there were faint smudges of eyeliner creasing the skin beneath her lashes. He experienced a stab of concern.

"Hey." He reached out and touched her hand, stilling her movements as she prepared the coffee. "Don't take this the wrong way because I really am thrilled to see you, but you look a bit of a mess. Are you all right?"

She avoided looking at him. "I had a long drive. I'm just a little weary."

"Did Sawyer come with you?" he asked, referring to Rory's longtime boyfriend.

She was quiet for a beat too long. "He couldn't come, had a conflict in performances. So I'm here to do the festival by myself."

His memory prodded him, and he felt a rush of embarrassment at having forgotten. As locals, Rory and Sawyer performed together at the Independence Festival every year for the July Fourth holiday. She always stayed with him and Molly when she was in town, but he'd forgotten she was coming. He stole a glance at the calendar on the fridge and realized the festival was in just a few days.

"I have to admit, I forgot that was this weekend. The summer's really flying by."

Rory finished preparing the coffee and punched the button to brew. "I also thought I'd better check in, see how things are going at the restaurant. Has business picked up over the season like you hoped it would?"

He flinched at this question and then slid a glance in Molly's direction. She had pulled out the stickers and printed menus Harper had brought her the evening before. His chest ached at the sight, reminded of Harper's thoughtfulness toward his daughter. When he looked back to Rory, he saw the concern in her eyes.

"We can talk later," she murmured, obviously understanding his reluctance to speak of such things in Molly's presence. She drew a deep breath and shifted toward the sink, busying herself with the few dishes there.

"In fact, I thought I might stay for a while, if you don't mind."

He blinked in the wake of this unexpected announcement. He'd come to think of his sister as a wanderer, one of those people who craves a life of travel. She'd been all over the States with Sawyer, playing various gigs and even opening for a couple of up-and-coming artists. He couldn't help being curious about her decision, but he also felt a wave of happiness.

"We're thrilled to have you around for as long as you care to stay," he reassured. "This is your home, too, you know."

He was utterly baffled when she suddenly wrapped her arms around his waist, hugging him fiercely. She buried her face in his chest but not before he saw the heavy tears she tried to blink back from her eyes.

"Hey." He squeezed her tight. "Are you all right?"

She sniffled. "I'm just…glad to be home."

Somehow, he suspected there was more to her the story than that. But he and Rory had always been close. He knew she'd tell him in her own time, and he'd just have to wait patiently until she did.

"Sawyer and I are finished."

Though Rory had never been given to melodrama, he nearly scoffed at this stark statement.

"Finished?" he repeated as he put his coffee mug down on the table between them. They were seated outside on the Anchor's deck overlooking the bay. He'd put Molly to bed thirty minutes earlier, and they'd stolen downstairs to the restaurant so she wouldn't overhear their conversation.

Rory cupped her own mug of coffee in her hands, staring down into its dark depths.

"He was offered a recording contract with a major record label. A talent scout saw him perform at a venue in Texas and called in a producer. They liked what they saw and made him an offer."

She was trying to remain detached, he could tell, but he knew her well enough to recognize the grief in her voice.

"But you and Sawyer usually perform together. Why him and not you?"

She shrugged. "They thought he had more appeal as a solo artist. I mean, this is a big deal. They're predicting he's going to be the next country music superstar. But the thing is, they made it clear that the contract was for him. Not me."

Connor felt his hackles rise in defense of his sister. "How can they think that? You've performed solo before, but you're both at your best when you make music together. Your Irish folk with his country. They'd be daft to take him without you!"

Rory didn't say anything, and Connor tried to rein his temper in. His sister was wounded, and his own anger wasn't going to help with that. He sighed and willed himself to be calm.

"You can still get your own contract. You don't need Sawyer—you're a true talent all on your own."

She was shaking her head before he'd even finished speaking. "No, Connor. You misunderstand. I'm not jealous of Sawyer—I'm happy for him. He's a talented musician, and he deserves this. I think they're right, he's going to be really famous." She cleared her throat. "But I won't be with him when it happens. They hinted they could leverage his appeal more if he didn't already have a girlfriend. Fans like to dream, after all."

Her voice wavered on this last part, and then she fell silent. She lifted the mug of coffee to her lips, but he saw her hands were trembling.

"Wait here," he commanded as he stood and headed back inside the restaurant. He took the steps up to the apartment two at a time and quickly gathered the items he needed. Once he'd finished what he was up to, he hurried back downstairs and out onto the deck. He placed the glass of chocolate milk he'd prepared in front of her and was gratified when she pushed aside her coffee mug, drawing the glass closer to take a sip through the straw.

"It's just as good as you used to make when we were kids," she declared after the first swallow.

It had been his way of caring for his sister when they were children. Chocolate milk with a straw had become their sibling tradition during their first year in the States, a custom they'd kept the alive as the years passed.

They sat in silence for a few minutes as Rory drained her glass. He studied her, noting the shadows beneath her eyes, and the way she seemed to struggle to hold herself up.

"What will you do now?" he asked, keeping his voice soft.

She toyed with the straw and avoided his eyes. "I thought I'd stick around for a while, like I said this morning. I had hoped you might need help at the restaurant, but it doesn't seem like that's the case."

He wanted to reassure her, to tell her he had a place for her no matter what. But given the bank's ultimatum, he didn't want to offer false reassurances. She sensed his silence and looked up.

"So, what's going on?" she questioned. "Has the restaurant not been as busy as you hoped?"

He refused to burden her with the restaurant's problems when she was dealing with her own. He tried to shift the topic.

"Well, I have a new employee. You'll never believe who it is."

"Oh?"

"Harper Worth."

Rory's eyebrows furrowed at the name. "Harper Worth… Why does that sound familiar?"

"You might remember her from that review she gave me some years ago. The *Worth It?* column?"

Rory sucked in a sharp breath. "The *harpy* is working for you? How did that happen?"

Connor cringed at the nickname. "Don't call her that. She's actually not so bad. I mean, we got off to a bit of a rocky start, but she's… wonderful."

Rory leaned back. "Wonderful?" Then she leaned forward and placed a palm against her brother's forehead. "Are you feeling feverish? You say that almost as if you like her."

"I do like her," he replied. "She's worked really hard the past month, and she somehow managed to win over Molly, who loathed her at first."

"How did all this come about?"

So he told her, carefully leaving out the events of the evening before, after they'd had dinner together. But even without that part, Rory was eyeing him curiously by the time he finished speaking.

"Connor, you seem almost as if you…have feelings for her."

He laughed, though it was strained, and turned his attention to the lukewarm remains of his coffee. "Don't be daft. It's just that we've formed a truce, that's all. She's a good employee, and she's been sweet to Molly. I like having her work for me."

Rory remained silent so he was eventually forced to look up and gauge her reaction. Her expression remained dubious.

"Hmm. I can't wait to officially meet her then. And now that I'm staying in town, I'll have plenty of time to get to know her."

She turned her head to look out over the water.

"It's true what they say, isn't it?" she murmured, so quietly that he had to strain to hear her. "There's no place like home."

CHAPTER SEVEN

HARPER'S STOMACH WAS twisted into a knot of nervous anticipation as she headed in for her shift at the Rusty Anchor on Tuesday. She'd spent the better part of Monday attempting to lose herself in plans for her restaurant, polishing her business plan, sketching out ideas for an interior remodel and brainstorming the menu. With each change she made, she imagined Connor looking over her shoulder, frowning in disapproval. Eventually, she'd put away her work and headed outside to the park for a much-needed break.

She'd strolled along the promenade that wound around the park perimeter and stretched for nearly three-quarters of a mile, offering an unobstructed view of the Chesapeake Bay. No wonder her sister had chosen to live here. Though Findlay Roads was not a large town, it had plenty to offer in the way of beauty, from the natural landscape and the lighthouse in the distance to the hum of Main

Street. It was sort of like having the best of both worlds, Harper realized—the summer season buzzed with energy from vacationers and tourists while the locals provided a sense of home and community.

Harper had settled herself on one of the park benches and lingered for so long that dusk had begun to fall before she'd headed back to the cottage. It had been the perfect respite from her frantic thoughts.

Until Tuesday morning dawned, and it was time to head into work.

Part of her had been extremely eager to see Connor again. She'd hoped she might hear from him at some point on Monday, but her phone had remained silent, and she'd mentally chastised herself for her girlish daydreams. Connor's Mondays were always spent with Molly. He'd explained before how it was their daddy-daughter day. She shouldn't have even considered he might interrupt that for her. And besides, he'd made it clear that kissing her was a mistake. Why did she think he would change his mind?

She attempted to put the kiss from her thoughts as she drove into work and then entered the Anchor through the back door. She retrieved her apron from her locker and then walked down the short hall to the kitchen. It was empty, so she headed for the dining area. Connor might have been in his office. She noticed the door was closed as she passed by, but she didn't stop to announce her arrival. She told herself she didn't want to interrupt him if he was busy, but in truth, she wasn't sure she could face him just yet.

She had just finished tying her apron on when she stepped into the dining room, and a voice drew her attention toward the bar.

"You must be her."

She turned to see a woman with long, black hair wiping down the counter. For a minute, Harper was confused, wondering if this was perhaps the server whom she'd replaced, the one who'd broken her leg a few weeks ago. But she quickly registered the Irish accent. Harper studied the woman, her dark hair and assessing green eyes. She had that same, mistrustful stare that Connor had once displayed when he'd looked at Harper.

"You're Rory," Harper deduced.

"That I am." Rory came around from behind the bar, wiped her palm on the jeans she wore and then held out her hand. "And you must be the harp—I mean, Harper."

Harper couldn't determine if this slip was

accidental or on purpose. She slid her hand into Rory's. "Pleased to meet you."

"My brother told me you've been working here. I wasn't sure I believed him at first. It seems a long way for a restaurant critic to fall."

Harper wasn't sensing outright hostility from Rory, but it was obvious the other woman wasn't sure what to make of her. She shrugged.

"It might have been a longer fall if your brother hadn't caught me when he did." She realized how this might sound and cleared her throat. "I'm grateful that he gave me a job. He's a good man."

Rory studied her intently. "He is," she softly agreed. "He's like our dad. Not too many men like that anymore."

"No," Harper concurred. "There's not."

"There's not what?"

She jerked around at the sound of his voice, her heart hammering against her ribs. She was becoming like one of Pavlov's dogs, she realized. As soon as she heard that Irish accent, her awareness heightened tenfold. She wondered if he felt the same, if his pulse raced when she was around. He met her eyes briefly and then quickly looked away. Her awareness turned into awkwardness, and Rory must have sensed it, too, because she whistled low.

"Harper." He said her name, but it was Rory he looked at with a warning scowl darkening his features. "May I introduce my sister, Rory?"

"We've met," Harper said, noticing that his accent had deepened, perhaps as a result of his sister being there.

"Yes, Harper and I were just getting acquainted," Rory said, not looking at all cowed by her brother's expression.

"Rory's in town for the Independence Festival this weekend. She'll be performing at the concert taking place later in the day."

"Oh, that's great," Harper responded with genuine interest. She looked at Rory. "I forgot that Connor told me you were a musician."

She inclined her head. "I play at the festival every year with…" she trailed off, looking stricken. Harper frowned, but Rory quickly recovered. "I'll be playing solo this year," she offered as she shared a look with Connor.

Harper felt left out. The glance Rory shot Connor was clearly a silent communication between the two.

"Well, it was a pleasure meeting you, Harper." The words sounded genuine enough, but perhaps that was for Connor's benefit. "Now, if you'll excuse me, I promised my niece we'd play restaurant together."

Harper felt a stab of disappointment that Rory had been invited to play restaurant with Molly. But that was ridiculous. She was Molly's aunt, and she was in town for a visit. Of course Molly would ask her to play.

Rory left the room, and Harper was suddenly aware that it was just her and Connor in the empty dining area. He cleared his throat.

"How was your Monday?"

"Um…good."

"Do anything special?"

She wasn't about to tell him she'd spent most of the day working on her business proposal for the restaurant. "Not…really. I took a walk on the promenade in the evening."

"Sounds nice," he said.

"It was. What about you? When did Rory get into town?"

"Early Monday morning. She spent the day with us yesterday. Molly was thrilled to see her. We had a lot of fun."

"That's good."

Harper nearly winced at the strain between them. She rubbed the back of her neck and avoided looking directly at Connor.

"So, what are the specials today?"

He seemed relieved to have such an easy question to answer. As he named the dishes, she only occasionally glanced at his face, but it did no good. No matter where her eyes landed, she was distracted. They fell on his hands, and she thought of how he'd held her, his fingers tracing her lips. She looked over his shoulder and remembered what it had been like to be in his arms. She glanced at his hair and her fingers twitched as she recalled the smooth feel of it.

Eventually, she released a tiny sigh and returned her attention to his face. He was frowning.

"You don't like the sweet corn and roasted pepper salsa?"

"What?"

He cocked his head.

"Oh." She had completely tuned out the specials he'd been sharing. "No, it's fine."

His brow furrowed.

"Great," she corrected. "It's great."

They stared at each other until Connor finally looked away.

"Why don't I just write them down for you?"

"Thanks. I'd appreciate that."

Because she didn't think she'd be able to focus on anything he said today.

Get your head back in the game, Harper. Do your job. Remember what it is that you want.

But just then, she couldn't have said for sure what that was.

THE WEEKEND OF the Independence Festival, the town was packed with tourists and locals alike. Tessa and Harper walked to the park, where most of the festivities were to take place, and Harper was glad they didn't have to fight for parking along the crowded streets. The day was warm, with temperatures edging toward the nineties, but a steady breeze off the bay served to keep the air relatively pleasant. Tessa waved to a few acquaintances and even introduced Harper a time or two. She was slowly getting to know a few of the locals. In the past week, she'd taken to hanging out at a nearby coffee shop before and after her shifts as an excuse to get out of the house as well as to continue working on her restaurant proposal. She didn't admit it to Tessa, but she liked having somewhere to go after work so she didn't dwell overlong on Connor or Molly. Since Rory had taken over babysitting duties, Harper didn't see as much of the little girl anymore.

And Connor was almost too polite these days. She missed his occasional irritation and the joy she'd found in teasing him. They were far too stiff around each other now, staying carefully within the lines of boss and employee.

She was looking forward to this day off and its distractions. A lot of the businesses closed down for the festival, and the Rusty Anchor was no different. Connor had put out the closed sign so all of his employees could enjoy the day. She'd promised to meet up with Leah later so they could get matching fake tattoos at the high school band's stand, and Rafael had pledged to buy her the "best crab cake sandwich" she'd ever eat from a local food truck. Erin would be there with her son, Kitt, and she'd told Harper not to miss the skipjack races on the bay. And Molly had made it clear she expected a funnel cake from the fire station's tent. It seemed the only person she hadn't made some connection with concerning the festival was Connor.

But that wasn't surprising, given how stilted things had become between them. They could barely converse about restaurant topics much less anything as interesting as the Independence Day events.

"Oh, we should check out the reenactment!" Tessa said, pointing off in the distance where Harper could make out a cluster of men and women in Colonial-period clothing gathered in an open area of the park.

Tessa was more of a history buff than she was, so she shook her head. "You go on ahead. I think I'll just walk around for a while."

"Oh. Do you want me to stick with you?"

Tessa was looking longingly at the tableau of bygone days.

"Don't be silly. I'm fine on my own. You go watch the reenactment and catch up with me later."

"Okay," Tessa agreed. "I'll meet you on the promenade to watch the skipjack races if I don't see you before that."

"Have fun."

Tessa set off in the direction of the reenactment, leaving Harper to wander the park on her own. She made her way through the crowds, stopping at various tents and stands. She purchased a bracelet made of leather cord and sea glass for Tessa as a thank-you for the past few weeks. She admired the work of local artisans, displaying their talents in a variety of media from carving to watercolors to sculptures. She tasted four different kinds of wine from a nearby winery and complimented them on the quality. She stopped at a demonstration on decoy carving, a time-honored tradition in the Chesapeake region, where decoys were once a booming industry among avid waterfowl hunters. She studied the artist's graceful movements as he painted feathers on a carved decoy, adding life to the inanimate object. She was thinking how easy he made it look with his deft and sure touch when a hand gripped her elbow. She jumped at the touch and turned to see Leah making a face.

"Come on, you can't watch that guy paint ducks all day."

Before she could protest that she was enjoying the display, the younger girl had already tugged her away from the tent and toward Rafael, who was balancing several plastic baskets on his arm.

"Best crab cake sandwich you'll ever eat," he announced as they approached, and he held one of the trays in her direction.

She laughed at his enthusiasm. "That's a pretty bold statement for this area, you know," she teased him. "It seems like every Marylander has a recipe for the best crab cake."

"Yeah, but this place has a secret ingredient."

"Old Bay?" she joked as she gathered the heaping sandwich in her hand. No sensible Maryland resident would even think about eating crab cakes without Old Bay seasoning.

"Of course it has Old Bay," he retorted, "that's not exactly a secret."

Harper took a bite of the sandwich and belatedly realized that Leah was watching her with amusement.

"What?" she asked around a mouth full of seasoned crab and potato roll. She realized what they were waiting for only a second later, as her tongue came alive with heat. Whatever this secret ingredient was, it must have contained a pepper scoring high on the Scoville scale. Her mouth was positively on fire.

"Hot!" she announced as she swallowed and then fanned her tongue. "Hot, hot, hot, hot!"

Rafael and Leah were beside themselves with laughter. Harper's eyes watered.

"Seriously, hot! Bring me milk. *Now!*"

They ignored her, still hooting.

Just then, Erin stepped up and held out a water bottle to her. Though it wouldn't take the heat away like dairy, she was desperate and grabbed it from Erin's hand.

"You should have known better than to trust the two of them," Erin lightly chided as she shifted her son, Kitt, from one arm to the other. "They did that to me two years ago. Now I carry plenty of bottled water with me to this festival every year."

Harper had uncapped the water and drained half the bottle as Erin took the plastic basket from her hand. The liquid barely took away the initial burn, and her tongue still smarted at the lingering heat.

"That is not a secret ingredient," Harper said, "that is a weapon of mass destruction."

Rafael and Leah leaned against each other, laughing anew. Erin shook her head. "The worst part is that you can't even get revenge. They're two peas in a pod and have stomachs made of iron."

To prove Erin's point, both Rafael and Leah picked up their sandwiches and took big bites.

"Mmm, spicy," Rafael declared.

"I don't know, I think it could use some more Tabasco," replied Leah.

Erin rolled her eyes.

"Just watching them makes me want to find some ice cubes to suck on," Harper said.

The group laughed at this.

"You're a good sport, Harper." Rafael nudged her.

"A good sport with a scarred tongue, but thanks, Rafael."

Leah polished off her sandwich and shoved the basket at Rafael. "Okay, now it's time for those tattoos," Leah announced.

"I'm not sure they'll have your style," Harper said. "I mean, do you really think they have any chili pepper tattoos?"

"Ha ha," Leah replied and threaded her arm through Harper's. "Come on, my treat to make up for Rafael's nasty prank."

"Don't you put this all on me, girl!" Rafael called as they wandered away.

Twenty minutes later, Harper left Leah at the high school band's tent. The younger girl had met up with several of her classmates there, so after receiving her tattoo, Harper decided to head off on her own to do more exploring.

Checking her watch, she noted that the skipjack races would be starting soon and decided to head over to the promenade to find Tessa and watch. She stepped off the lawn and onto the boardwalk and dropped her gaze to admire the falling star tattoo she'd just received on her upper arm. At Harper's insistence, Leah had chosen the design, and she had to admit it was the perfect choice. One of Leah's friends had even added a touch of glitter so that the star really looked as though it were falling, trailing a cloud of stardust behind it.

She was so busy concentrating on the star that she would have run right into another pedestrian if a hand hadn't reached out to catch her.

"Whoa, you need to watch where you're going there, love."

She looked up and started as she found herself staring into Connor's amused green eyes.

"I'M SO SORRY," she said and flushed a deep red shade. Was she truly that embarrassed or was his touch causing the blush that stained her cheeks? He removed his hand from her arm, and his fingers nearly ached from the loss of contact.

"It's all right, but you looked like you were in another world." He tilted his head to see what she'd been looking at. "Ah, so you bit the bullet, did you? Let's take a look."

He didn't wait for her to present the tattoo. Instead, he took the opportunity to touch her again by resting his palm beneath her elbow and taking a look at the star on her upper arm.

"Did you pick that out?"

"Leah did," Harper said. He could feel the tension in her arm and reluctantly released her.

"It suits you," he stated.

"Thanks. I kind of like it."

They paused, and Connor rushed to fill the silence.

"Are you enjoying the festival?"

"I am." She made a face. "Well, except for the part where Rafael and Leah convinced me to eat a spiced crab cake sandwich."

He laughed loudly. "You fell for that?" He clucked his tongue. "I'd have thought you knew better by now. Never eat anything that Rafael says contains a secret ingredient."

She cocked her head. "So you've fallen for it, too?"

He grimaced. "Worse. And don't ask because I'm not telling."

This put a smile back on her face, and he couldn't help grinning at the sight. She tried to peer around him.

"Where's Molly?"

"With Rory," he answered. "She's spoiling her more than she should. Every time I turn around, she's given her another sweet. Cookies from the church bake sale. Cotton candy. Saltwater taffy. I think the two of them even snuck a few Smarties from the senior center volunteers when I was talking to the mayor. I worry Rory is out of control."

Harper laughed. "Don't forget Molly got me to promise her a trip to the funnel cake stand."

He groaned and threw his head back. "What's a poor bloke to do?"

"Well, it is a holiday," she reminded him. "And it's an aunt's job to spoil her niece."

He pulled his head forward. "Ah, you're an aunt, too, then?"

"I am," Harper confirmed. "My older sister, Paige, has a daughter, who turned one not too long ago."

"And you spoil her shamelessly?"

"When I can. I don't see Paige and her family very frequently."

"But didn't you say she lives in DC? So you both lived in the same city. How did you not see her more often?"

Harper shrugged. "We were both busy with our careers and stuff."

He moved, leaning against one of the promenade's wooden posts and eyeing Harper. He sensed she didn't want to talk about Paige, so he decided to drop the subject. For now.

She looked past him and straightened, lifting an arm to wave.

"Speaking of sisters, here comes my younger one." He turned to see a young woman with blond hair returning Harper's gesture as she approached.

"Hey, I've been looking for you," the woman said as she reached them.

"Sorry, I meant to come find you," Harper said, "but I ran into my...boss." She gestured toward him.

"Literally," Connor noted. "She really did run into me."

"Don't listen to him," Harper cut in. "He's just giving me a hard time. Connor, this is my sister, Tessa. Tess, this is Connor."

"So you're the Irishman," Tessa observed.

Connor crossed his arms. "That all depends on what you've heard."

Tessa laughed. "Well, if you don't mind, Connor, I promised Harper we'd watch the skipjack race together, and it's going to start any minute."

He was surprised when Harper spoke up, looking at him with something close to wistfulness. "You can join us, if you like." She paused. "That is, unless you were supposed to meet Rory and Molly?"

Connor looked around, wondering where the two of them had gotten to. Rory would be performing later, so maybe she'd taken Molly with her to do a sound check. He wasn't worried as long as they were together.

"I wouldn't want to intrude on you and your sister," he commented, but it was a lie. He'd like nothing more than to watch the race with Harper.

"Oh, we don't mind," Tessa said. "If you're planning to watch the race anyway, then the more the merrier."

And even though Tessa had been the last one to speak, he looked at Harper as he answered, "I'd like that."

HARPER WAS GLAD she'd asked Connor to join them. While Tessa knew a little bit about the skipjack boats, Connor knew far more, and he filled her in as they took their places with the other people lined up along the promenade to catch the race.

"They were oyster boats," Connor explained as they waited for the race to get underway. "Skipjacks were introduced in the late nineteenth century as a fast, light boat to dredge the shallow bay waters for oysters. They were easy and cheap to build, and at their peak, there were something like two thousand of them in existence. Now it's around thirty or less."

"What happened?" Harper asked. "Why are there so few of them left?" She was doing her best to concentrate on Connor's words but found it difficult when he would lean in, his shoulder brushing against hers. The breeze off the water shifted his scent her way, and she savored how he smelled of peppermint and sunshine.

"The oyster boom died off at the beginning of the twentieth century, and the ships were no longer used. They made a bit of a comeback after World War II when oyster prices rose, but the market soon fell again. Now their heritage is mostly kept alive through a couple of museums and races like this one. All the ships you see out there are original skipjacks, lovingly restored to preserve the heritage of the past."

Harper watched as the single-masted vessels edged away from the marina and out onto the bay, gliding across the choppy waters with slow purpose. The white canvas of their sails stood out sharply against the cloudless blue of the sky, their hulls riding high upon the silvery gray water.

"How did they get their name?"

"From the bluefish, which is also called a skipjack. It's said they resemble a fish when they skip back and forth over the water, making their licks."

"Licks?"

"That's what it's called when the ships pass over the oyster beds."

She admired the graceful way the skipjacks skimmed along the bay, their sails taking the breeze that helped propel them toward the shore.

"They're beautiful," she remarked, more to herself than Connor, but he heard and nodded.

"They are indeed. Dad always loved them. He hoped to buy one when he retired and restore it to its former glory."

She tore her gaze from the race to look at him. He was staring out at the water, and he didn't seem bothered by the memory.

"I wish he could have lived to make that dream a reality," she remarked.

He turned his head, catching her eyes in his. He seemed startled at this sentiment from her.

"Aye," he murmured, his words nearly lost in the breeze. "I wish that, too."

"He must have been a pretty special man to have raised you and your sister single-handedly."

Connor dipped his head in acknowledgment. "That he was. Sometimes, when I'm feeling completely out of my depth with Molly, I think of the challenges he faced—coming to the States and starting over with two young children. Building his business and trying to raise us on his own. Not to mention how he grieved over the loss of my mom."

Harper tucked a strand of hair behind her ear as a surge of wind swept by. "If you don't mind my asking…how did she die?"

"Breast cancer," he responded, his tone matter-of-fact.

"It must have been very difficult, for all of you."

"It was. But worse for Dad, I think. He loved her so well that he didn't ever really heal from her loss. He never looked at another woman the way he looked at her."

"So there was no one else after he left Ireland?"

Connor shook his head. "No one. He didn't even date, though I'm sure there were women who would have been interested. He wasn't a bad-looking man." Connor grinned, but it soon evaporated. "Sometimes, I think he left Ireland because of her death."

"What do you mean?"

He gave a little shrug. "I wonder if it was too difficult to be there, without her. Like maybe he needed to start fresh where there were fewer reminders of their life together."

"That's both terribly sad and very romantic."

He nodded his agreement. "I asked him about it once—why he chose to move to America. He just said it was the right thing to do, and I never got any more out of him than that. So I've always suspected his grief played a large part in his decision."

"Do you have family still, in Ireland?"

"We do. Some cousins, and an aunt on my dad's side. A few extended relatives. We exchange the occasional email and such, and Dad used to ring up his sister a few times a year before he passed. We stay in touch, but we're not extremely close. Rory calls our aunt now and again. I think it helps her to have a female relative she can reach out to. It was difficult for her, growing up without our mom. Her struggles when she was younger make me acutely aware that Molly doesn't have a mother in her life."

He looked away following this admission, as though embarrassed to have revealed such a personal detail. Harper flicked a glance at the skipjack race to check the progress. Beside her, Tessa had fallen into conversation with someone she apparently knew. From the few words she caught, it sounded as though they were discussing races from previous years.

"Do you ever miss it?" Harper asked as she turned her attention back to Connor. "Ireland, I mean?"

He considered the question. "It's not that I miss it, exactly. But it's a part of me. It was difficult to reconcile that for a while—to embrace being born Irish but raised in America. When we first moved here, Rory and I had some trouble fitting in. It made us close, but it also was a challenge to establish a sense of identity. Dad was a great help with that, though. He encouraged us to embrace our Irish roots while establishing American ones."

"Well, I'm glad," Harper said. "There's something special about having a dual heritage like that."

He looked thoughtful, then nodded. "I suppose there is." His gaze fastened on her face, searching her features for the span of several breaths. She didn't look away.

"You have…"

He lifted his hand, as though he was going

to touch her cheek. She lowered her head self-consciously.

"Here." He tipped her chin back up and then touched his index finger in a featherlight touch to the bridge of her nose. "An eyelash."

He pulled his hand back so that she saw it resting on his finger.

"Aren't you supposed to make a wish now?" he prompted. "That's what Molly says is the thing to do with eyelashes."

Harper nodded at this suggestion. "Sure. I suppose so."

"Well then?"

She closed her eyes, not forming her wish into words but rather just a feeling of happiness for this perfect day and the comfort of this moment with Connor. She opened her eyes and then blew the eyelash from the tip of his finger.

When she looked at him once more, she noticed he had moved closer, his head tilted toward hers. For a moment, she thought he just might kiss her again. His gaze was fastened on her lips, and she felt herself leaning into him.

And then the intimacy was shattered as people around them broke into cheers, whistles and clapping. She and Connor jerked apart and looked out on the bay as the lead ship reached the opposite shore and won the race.

When she looked back at Connor, she noticed he had put a little more distance between them.

FOLLOWING THE SKIPJACK RACE, Connor, Harper and Tessa wandered the festival, trying different foods, playing a few carnival games, shopping different craft and artisan stands and generally enjoying themselves. Rory and Molly caught up to them, and Molly immediately demanded Harper fulfill her promise of a funnel cake. Connor didn't try to stop them. It warmed him to watch Harper and his daughter stroll away, hand in hand, to the funnel cake stand and return with powdered sugar coating their lips. Harper brought back two more funnel cakes to share, and he was gratified to see Rory make an effort to be gracious where Harper was concerned. He knew she had struggled with the idea of Harper as someone other than a spiteful restaurant critic, but he was pleased that she seemed to be thawing slightly in that regard.

When his sister left them to head to the concert stage and perform her final sound check, he invited Harper and Tessa to join him and

Molly as they walked to her performance. They agreed, so the four of them made their way to the concert stand at the other end of the park.

Erin had made sure to stake out a good spot for the lot of them early on in the day, so he and Molly, Harper, Rafael and Leah were all able to line up near the front to watch. They managed to squeeze Tessa in as well, and Erin was happy to hand Kitt into Tessa's capable arms.

Connor was soon distracted as Rory's name was announced. He whistled so loudly when she appeared onstage that she immediately found him in the crowd and waved a hand in his direction. He clapped in reply and gave her two thumbs-up. As a local girl, she was one of the most popular acts at the festival, and the tiered seats in front of the stage were crowded with people who had come to watch her perform.

Those in the crowd who knew Rory cheered every bit as loudly as Connor, and those who didn't realized they must be in for something special and joined in so that the entire concert area thundered with applause.

Rory waited patiently for the deafening greeting to fade. Connor couldn't help noticing a tenseness about her shoulders, one he couldn't remember seeing the last time he'd watched her perform. She'd always seemed at home onstage, comfortable with her music and confident in herself. It appeared that some of that poise had diminished now that Sawyer no longer stood beside her. He felt a pang of sadness at the realization as well as a flash of irritation that Sawyer had dumped her as he had. Connor could relate to that feeling of abandonment after the way Chloe had left him and Molly. He wished he could have spared Rory similar pain. In the few days she'd been back home, she'd seemed a little...lost. He could only hope it was a state that improved with time.

"Daddy! Lift me up so I can see!" Molly was already standing on her seat and seemed to have a good view of the stage, but he indulged her and lifted her into his arms. His eyes caught Harper's as he hoisted Molly higher, and she grinned. She appeared to be enjoying herself, and he was glad of it. It had been fun to watch the skipjack race together and share a bit of cultural history from the area. And though he'd never say it aloud, he had to admit that half his pleasure had come from watching the interest that lit up her eyes as she admired the ships gliding over the bay and the way she kept leaning in his direction to catch whatever he had to say.

Now he watched her as she joined in with the rest of the crowd clapping for Rory.

"Thank you, thank you," Rory was saying from the stage as she raised a hand to silence the crowd. Connor shifted his attention in her direction.

"You all certainly know how to make a girl feel special."

The crowd laughed, and Connor felt a swell of pride. Rory had a way of charming people with her onstage persona. She and Sawyer used to banter back and forth until an audience was shouting for more, entertained by their dialogue as much as their music.

"It's good to be back home," Rory went on. "Sometimes, when I'm on tour, I forget the little things that make Findlay Roads special. Like the colors of the sunset over the bay. There's a fantastic view of it from the deck of my brother's restaurant, the Rusty Anchor. You can sit there at dusk, listen to the ducks and watch the entire skyline turn shades of amethyst and topaz."

He grinned, noting how Rory was trying to gain him a little free publicity by mentioning the restaurant. Harper leaned in to whisper, "Oh, she's good."

He nodded. "And you haven't even heard her sing yet," he quietly replied.

Another smattering of applause rippled through the audience.

"We are truly blessed to live along the Chesapeake. I've traveled all over the nation, and I can promise you that this is still one of the most beautiful places on earth."

There were a few cheers from the crowd. Rory began to strum her guitar, effortlessly checking to be sure it was in tune and ready for her first song as she continued to speak.

"One of the things I like best about Findlay Roads is that it was founded by an Irishman. Donal Findlay came over before the start of the French and Indian War and brought his entire family with him. They settled this area, and old man Findlay's descendants have been a rich part of this town's history, participating in the Revolution, the War of 1812 and even ferrying slaves across the bay so they could escape to Canada and find their freedom."

She was nearly warmed up now, and Connor recognized the opening minor chords of an old Irish folk song, "Lanigan's Ball."

"So, in honor of Findlay Roads' founder, I'd

like to dedicate this first song to the descendants of Donal Findlay."

And then she was off, her fingers flying over the strings, her voice clear and sharp as she dashed through the lyrics, singing the song of Jeremy Lanigan, who threw a party with bacon, cakes, potatoes and tea after coming into his inheritance. It was a lively tune with minor chords, and Rory's energetic performance soon had the entire crowd clapping in rhythm with her guitar.

Connor shifted Molly in his arms and glanced at Harper. She was clapping along with the rest and swaying from side to side in tempo with the music. Her cheeks were flushed with excitement, her mouth stretched in a wide smile. And Connor suddenly wondered what it would be like if it were always this way—Harper beside him, a part of him, permanently woven into his heart, his life. Molly liked her—after she'd gotten over her initial mistrust, she'd gradually warmed to her. Now, her eyes lit up whenever Harper came into a room. She was still trying to play it cool, Connor noticed, by not seeming too eager for Harper's attention. But he hadn't failed to observe how often she gravitated in Harper's direction when she was nearby. Though Rory had distracted her for the past few days, he still knew Molly was forming an attachment.

Was that something he wanted to have happen? After all, he didn't know what the future held. And he didn't want Molly becoming too fond of someone who might leave her, as Chloe had done. But Harper seemed to love this town, and she'd said she planned to stick around for a time. What if that future could include him?

But then there was still the Anchor to consider. He wasn't exactly what a woman might think of as a "catch." Between trying to keep the restaurant afloat and the hours demanded of him as chef and restaurateur, how could he find time to invest in a relationship? Besides, he should be focusing his efforts on saving his restaurant, not romance. If he didn't start bringing in more business, he was going to lose everything. He had to at least try to turn things around. That should be his priority right now, not his interest in Harper.

But still, he couldn't completely ignore his growing attraction to her. He wanted to keep her close to him, get to know her even better.

She looked at him then as Rory strummed into the final stanza of the song. Whatever expression he had on his face, it caused her to immediately stop clapping, her eyes turning serious. She reached out, her hand coming to rest on his. Molly was swaying in his arms as she joined the rest of the crowd in cheering Rory toward the finish.

The feel of Harper's fingers on his hand was electric, her touch making his skin tingle. He leaned down, his forehead nearly resting on hers.

"Harper," he murmured, not even sure she could hear him amid the noise.

But she must have because he saw her lips move slightly in question. "Yes?"

"I…" He didn't know how to find the words, didn't even know if this was the right time or place.

And before he could decide how to give voice to his feelings, he became aware of a shift in the crowd's mood. In another heart-beat, he realized Rory had stopped playing. Not that she'd finished the song, but that it had abruptly cut off. He didn't want to turn away. Harper was looking at him, her eyes intent on his, willing him to continue.

Then he heard it. Someone calling his name. And words that rippled through the crowd, dousing his longing for Harper and bringing him sharply back to reality.

The Rusty Anchor was on fire.

CHAPTER EIGHT

THE FIRE MARSHAL had yet to make an official determination, but the general consensus was that an electrical short in the restaurant kitchen had caused the conflagration. Connor explained he'd been hoping to upgrade the kitchen and install a new sprinkler system at the restaurant, but lack of funds had caused him to put it off. He'd had no idea there was a short in the wiring, and Harper could tell by the haggard guilt lining his face, that he would never forgive himself for the oversight.

Because most of the fire department had been working the festival, the response time wasn't quite what it should have been. Fortunately, however, most of the damage had been restricted to the kitchen. The dining room, deck and apartment on the second floor had escaped relatively unscathed. But sections of the back, including a large portion of Connor's office, were charred black with layers of ash coating most of the equipment.

Harper could tell by the way Connor hugged his daughter to him, that he was thinking, as she was, how much more devastating the incident might have been had they all not been attending the festival. If anyone had been inside the building, if Molly had been there…it didn't bear thinking about.

Molly clung to her father, her arms wrapped tightly around his neck as he surveyed the damage. Though the upstairs apartment remained intact, the fire marshal decided Connor and Molly couldn't stay there until the structural integrity of the floors and ceiling could be assessed. At this news, Erin spoke up, offering to let Connor, Molly and Rory come and stay at Gavin's great-aunt's bed-and-breakfast, the Moontide Inn, for as long as necessary.

Molly began to cry at this news, and Rory moved in to try to take her out of Connor's arms. But the little girl resisted, gripping her dad all the tighter as tears rolled down her cheeks. Connor shifted away, holding Molly to him, and Rory gave up. Erin said something to Rory and then wrapped her in a hug as they moved a few steps away.

Harper hung back, uncertain whether she should be at Connor's side or give him his space. She ached at the ill fortune that seemed to follow him like an inescapable storm cloud. Whoever had coined the phrase "luck of the Irish" had clearly never met the Callahan family.

As the fire marshal approached Connor once more, he tried to put Molly down, but she squirmed, clinging to him as she cried out in protest. Her frustrated sobs propelled Harper forward. She didn't really expect Molly to let go of her father, but as soon as the little girl saw Harper, she stopped struggling and reached out her arms. Connor looked startled at her sudden calm, and he willingly passed Molly into Harper's embrace with a grateful nod. He turned to speak to the marshal, and Harper carried Molly a few feet away, out onto the docks and away from the onlookers and firefighters.

Harper waited to see if Molly would speak, but when the little girl remained silent, Harper didn't push her to talk. She set her on her feet, and they walked hand in hand down the dock before settling onto the wooden boards. Molly dangled her legs over the pier and lowered her head as she sniffled. Harper sat beside her and rubbed soothing circles on her back as the tears gradually receded.

The late afternoon was waning toward early evening, and the golden summer sunshine had blurred to a deeper bronze. With the sun's gradual descent, the air had cooled, and the evening heat was tempered by the pleasant breeze off the bay. Harper continued to run her palm along Molly's back until the child relaxed and even leaned into Harper, sagging against her with a sigh.

She mumbled something that Harper didn't catch. Leaning over, Harper placed her cheek against the crown of Molly's head.

"What did you say?" she asked.

Molly sniffed. "Does this mean we can't live above the restaurant anymore?"

Harper didn't want to lie to Molly. She didn't know what this tragedy meant for Connor and the restaurant, but she recognized it didn't bode well for him.

"Not for a little while at least," she chose her answer carefully. "But you'll get to stay with Erin and Kitt for a few days. That will be fun, won't it? Sort of like a sleepover."

Molly shrugged and swung her legs with more force, back and forth over the dock's edge. Harper sensed this wasn't the only thing on her mind.

"I know it seems pretty scary, but everything's going to be all right. You know that, don't you?"

Molly turned to her with puffy eyes, her cheek still stained with the tracks of her tears. Her little nose was pink from her sniffles, and her lips quivered slightly. "Will they take the restaurant away now?"

Harper felt a prick to her conscience with this question, even though the restaurant fire had nothing to do with her. She supposed it was the idea that, even if Connor kept the Anchor following this tragedy, he'd likely have to give it up at summer's end. And then, if all went according to plan, she'd step in and purchase it for herself. How would Molly feel about that? She treasured the tentative relationship she'd formed with Connor's daughter and hated the thought of Molly seeing her as some sort of bad guy.

"Molly. Listen to me." She looked into Molly's face and held her eyes. "You don't need to worry about that. You're just a little girl. Let your dad take care of that stuff, okay?"

Though Harper tried to hold Molly's gaze, she dropped her eyes and toyed with a stray thread on the hem of her shorts.

"But I heard him talking to Aunt Rory. He said the bank's going to take the restaurant away from us unless he can pay thousands and thousands of dollars."

Harper felt a deep ache for the child. It was tough to be a kid, knowing there were problems in your family and feeling unable to do anything about them.

"Oh, Molly." She wrapped her arms around Molly's shoulders. The little girl scooted closer and crawled onto Harper's lap, clearly needing to be comforted. "Maybe you should talk to your dad. Tell him how concerned you are."

Molly shook her head. "He'll just say little girls shouldn't worry about grown-up things. That's a daddy's job."

Molly might be right. That did sound like something Connor would say to reassure his daughter. She wondered if she should mention Molly's fears to him and see if he could help her understand. Harper didn't want to betray the child's confidence, but shouldn't Connor know his daughter was aware of the situation? Then again, speaking to Connor would alert him that she knew the Anchor was in trouble. Harper hugged Molly tighter.

"Well, what would you do, if you could help your dad with the restaurant?" she asked, hoping to redirect Molly's thoughts.

"I'd open a lemonade stand," she promptly

answered, obviously having put some thought into this already. "And I'd give all the money I made to Daddy, so he could keep the restaurant."

Harper ran her palm over Molly's forehead, brushing back her hair. "That's a wonderful idea, Molly, but I'm not sure it would be enough."

"But Billy Stevens has a lemonade stand, and he said he made hundreds of dollars!"

Harper didn't know whether to laugh at this childlike logic or weep for how much Molly didn't understand.

"I think Billy Stevens might be exaggerating things a bit."

She stole a glance at Molly's face and saw her frowning sadly.

"But I think you're a very generous girl, to want to give that money to your dad. You love him a lot, don't you?"

Molly nodded.

"And I know he loves you, too. More than anything else in the world."

Molly burrowed deeper into Harper's midsection and wrapped her arms around Harper's waist. They rocked back and forth on the dock for a long time. Harper stroked Molly's back until the little girl relaxed, becoming lethargic in her arms. She didn't know how much time passed, but the sun gradually dipped toward the horizon. Molly's breathing became even, and Harper realized the little girl had fallen asleep in her arms. She felt a rush of maternal affection for this child. Though she'd never considered herself to be good with kids and had doubted she'd ever have children of her own, Molly had made her rethink such assumptions. Her experiences over the past few weeks made her wonder about motherhood and whether it was something she wanted, after all.

Or maybe it wasn't just the idea of motherhood. Maybe it was Molly herself. In spite of the initial clashes between them, Connor's daughter had worked her way into Harper's heart. From her frizzy braids to the way she looked at Harper sometimes, so like her father, Harper felt a deepening affection for the little girl. And she had to admit that when Molly had reached for her, something in Harper had opened up, as if she'd been waiting for Molly to need her in just this way. Now, rocking the child in her arms, she allowed herself to imagine that Molly was her daughter, that the three of them were a family. The thought flooded her with warmth, a feeling of belonging to someone else, of being connected and embraced.

She didn't allow herself to dwell on this dream for too long. She feared that if she did, returning to reality would be that much harder. And return she must. She couldn't risk all her plans for a temporary infatuation. She wasn't that kind of girl. She'd been raised to always keep the end goal in sight. And despite any damage resulting from the fire, Harper was determined to resurrect the Anchor and make it her own. That was the true prize.

Connor was a lovely daydream, but that's all he could ever be. Because she knew, in her heart of hearts, he would never be content to work for her once she owned the Anchor. Just as she knew that she couldn't give up her plans for the possibility of a summer romance.

Unless…what if she and Connor could find a way to work together? Maybe all they needed was a common goal, such as saving the Anchor. Perhaps they could become partners, rebuild from the fire? She felt a swell of excitement. It could solve everything—she'd still have her piece of the restaurant, and Connor could hold on to his dream. They could have a future together. If her father lined up the investors…

At this thought, her runaway daydream came to a screeching halt. Her father would never approve of investing in the Anchor as it was right now. Especially not after this fire and the damage it had likely caused.

There would have to be changes, a fresh start and innovative business plan, before it could be considered a viable venture. Could Connor commit to the necessary evolution of his business? Or would he dismiss such suggestions from her as interference?

Proposing they team up could very well drive a wedge between them.

Was she willing to risk that? And even if he was agreeable, what if they failed? Would he blame her if their partnership flopped, just as he'd blamed her for tainting his first restaurant with her review? She couldn't bear to have Connor think she was meddling or trying to undermine him. She suspected his pride wouldn't allow for her stepping in.

No, it was a bad idea. He may have forgiven her for her critique, and they may have become friends bordering on something more. But that's all they could ever be. Hiring her as an employee was one thing but becoming partners? He would never agree to it.

She might as well get used to the fact that

there could never be anything else between her and Connor.

So, sadly, Harper closed her thoughts to these feelings. But even her body seemed to protest at this as her legs fell asleep with Molly in her lap, and she let them go numb rather than risk moving the little girl.

And though she told herself she had to place some emotional distance between herself and the child in her arms, to safeguard both their hearts from disappointment, she also knew that wasn't likely to happen.

IT SEEMED AS though it was hours later when Harper spotted Connor coming down the dock toward her. She still held a sleeping Molly in her lap, so as much as she wanted to stand and go to him, she remained seated as he approached. She watched as he drew near, his dark hair mussed and his face grave. Though the sun had dipped over the horizon, the glow of the moon and the lights along the harbor allowed her to see him clearly. She thought he would gather Molly in his arms to take her away, but she was surprised when he sank down onto the pier beside her.

He looked at her before his eyes settled on

Molly. Harper didn't move. They sat in silence for a few minutes until Connor spoke.

"Thanks for taking care of her," he said, his voice heavy with the strain of the past few hours.

"You're welcome," she replied, the words nearly catching in her throat. How she wanted to draw him into her arms, as she'd done with Molly, and kiss away the lines of stress carved around his eyes. But since she couldn't, she chose to give him the option to unburden himself. "What's the damage like?"

He sighed, and in that sound, she heard every ounce of the weight he carried.

"It's not too bad but…bad enough. It'll be at least six weeks until I can reopen, probably longer."

"You have insurance, right?"

"Oh, sure, it will cover the costs to rebuild the kitchen, but…" He trailed off, and Harper waited, not wanting to push him but rather hoping he'd open up to her on his own. He caught her eyes with his, and she felt her pulse speed up at the intensity there.

"The Anchor is mortgaged to its rafters. My dad used the money to pay for my schooling, and it's been a rough go to make the payments each month. All of his dreams for me, for this place…" He glanced over his shoulder and then turned back, looking past her and out over the water. "He should have known better than to gamble his legacy on me. I don't think I have what it takes."

Harper could understand how he felt, in a way. She'd always thought her dad must have known Paige was a safer investment. She would follow in their father's footsteps and make him proud. But Harper? She was a risk. She didn't have Paige's talents or her efficiency or even her sharp intelligence. All she had was a way with words and a love of food.

"Connor, please don't talk like that," she found herself saying. "Your dad believed in you. From everything you've told me, the things he did were about love, not his legacy."

Connor dropped his stare to the dock's boards. "Well, it doesn't matter now, does it?"

"Of course it matters," she softly replied. "Love like that always matters."

He raised his head again and looked at her.

"You realize you're out of a job, don't you?"

She blinked. That thought hadn't occurred to her. She'd been so concerned for Connor and Molly that she hadn't considered how the situation at the Anchor might affect her. She felt a ripple of dismay. She wouldn't be able to go into work each day and see Connor. There would be no more pretend restaurant games with Molly, no banter between her and Rafael. Leah wouldn't trail after her, asking questions about living in the city, and she wouldn't get to tease Erin for how much she talked about her son and husband. Obviously, she could still see each of them but not like she did now.

She hoped, if she was able to reopen the restaurant one day, that they'd all come work for her. But then it would be different. She'd be the boss instead of Connor. They'd be her employees and not her coworkers. And that was if they even chose to stay. What if they didn't like the idea of her taking over the Anchor? What if they quit when it no longer belonged to Connor?

And on the heels of all this, she realized she'd probably have to find another job to carry her until she purchased the Anchor. That was, provided she could secure the necessary investors.

Her head began to pound until she felt a reverberation deep within her eardrums. Seconds later, she realized the echoing boom she'd felt was not the start of a major headache but rather the beginning of the fireworks display that would wrap up the Independence Day Festival.

As sparks of color bloomed across the sky, the dull explosions woke Molly from her sleep. She sat up and blinked at the streaks of red, white and blue that filled the expanse above them, but then her face glowed with awe. Harper gave herself over to the moment and let her eyes wander upward to soak in the sparkling displays. The three of them sat in silence, watching as flashes ignited throughout the night. She soaked it in, refusing to think about what would happen tomorrow or a week from now or at summer's end. For now, she was content to hold Molly in her arms and feel Connor's warmth beside her.

After several long minutes, she finally dropped her eyes and realized that while she and Molly had been enjoying the fireworks, Connor had been studying her. They locked eyes and held each other's gaze as the light cast shadows of red and blue across his features, adding to the lines of strain he wore from the day's events. He was looking at her thoughtfully, as if he had something quite serious on his mind.

Eventually she couldn't bear his open perusal any longer, and she turned away. Part of her willed him to speak, to offer her some clue about his thoughts. But he remained mute as the roar of fireworks filled up the silence between them and reverberated in the hollow space of her heart.

ON SUNDAY AFTERNOON, the Rusty Anchor staff met in the dining room of the Moontide Inn to learn Connor's plans for the future. They gathered around the large oval table where Erin had laid out a modest spread of coffee and scones. After Connor had called Harper to tell her about the meeting that morning, she'd immediately set to work on a batch of cookies to add to Erin's refreshments. Now she sat with a scone on her plate and a cup of coffee at hand as Connor looked around the table.

Rory was watching Molly and Kitt while Aunt Lenora, the B and B's proprietress, was taking a nap after seeing off the last of her guests that morning. The inn had experienced a full house thanks to the Independence Day Festival and at seventy-two, Lenora had earned an afternoon break. Rory and Molly had bunked with Erin the night before while Connor had been forced to take a couch in the private living room. But now that the guests had cleared out, they'd each be given their own room. Erin had shared all this seemingly in an effort to dispel the thick cloud of uncertainty that hovered in the room as they settled into their chairs.

"Thank you all for coming today," Connor began. "And, Erin, I want to again offer my thanks to you and Lenora, not only for putting up Rory, Molly and me for a while but for giving us the use of the dining room for this meeting."

"That's what friends are for," she assured him.

Harper watched Connor carefully as he spoke, checking to see if an evening's rest had done him any good. He looked a bit more refreshed than he had when they'd parted ways the night before, but there was a thicker layer of stubble than usual shadowing his jaw and his eyes were faintly pink, perhaps from sleeplessness?

"It looks like the Anchor will be closed indefinitely until the necessary repairs to the kitchen have been made."

"What do you mean...indefinitely?" asked Leah. "Will we be open again before the summer ends?"

Connor scratched the back of his neck, keeping his face lowered. Harper felt herself tense in the long silence before he replied, "It's not likely."

His answer served to make the silence that followed feel even weightier as they all absorbed what this meant. The Anchor had already been in precarious straits before, and without the summer income, there was absolutely no way it could survive through the off-season. Though Harper knew it was unlikely Connor could have pulled together the money required by the bank, this loss of revenue was a double blow. Even if the others didn't know about the impending foreclosure, hearing that the restaurant would be closed throughout the season brought the grim reality of the Anchor's demise to the forefront of all their thoughts.

"Does that mean…" Leah trailed off, unable to voice the thought aloud.

Connor didn't flinch. "I'm meeting with the insurance company tomorrow. I'll know more then." He drew a breath. "In the meantime, I have to advise you each to look for other jobs. If there's any way I can help you—reference letters or phone calls, please let me know. I'll do whatever I can to assist you."

His cool formality made Harper want to cry. Already, this tight-knit group she'd come to love seemed to be growing apart. She appreciated how Connor had offered to do what he could for his employees, but she wished he wasn't behaving so distantly. But then, she couldn't imagine how difficult this must be for him—to tell them all to look for other work. She imagined his aloofness was a defense mechanism to help him hold it together.

"Don't worry about us, Bossman," Rafael said. "We'll land on our feet."

Harper crumbled her scone into bite-size pieces, needing to do something with her hands to distract herself from staring at Connor.

"And when the Anchor reopens, we'll be ready to go back to work," Leah declared. Though this statement was brimming with optimism and loyalty, it only served to dampen Harper's mood even further.

Connor remained silent after this declaration until all eyes were on him. Harper wondered if the rest of them had the same sense of impending doom.

"While I appreciate that sentiment, Leah, more than you can imagine, I have to inform you all…" He hesitated, and Harper started when his eyes fell directly on her. "It is unlikely the Anchor will be reopening under my ownership."

At first, they were so quiet so that the only sound in the room was the measured tick of the grandfather clock in the corner. Connor's eyes finally moved from her face and to each of the other members of his staff. After nearly sixty clicks from the clock, Erin, Rafael and Leah began speaking all at once, their voices layering over one another so that Harper could only make out fragments of what they were saying.

"—if it comes to that—"

"—have more faith in—"

"—we could always try—"

In the midst of their dialogue, Connor's gaze sought hers once more. The sadness buried deep in his eyes was almost more than she could bear. She wanted to say something, but she knew she wouldn't be heard above her friends. And besides, what was there to say?

Don't worry, Connor, I'm going to buy your restaurant as soon as you fold, and everything will be okay.

Not likely. She shuddered to imagine his response. What if he hated her for this? Was losing Connor's affection worth the fulfillment of a childhood wish? But then, it wasn't as if the two of them were in a relationship. They'd danced on the fringes of attraction, but no commitments had been made. And after their kiss, he'd seemed happy to keep things as they were. It would be foolish to risk her heart and dreams on a man who might not have feelings for her at all.

She purposely looked away from him. Seconds later, he spoke again, raising his voice to be heard over the arguments the others were still bandying about.

"The Anchor is going under," he practically shouted.

Silence followed this ear-ringing announcement. Harper kept her eyes fastened on the crumbled remains of her uneaten scone, but she could tell the others were staring at Connor.

"With how slow business has been the past two years, I fell behind in the mortgage payments. The bank declared I'd have to put ten thousand dollars against the loan by summer's end or the restaurant would go into foreclosure. I had little hope of raising that kind of money in the next couple of months, but now I don't have a prayer. So unless a miracle happens, I'm going to have to turn everything over to the bank."

"Oh, Connor," breathed Erin. Harper stole a glance at her face and saw the anguish there. She was obviously devastated for her boss and friend.

"Isn't there anything we can do?" Leah asked. "Can't you take out another loan or something?"

"It's unlikely I'd be approved given the situation. I've already refinanced multiple times. I had hoped, with the town's increased tourism, that things would turn around eventually. It was wishful thinking, I suppose."

"Nah, man," said Rafael. "You were holding on to the dream. There's no shame in that."

Connor cleared his throat. "Aye. Well, there it is. It pains me to think that this is our last time together as a team, but I fear that may well be the case."

Harper fidgeted in her seat. Part of her wanted to speak up and tell them her plans, give them the hope that they could still work together. But she didn't dare.

Following these last words from Connor, a gloomy pall fell over the room.

"We're not giving up, Connor," Erin suddenly said. "And neither should you. I won't lose hope until you sign it over for good. And until that happens, I'm going to keep the faith that things will turn around, and the Anchor will become the place your father always dreamed you'd make it."

Harper couldn't help but admire the fierce determination Erin exhibited. She was the kind of friend everyone needed—the one who wouldn't give up on you even when you gave up on yourself.

"Erin, I appreciate that, but I think—"

She waved away whatever he was about to say. "Oh, I know. I'm daft or a blithering eejit or whatever it is you want to call me." Leah snickered at Erin's Irish accent as she mimicked how Connor sounded saying these words. "But I don't care. We're behind you, Connor. All of us. So while I appreciate your offer to help us find other jobs, you also need to let *us* know what we can do for *you*."

Harper didn't think Connor was the sort of man to become emotional in front of others. The occasional feelings she'd seen from him, when speaking about his dad or his failed marriage, were rare glimpses into his very heart. But now she noticed that he struggled to contain his reaction, his jaw working furiously following Erin's speech.

"I second what Erin said," said Rafael.

"And me," Leah added.

Harper felt awkward, given her own plans, but she agreed with the rest of them. As much as she wanted her own restaurant, she also wished the very best for Connor. She wasn't lying when she said, "Me, too."

Though each of them had voiced their support for their boss, she was the one Connor looked at.

"Okay," he said and then leaned back in his chair. His eyes were still resting on her face until she felt his perusal was just a little too obvious, and she had to look away. Did he doubt her sincerity? Was that why he was watching her so intently? Or was it something else?

"The fact still remains that I can't pay you anything while the Anchor's kitchen is being rebuilt."

Rafael spoke up first. "Don't sweat it. I'm sure I can pick up some shifts around town. Plus, my food truck buddies said they've been working like crazy. I bet they can give me some hours."

"And I don't really need to work," offered Leah. "I can just take the rest of the summer off and spend it with my friends. It'll be a nice excuse to slack off."

They all looked at Erin, who shrugged. "Lenora's been working pretty hard with the B and B. It doesn't get a lot of business through the week, but the weekends have been filled up. She'd probably appreciate it if I helped out a little more."

That only left Harper. She didn't have the solutions the others did, but she tried to appear optimistic. "I'll figure something out. I don't think Tessa plans to kick me out anytime soon." She chuckled, but from the corner of her eye, she noticed Connor frown.

"See?" Erin said. "There's no need to worry about us. You just concentrate on doing what you need to do in order to get the Anchor back up and running."

Harper didn't think Connor looked quite convinced, but he nodded anyway.

"All right." Erin got to her feet. "Now, there's still a bunch of leftovers from breakfast the past two days, so if the scones and cookies didn't fill you up, let's head into the kitchen, and everyone can grab a plate. Rory can bring the kids in, too."

Rafael and Leah stood as well, bantering with each other as Erin led the way out of the dining room. Harper didn't rise. Neither did Connor. They sat in silence until the others disappeared through the door.

"You haven't said much," Connor noted.

She looked his way, uncertain how to respond to this.

"I'm really sorry, about your job. I wish…" he trailed off, leaving her wondering what he'd been about to say.

"It's okay," she finally said, when it became evident he wasn't going to finish his thought. "It's not your fault, after all. And I'll be all right."

She was worried about him and Molly, more than anything, but she didn't speak this thought aloud.

"Harper, I…" He looked thoughtful. "I want you to know that despite how things started off between us, I've really enjoyed working with you." He met her eyes, and she nearly shivered at the seriousness in his expression. "It's been a pleasure."

"I… I feel the same way," she admitted.

"You've been good for Molly, too. Thank you for the attention you've paid her. It can be difficult, at times, since she hasn't had a mother figure in her life. She doesn't always behave as she should. But you've been so kind to her, helping with that pretend restaurant of hers and especially sitting with her yesterday, after the fire. You really seemed to lift her spirits."

These compliments warmed her. "She's a sweet girl. You should be proud of her. Even without a mom, you're doing a wonderful job raising her."

His expression softened. "Thank you," he quietly murmured. "If I do lose the restaurant, it will be hard on her. It's the only home she remembers, and there are so many memories for her there with her grandfather and all. When the bank forecloses." He paused and corrected himself. "*If* that should happen, I hope…" He swallowed. "Well, you seem to know just how to comfort her. So if we lose the restaurant… I wondered if you could talk to her about it and help her understand?" He rushed ahead before she could answer. "Of course, I'll speak to her first and encourage her that things will be all right. But she looks up to you, and I just thought…well, that talking to you about it might soften the blow a bit."

Harper's breath caught at this request. It meant so much that Connor would ask such a thing of her. She should tell him, she knew. She should let him know what she was planning. Better for him to hear it from her now than to find out later.

But she imagined his reaction, thinking of how his expression would change from one of affection to betrayal. She feared he wouldn't be asking any favors from her where Molly was concerned if he knew she'd try to take over the Anchor after it was no longer his. And besides, what if none of it panned out anyway? She'd have angered him for nothing.

"Harper?"

His voice cut through her thoughts, bringing her sharply back to attention.

"Of course," she automatically answered his question. "I'll do whatever I can."

She left the rest of her thoughts unspoken.

If you can forgive me when you find out my plans for the Anchor.

ON SUNDAY EVENING, Harper gave her business proposal a final polish and decided that rather than emailing it to her father, she'd deliver it personally to his office. She didn't arrange an appointment but rather set out for DC on Monday morning without informing him of her intentions. She feared that if she alerted him she was coming, he'd want to make it a family affair and include Paige. She didn't think she was quite ready to face both her father and her sister at once. She knew she risked a long wait and the possibility of him being out of the office, but she decided to take the chance rather than tip her hand.

Luck, as it turned out, was on her side. When the secretary learned who Harper was, she put an immediate call in to her father, who had some free time before lunch. Her good fortune continued when her father came out to greet her, gushing his pleasure at her unannounced visit but regretfully informing her that Paige was out for the day.

She was ushered into her father's office as he directed his secretary to bring some refreshments. Harper tried to explain that it wouldn't be necessary, but her father brushed off her protests.

"It's a rare day when one of my daughters pops in for an unexpected visit. Let's treat it like a holiday."

He gestured for her to be seated on the sofa in the center of the room, and after she sat, he took the place beside her.

She was on edge as they exchanged pleasantries, her tension mounting when the secretary brought in a tray of coffee and French pastries. Her father poured her coffee, but she took it upon herself to add a touch of cream. He offered her a croissant, but she passed. Her stomach was far too twisted into knots to consider food.

"I'm glad you came to see me, Harper. I had planned to call you in another day or two to see how you're making out with that restaurant proposal of yours."

"That's why I'm here." She reached into her bag and withdrew the thick folder containing her business plan. "This is my proposal. I thought I'd deliver it in person." She passed the folder to her father and he took it from her hands, flipping it open and perusing the contents.

She tried to maintain her poise as she waited in the silence. Her dad was nothing if not thorough, so she knew it would be a few minutes until he spoke again. She sipped her coffee and noticed her fingers trembling slightly. She was nervous. If her father didn't approve of her plans, she'd have to seek out her own investors. And while she had plenty of industry contacts, she didn't have a lot of time to approach each of them on her own. Her father's assistance would move things along much more quickly—he would already know what sort of clients would be looking to invest in a venture such as this.

And it wasn't only that. Her father's approval meant so much to her. If he liked her ideas, it would buoy her confidence, give her the faith she needed to know she was capable of pulling this off. His criticism, however, would rock the foundation of her dream, ushering in a flood of doubt.

She tried to avoid any agitated movements, keeping her fingers wrapped around her coffee cup to still them. She thought his review of the proposal would never end, but after what felt like twenty minutes (though it was probably only five) he closed the folder.

"I have to say, Harper, that I'm impressed with the attention to detail you've put into this."

It was a compliment but not necessarily confirmation he'd help her. She waited to see what he said next.

"I did some homework on the Rusty Anchor," he went on, "and I noticed a steady decline in profits over the past few years. Why do you think that is?"

She knew he was testing her and took a moment to compose her thoughts before she answered. "The location is currently an issue," she admitted. "Main Street has been built up with shops, boutiques and other restaurants, and that's where most of the foot traffic is."

"And how do you plan to drive more customers in the direction of this restaurant?"

She drew a breath and willed a note of confidence into her voice. "There's advertising, for a start." She explained her ideas to partner with other businesses in town, gaining the Anchor more attention than it had previously been given. It was all in her proposal, but she knew her father likely wanted to hear her present her ideas in her own voice, since she'd be doing that very thing when she met with the investors. She expanded on her idea to draw in the locals once more—which was a surefire way for word of mouth to spread.

"I also think it's important to look at what the Anchor has that other restaurants don't. One of the ways I can leverage its location is the view of the bay. None of the establishments on Main have that. Their view of the water is obscured, but the option for waterfront dining at the Anchor is one of its greatest assets."

He nodded in approval, and she felt herself relax marginally.

"This Irish pub theme of yours has a lot of promise. There would be some initial costs to renovate, but it's nothing that should deter investors. And your sketches of the proposed interior and exterior are impressive. I'm not sure about this name change you've suggested, though."

"The name is nonnegotiable." She was firm on this point.

"Well, I agree the Rusty Anchor has to go. It doesn't fit with what you'd be doing."

"Yes, but I'm not budging on the new name."

Her father sighed. "Fine," he relented, "provided none of the investors criticize your decision."

He placed the folder on the coffee table in front of them. Harper set her coffee cup down, as well.

"You have some grand ambitions," he commented.

She wasn't sure if he meant this in a positive way or a negative one.

"I'd like Paige to review your proposal, and then—"

"Paige? Why does Paige have to be involved?"

His expression didn't waver. "Because this is what I pay her for, to analyze the inherent risks in investments before I present them to our clients."

Harper tried to remain calm, but the

mention of her sister's involvement put her on edge.

"Dad, if there's anything in the prospectus that worries you, I wish you'd tell me."

"Harper, this isn't a criticism of your plans. This is just standard procedure."

Standard. Fine. "Does it have to be *Paige* reviewing the documents?"

He sighed, and she tried not to wince. She shouldn't have voiced that aloud.

"Harper, I trust your sister's opinion. This isn't about a lack of belief in your abilities. I know that if given this opportunity, you'll work as hard as possible to make your restaurant a success."

She felt a tingle of joy at the words *your restaurant*. Her restaurant. Hers. Harper Worth, restaurateur. She tried to keep from grinning at the thought.

"Okay. So, if Paige thinks the risks are acceptable...what then?"

Her dad folded his hands in front of him. "Then I'll give you a call, and we can start talking to potential investors." He paused. "I did some investigating and learned that this restaurant is facing foreclosure in the near future. Is that why you were so evasive with details on the sale of the property?"

Harper swallowed. Given that Connor had revealed as much to his employees the day before, it wasn't exactly a secret anymore. But she still felt uncomfortable discussing his finances behind his back.

"Yes," she admitted. "I wasn't at liberty to say more at the time."

"I see." He was quiet for a long stretch, and Harper did her best to remain patient.

"Harper," he finally began, and she tensed. "I want you to know that even though you and I have had the occasional disagreement over your future… I'm proud of you. This idea, this passion of yours has made me wonder if I've perhaps been too hard on you in the past."

She felt her mouth hanging slack and willed herself to close it.

"You've shown real initiative and innovation here," he continued, "and I want you to know that I think this idea…that *you*…have a lot of potential."

Much to her embarrassment, Harper felt tears prick her eyelids. She cleared her throat and looked down, busying herself by smoothing the hem of her skirt. "Thanks, Dad," she murmured finally. "That means a lot."

Everything. It meant everything to have his approval. But inwardly, her conscience chafed.

The loss of Connor's restaurant would surely devastate him and make him feel as though he'd let his own father down.

Was fulfilling her dream worth destroying his?

She didn't have the answer.

BEFORE HEADING BACK to Findlay Roads, Harper decided to stop at her favorite coffee shop and celebrate her successful meeting with her father by ordering a triple mocha with extra whipped cream. After placing her order, she settled herself at the bar to wait and tried to balance her conflicting emotions.

Though she was thrilled by her father's support of her proposal, she was still wondering how Connor would react to the loss of his restaurant. She wished there was some way they could both have what they wanted. It felt wrong for Connor to lose the Anchor. And yet, that's what needed to happen to see her plans fulfilled.

As the barista pulled the shots for her drink, she noticed an abandoned copy of the *DC Ledger*, her former paper, on the counter and pulled it closer. It was the weekend edition, left from the day before. Her articles had always run on the weekend. She knew she shouldn't torture herself by looking up her old column. What did it matter how the new reviewer was doing? That part of her life was over, and she had a new purpose for the future.

Nevertheless, she folded the front page and sports sections, placing them aside in favor of the food-and-living segment. She skimmed a few of the articles before her eyes fell on the restaurant critique column.

The reviewer had chosen a high-profile restaurant in DC, owned by a well-known actress. The executive chef was her husband. They owned three different establishments— one here in DC, another in New York City and the most recent, Celadon, had opened in Findlay Roads last summer. Harper hadn't yet visited their Findlay Roads venture, but she'd once reviewed their DC restaurant and was forced to admit it was one of the few establishments she'd been unable to find anything negative to write about.

She devoured the article so intently that she barely heard the barista call out her drink. It was a glowing recommendation that praised the chef's skills and raved about the food. She supposed it was her own bias, but the gushing review annoyed her. How was it that a restaurant like this could receive so much exposure when a place like the Rusty Anchor barely brought in enough business to make it worth turning on the lights?

Her eyes dropped to the end of the column to note the perfect, four-star review. And then she noticed an editorial note.

Celadon's executive chef and owner, Daniel Roth, will be competing in Baltimore's upcoming Best of the Bay competition, featuring chefs from all over the Chesapeake Bay region. Roth is the favored entrant and is thought to be most likely to win the $25,000 prize. To learn more about the competition, see the article on page D4.

Harper quickly flipped the newspaper page to D4 and began reading the details of the competition. Her heart beat faster with every word. She hesitated at first and thought about tossing the paper in the recycling bin at the end of the counter. It was counterproductive to her own goals to show this to Connor. And yet...this might just be the lifeline he needed.

She knew she'd never forgive herself if she didn't at least show it to him. If the Anchor was meant to be hers, then it would be. But

Connor deserved the chance to save his restaurant.

Standing, she folded the newspaper and tucked it into her bag. She hurried from the coffee shop to her car, not even realizing until she was halfway home that she'd forgotten her mocha.

CHAPTER NINE

CONNOR HAD JUST hung up the phone with the insurance company when Erin popped her head around the corner of the B and B's sunroom, which also served as an office area for guests who might need to focus on business while visiting town. She took one look at his face and frowned.

"You okay?"

He forced himself to nod and smile, though it felt tight and awkward on his lips. "Just busy sorting out the details of the Anchor's reconstruction." After Erin's hopeful speech the day before, the last thing he wanted was to let on how discouraged he felt. He was grateful for the loyalty of his employees, but it didn't change the fact that he still didn't have any way to meet the bank's demands. He hadn't entirely given up just yet—he was going to hold on until the August 31 deadline rolled around. But after hours of trying to figure out how to keep things going, he was gradually coming to accept that it was only a matter of time until the Anchor was no longer his.

"Well, do you have time for a break? Harper's here to see you."

His spirits immediately lifted. "Harper's here?"

Erin looked amused as she nodded. "Yeah, she's waiting in the parlor. Why don't I send her in here, and I'll bring you guys some iced tea."

He appreciated Erin's attempt to give them some privacy, but it was also a little strange to be treated as a guest since he was staying at the B and B for free. He felt as if he should be doing something to earn his keep. It was a discussion he'd had with Lenora, who'd snorted at his concerns and told him that at her age, it was good to have as many young folks around the place as possible. She adored Molly and bantered with Rory all day long. He felt indebted to both her and Erin.

"You don't need to wait on us," he reminded his friend, but Erin shrugged.

"It gives me something to do. Plus, I kind of like how uncomfortable you are when I treat you like a guest. You get this weird little twitch at your left eye."

His expression went flat at Erin's teasing. "Just tell Harper to come in here, would you?"

Erin grinned as she departed. Seconds later, Harper appeared in the doorway. Erin was nowhere in sight. He stood at Harper's arrival, his entire body feeling as though it were waking up. It had only been about twenty-four hours since he'd seen her last, and yet, it felt as though days had gone by. How had he gone from loathing the sight of this woman to wishing he could keep her nearby all the time? Things had certainly changed.

"Harper," he breathed her name and stepped forward to greet her. He wanted to draw her into his arms, to inhale the scent of her citrus shampoo and bury his face in her neck. With all the difficulties of the past few weeks, the one bright spot through it all had been her: her smile, and the way her eyes scrunched up when she found something amusing. He liked observing her with Molly, seeing how she cared for his daughter. It entertained him to watch her eat, the way she savored the flavors carefully at first, as if trying to figure out how she might describe them if she were still writing her critique column.

The change in his feelings had occurred gradually, so subtly he hadn't realized how much he was coming to care for her. She was no longer "the harpy" in his eyes. Instead, next to Molly, she had become the person he looked forward to seeing most.

He wasn't blind to the way he felt about her but neither was he naive concerning the future. If he lost the Anchor, not only would it be the end of his, and his dad's, dream, but it would leave him in a predicament. What did a failed restaurateur and lackluster chef have to offer a woman like Harper?

The question reminded him of the ratings system in Harper's column. Perhaps she'd been right when she dubbed him *not worth it*.

He swallowed as he stepped closer to her, tamping back his dismay at such thoughts.

"Connor, I'm glad you're here."

He made a face. "Where else would I be?"

She was fairly jumping in agitation he realized. There was an air of energy around her as she brushed by him and stepped farther into the room. She turned to face him once more and held up a piece of paper.

"I think you'll want to see this."

He squinted at what appeared to be an internet printout of some sort. "What is it?"

"It's an entry form for the Best of the Bay

competition in Baltimore," she answered. "And it's how you can save the restaurant."

She was obviously excited, fidgeting restlessly and shifting her weight from one foot to the other.

"Slow down, love, and tell me what you're talking about."

She moved closer, and his pulse jumped with a will of its own at her proximity. "Look." She stood beside him and held out the paper, but he was so distracted by her nearness that he didn't immediately look at it. She was dressed professionally, he suddenly realized, in a cream-and-navy-striped skirt with an off-white blouse. It was a business sort of ensemble, and he wondered why she was so dressed up. Perhaps she'd had a job interview, he realized, and his heart sank. Of course, what did he expect? He'd made it clear that she needed to look elsewhere for work. She seemed to have moved along quickly, however, if she was interviewing already. Unless she'd had an appointment scheduled before the fire happened…

"Connor?"

"Hmm?" She was looking up at him impatiently, so he turned his attention back to the paper she held.

The words *12th Annual Best of the Bay Chef Competition* were emblazoned along the top. The form was pretty standard, so he didn't immediately grasp the significance of what she was trying to tell him. He took the paperwork from her hands and flipped to the next page, which required more intimate details, including where he'd trained, the establishments he'd worked at, a space to write down any awards he'd won, his signature dish and its ingredients and so forth. He flipped through several more pages outlining the contest rules and sponsors before he looked at Harper once more.

"You want me to enter a competition?" He shook his head. "Harper, I don't have time for this sort of thing right now. I'm dealing with the bank, and the insurance company, and I have to meet with a contractor and code inspectors—"

She shook her head impatiently. "Yes, you do have time. You need to do this." She grabbed the papers out of his hands and flipped to the last page, the one he'd glossed over.

"Read this."

He took the paper back and ran over the fine print.

First place...grand prize... $25,000...feature on EATS television...

He straightened as he finally realized what she was saying.

"See? That's what I'm telling you. Enter this, win the grand prize and you'll have enough to hold off the bank *and* keep the Anchor going awhile longer, until we can figure something out."

She was right. Twenty-five thousand dollars might not bail him out completely, but it would buy him more time to get things together. He began rereading the competition details that he'd only skimmed minutes before.

As he read, he wandered over to the sunroom's wicker settee and sank into it. Harper came to sit beside him.

"Technically, the cut-off for entries was yesterday, but I made a call, and they said they'd be happy to include you if we send in the form and fee by the end of the day."

He turned to the competition requirements.

"Each chef needs to create three dishes. An appetizer, a soup and an entrée, all using ingredients that highlight the flavors of the Chesapeake Bay region. The event will be televised on the EATS Channel. That's a *national* cable channel," he noted.

Harper was nodding. "It's a crazy amount of exposure. And the prize money… Connor, this could be exactly what you need."

He let the form rest in his lap as he looked at her. "The competition is less than a month away. I don't know where to begin, what I'd prepare."

"Make something your dad would have liked," she replied and reached out a hand to rest her fingers over his. The warmth of her touch set off sparks of pleasure in his stomach.

"But you don't understand, the competition for this…it will be the most well-known and prestigious chefs in the area."

"I know that, but, Connor, you can do this. I know you can. I believe in you."

He could have leaned over and kissed her right then and there, not just for the words but for the conviction behind them.

"I have no kitchen to practice in," he said. "I can't just take over the Moontide's. Lenora will need it for guests, and I don't want to be in the way."

"You can use the cottage kitchen," Harper immediately replied. "Tessa won't mind. She doesn't cook that much anyway. I've been making most of the meals since I came to town. And she's at work all day so you can practice without interruption."

He considered this offer and then nodded. It was a perfectly practical solution.

"If I do this... I won't attempt it without you," he replied. "I'll need your help. If I'm going to come up with award-winning dishes, I'll need someone who knows what it takes to win. I'll need my very own restaurant critic."

Her eyes widened. "Really? You want *me* to help you?"

"Who else will tell me the truth, even when I don't want to hear it?"

She hesitated at that. "Are you sure that's what you really want, though? After all, things didn't go so well between us the last time I critiqued your food."

"That was different," he said. "This time we're working together, toward the same goal— keeping the Anchor open."

Something in her eyes flickered at that, and she looked away. Before he could wonder about it, Erin stepped into the room, carrying a tray of iced tea and cookies. Molly was right on her heels, nibbling on a cookie.

"Sorry it took me so long. I had a little extra help, if you know what I mean." She inclined her head in Molly's direction.

When his daughter saw Harper, she hurried forward and climbed onto her lap without asking permission. He opened his mouth to chastise her and then stopped when Harper spoke.

"Hey, kiddo. How are you doing?"

He watched as Molly stuffed the last of the cookie in her mouth and curled against Harper, who tugged at the French braid she wore. Rory had taken over Molly's hair since they'd come to stay at the Moontide, and she did a considerably better job of it than he had.

"Good," she answered Harper's question. "Lenora and I are going to have a tea party later with real tea and everything! Can you come, too?"

Harper dropped a kiss on Molly's temple, and Connor felt his heart swell at the sight. "I don't know yet, but we'll see."

"Okay." Molly scooted off her lap then and moved toward the tray with the cookies. Erin handed both him and Harper a glass.

"Here." Connor held the entry form out to Erin. "See what you think of this."

She took the paper and began to read over it.

"Make sure you read the last page."

While she studied it, he watched as Molly took a cookie from the tray and then gravitated back to Harper, crawling onto her lap once more. Harper wrapped her arms around his little girl. Erin's voice drew his attention away from the sight.

"Connor, this is an amazing opportunity. I mean, I know it's likely to be a tough competition to win, but if you could...it would solve everything."

"Maybe not *everything*," Connor corrected, "but it would certainly help us out."

Erin looked to Harper. "Was this your idea? Is that why you came by?"

Harper nodded, and Erin's face split into a wide grin.

"I knew you'd be good for Connor."

He felt Harper's startled reaction to this statement as much as he experienced his own surprise over Erin's confidence.

"Well, what's the next step?"

Harper explained about missing the entry deadline and how they would need to get the form submitted by day's end.

"Well, what are you sitting here for? Start filling out this entry form," Erin prodded.

"I can't," Connor said.

Erin blinked. "Why in the world not?"

His gaze settled on Harper. "Because Harper hasn't agreed to help me. And I won't do it without her."

Molly sat up straighter and looked from him to Harper. He doubted she understood what was going on, but she had picked up on his expectation.

"Harper, why won't you help Daddy?" she asked.

Harper shot him a look. "I'm afraid I'll say something that might upset your daddy if I try to help him."

Molly didn't seem at all concerned by that. "When I upset Daddy, I just say I'm sorry, and then he's not upset anymore."

He grinned at Harper. "See? It's simple."

But she didn't quite share in his amusement. "Are you sure, Connor? I mean, really sure?" she softly asked, her eyes searching his.

He held her stare and gave a nod. "I'm sure."

She released a breath. "All right. I'm in."

HARPER TRIED TO ignore the butterflies in her stomach as Connor watched her fork into the rockfish fillet he'd prepared. She brought the bite to her lips and chewed, testing the flavors of the flaky white fish against the cream sauce. She swallowed and then reached for her water glass. Connor's eyes were intent on her face.

"It's not...bad," she tentatively offered.

He groaned and then picked up the plate in front of her to slide the entire contents into the trash.

"Connor, you didn't have to do that. It wasn't terrible."

"But it wasn't a winner," he replied. "I could tell the second you put it in your mouth."

"How?"

"Because you always lick your lips right away if you like something, and when you don't, you get just a bit of a line between your eyebrows." He reached out and tapped his finger against the spot. "Right here."

She was a little flustered that he paid so much attention to her when she was eating. But then again, they'd been at this for over two weeks, trying recipes and variations, attempting to find the dishes that would stand out at the Best of the Bay. They'd discussed ingredients, labored over techniques and argued over the type of dishes to serve. Harper insisted Connor try dishes native to his homeland, such as his dad's shepherd's pie, but he feared such humble fare would lose points on technique. He wasn't wrong, Harper knew. Simplicity wouldn't be likely to rank him high in technique, but she believed the superior flavors would win back any points he might lose.

They had gone round and round on these discussions, long into the night. In fact, just two days ago, Tessa had come into the kitchen at midnight, asking if they could please wrap things up so she could get some sleep.

They hadn't only debated about the competition, however. In the course of the past week, she had talked about food more with Connor than she ever had with anyone. They'd shared views on everything from food history to social impact and the future of modern cuisine. They'd argued a few times but never in a malicious way, and Harper had to admit—she'd never had so much fun. Having Connor mostly to herself was a delight. Molly had come over once or twice, but she'd proved to be too much of a distraction as they'd tried to work. So Connor usually left her at the Moontide, in the care of Lenora, Erin or Rory, when he visited the cottage.

Connor picked up the notebook with the list of potential dishes and crossed out the rockfish entrée. He ran a hand through his dark hair, and she sighed at the sight. He was endearing when he was distracted like this. But she felt guilty for having shot down his most recent attempt at a winning entry.

"The sauce was too much, I think," she offered, trying to keep her tone gentle. "It didn't allow the fish to stand out on its own."

He leaned against the kitchen island where she sat on a stool. "You keep saying that— how I need to let the ingredients speak for themselves."

"Well, yeah. I think simplicity is best."

He eyed her. "You think getting in touch with my Irish roots is best," he shot back.

"I'm not going to deny it." She refused to give in on this point. "Connor, I've tasted a lot of your food by now, and I'm telling you...your best dishes are the simplest ones, the ones that are true to your heritage. Like the shepherd's pie. Or your Irish stew. Or that colcannon you made last week."

He sighed. "You may find them good, but they're not winners."

"You just think that because of your training. You've got it in your head that the best food has to be complicated. And that's not true."

He sank onto the stool across from her, his expression weary. Perhaps they'd been at this too long. After all, while Harper had been enjoying herself, Connor had been doing most of the work. She was offering suggestions and input, but the only thing she really had to do was taste the food and give her opinion. Connor was the one putting his future on the line and striving to make each dish something special.

"Maybe you should take a break," she suggested. "You've been in this kitchen every day for over a week. Perhaps it's best if you just step back and ease up on yourself."

He was shaking his head before she even finished speaking.

"I can't. The competition is less than two weeks away. I don't have a single dish of the three I need. If I want to win this, I have to keep going."

"Connor, you're driving yourself crazy."

He scrubbed a hand over his face, the stubble on his jaw rasping against his palm. "I don't have a choice."

Harper frowned. She wished there was some way to ease this burden. She felt as though she was responsible for placing it on his shoulders, and she began to doubt her own motivation. Was she really trying to help Connor by getting him to sign up for this competition? Or was it just a way to lessen her guilt for wanting his restaurant? But no, she believed he could win this. And if he did, the restaurant might be beyond her reach…but at least she'd still have a job…and maybe Connor.

Besides, didn't he deserve the opportunity to salvage his father's legacy and save his restaurant? She might have wanted the Anchor for her own, but Connor should have every chance to save his business. He'd certainly earned it with how hard he'd worked.

Harper hopped off her stool as an idea came to her. "You know what we need?"

He slid a glance her way. "What?"

"We need to check out the competition."

He scoffed and stood, gathering up her empty plate and carrying it to the sink. "As if my ego isn't bruised enough. You want me to visit one of my rivals?"

"Come on," she pressed. "Maybe you'll find it inspiring. If we taste what sort of dishes Daniel Roth is serving at Celadon, it might help you find your own direction."

"So you want to have dinner? At Celadon?"

She nodded. "On me. My treat," she offered.

She expected him to protest or just flat-out announce that he refused to visit his competitor's restaurant. So she was surprised when he suddenly agreed.

"How about tomorrow night?"

"Really? You'll go?"

"If you think it will help." He began rinsing the dishes at the sink. "I'll see if Rory minds keeping an eye on Molly. Pick you up at seven?"

Why did the thought of spending an intimate dinner with Connor at a fine restaurant leave her feeling unexpectedly flustered? After all, it had been her suggestion.

"Sure. Seven sounds good."

His back was still turned, and she experienced a shiver of anticipation. An evening out with Connor, almost like a date.

No. Not a date, she told herself.

But even so, she was already giddy at the thought.

CHAPTER TEN

"Is it a date?"

Connor looked over his shoulder at Molly, who lay curled up on the bed, watching him get ready for his evening out with Harper. It wasn't the first time she'd asked this question, and every time he had to explain things to her, he felt a touch of disappointment. Perhaps because he wished this was an actual date—that he could take Harper out and get to know her properly. His dad had been old-fashioned, and his classic values had rubbed off on Connor. He wanted to formally ask Harper out, to bring her flowers and take her to dinner. He wanted to walk her to the door and share a kiss...

"Well? Is it?"

Connor sighed. "I keep telling you, Molly, that no, it's not a date."

"But you're going to dinner at a fancy restaurant. Isn't that what people do on a date?"

"Well, this is different."

He went to the closet. A lot of his clothing had suffered smoke damage from the fire, but he had managed to salvage a few usable shirts that he'd brought to the B and B. Now he sorted through them, trying to find one that would suit for the evening. He pulled a plain white T-shirt off a hanger and tugged it over his head. Then he added a black blazer. He straightened it and studied himself in the mirror.

"What do you think?" he asked Molly. "Do I look all right?"

She nodded. "You look beautiful, Daddy."

"Why thanks, my love."

Moving to the bed, he leaned down and lifted her into his arms. He kissed her cheek as he held her close.

"Erin said Harper is helping you taste recipes for a contest."

"We're working together on it," he affirmed.

Molly looked thoughtful. "Does this mean Harper is your official taste tester now?"

His face grew serious. "Absolutely not. That's your job." He tapped the tip of her nose. "Harper's helping me figure out which dishes will help me win. But you still get final approval on all recipes."

"Okay." Molly smoothed the sides of his

hair back and into place. "But, Daddy, it'd be okay if Harper was a taste tester, too. I don't mind sharing."

His mouth parted in surprise. "You don't?"

"Not with Harper," she informed him. "I like her. She's nice."

"She is nice," he agreed and then set Molly down on the floor. Before he could release her, she smacked a kiss against his cheek.

"I hope you and Harper have a nice date, Daddy," she said before skipping from the room.

This time, he didn't bother correcting her.

CONNOR TRIED TO ignore the case of jitters he experienced as he pulled into the cottage driveway to pick Harper up for their dinner. Molly's constant questioning about whether this was a date or not hadn't helped with his nerves. Even if this was meant to be about the competition, it certainly had the feel of a date. He almost felt empty-handed as he stepped onto the porch, wondering if he should have brought flowers. But then what would Harper think of him? She'd suggested this outing, after all. And he didn't think romance was what she'd had in mind.

Connor made an effort to remind himself

once more of the purpose of the evening before he rang the doorbell. This was about the competition, and his restaurant and doing whatever was necessary to save it.

Seconds later, Harper opened the door, and as he prepared to offer a greeting, he found no words would come forth.

He'd never seen her dressed up before. Sure, she'd been wearing that nice business number when she'd first come to see him about the competition. And he remembered she'd been dressed in something cute when she first showed up at the Anchor looking for a job. But those instances paled in comparison to how she looked now. She wore a teal-green, scoop-necked sundress and had let her hair down for the evening. Her makeup was simple, accentuating her natural beauty. The only jewelry she wore was a plain pair of gold hoop earrings. Even without any embellishment, he found her breathtakingly beautiful.

"You look lovely," he managed to get out.

She smiled. "Thanks. You clean up pretty nicely yourself."

He relaxed a little and wondered if she felt as off-kilter as he did at the moment. After being in each other's company so much of the past week and a half, it felt strange to be fumbling over words and feeling awkward in her presence.

"Well." He cleared his throat. "Are you ready to go?"

She nodded and reached behind her to close the cottage door. He offered his arm to help her down the steps, and she hesitated for a moment before taking it. He walked her to his dad's truck, suddenly conscious of picking her up in the battered old vehicle. But Harper didn't blink an eye as he led her to the passenger side. He held the door open as she climbed inside, making sure she was tucked in before he closed it. He allowed himself to pause, just for a moment, to look at her before he went around and climbed into the driver's seat.

They drove to the restaurant in strained silence while Connor fiddled with the radio at every stoplight along the way. He kept the air conditioner cranked up to offset the heat of the summer night but then he saw Harper shiver, and he turned it off. By the time they reached the center of town, he was overly warm—whether from the evening air or nerves, he couldn't say. He found a parking spot along the main drag, only a few doors down from Celadon, and then hurried to help Harper out of the truck.

"You said you booked us a reservation?" he asked as they approached the line of patrons spilling out of the doors. The sight stunned him. He knew other restaurants were far busier than his, but what he wouldn't give to see a crowd like this at the Rusty Anchor.

"I did, but it looks like we may have to wait a bit anyway."

"I don't mind, if you don't," he said. The evening was warm and sticky, but standing around outside didn't bother him in the least. He would have gladly stood in blazing sunlight for hours if it meant he could spend more time with the beautiful, intelligent woman next to him.

She looked up into his face and didn't seem the least bit perturbed. "I don't mind at all."

They gave their names at the outdoor hostess station and were told it would just be a few minutes until they were seated. Connor placed his hand on the small of Harper's back and felt her tense for a moment as he steered her away from the worst of the crowd. She soon relaxed under his touch, and he found himself reluctant to take his hand away when they finally reached a more secluded spot to wait.

"You know, I think you might have been right. This is a good idea, checking out the competition. It'll help to know what I'm up against."

He was surprised when she reached out and squeezed his arm in reassurance. She didn't have to say a word. He knew it was her way of offering support.

"So." He cleared his throat and decided to change the subject. He knew the competition was the entire point of the evening, but he'd had enough of discussing it the past week. He wanted to talk about something else. Namely Harper. "How have you enjoyed living in Findlay Roads so far this summer?" he asked. "It's quite different from the city."

She brightened at this question. "It's a sweet little town. I always liked visiting here when I was younger, but now, as an adult, I can appreciate even more of it than I did as a child."

"Such as?"

"Its charm and beauty. The way it feels like a small town but has all these things to offer, what with the rise in tourism. It's a great place to raise a family. I can see why your dad chose it when you emigrated to the States."

He nodded. "He picked it mostly because of its history. The Irish helped build this town, back in the day."

"How so?"

"They were ferrymen who settled here in the early nineteenth century. Of course, the Irish weren't very welcome at the time, but they did a lot of good for the community, and eventually they were accepted as a part of it. Dad was always a bit of a history buff. He had a real appreciation for American history."

"He sounds like he was a wonderful man. I wish I could have met him."

Connor felt the familiar pang of loss at the thought of his father. "I think he'd have liked you. He always said the best kind of girl was one who kept you on your toes."

He frowned at the memory. He'd forgotten about that.

"I'll take that as a compliment."

"You should. It was meant as one."

She blushed, her eyes darting away. "Was Chloe like that? Did she keep you on your toes?"

He sighed, not wanting to think about his ex-wife when he was here with Harper. "I suppose so. Just not in the way my father meant."

Harper took a step closer, so that the two of them were huddled together in their own private space. "I have to admit I'm curious about her. I can't imagine…leaving your daughter like that Especially a little girl as precious as Molly."

He felt a swelling of tenderness toward her for these words. "I've tried very hard to understand how she could leave as she did…and to forgive her for it. I try to tell myself that in some ways, it was a blessing. It allowed me to get to know my daughter in a way that a lot of fathers never do. But I worry for Molly, growing up without a mother in her life. There are some things a father can never be to a little girl, you know?"

"I know," Harper quietly admitted. "I love my own dad, but he's not…soft. I don't think he'd have any clue how to be. My mom, she's the one who knew how to set the hurts of childhood right. Not that you don't know how to do that." She rushed to cover any offense. "I think you're a great dad."

He was taken aback. "You do?"

"I do. I've seen how you are with Molly— you're patient even when she exasperates you, but you're firm when you need to be. And mostly, you're trying, harder than many parents, to see that she grows up right."

He tried to swallow but found a lump in his throat. Molly was his world, and he'd convinced himself he didn't need anyone to help him with the doubts he had about raising her. But after all the "advice" he'd received from well-meaning friends and acquaintances after Chloe left, he hadn't realized just how much he needed to hear someone say he was doing things right.

"Thank you," he said, his voice choked. "That means more than…it means a lot."

Harper squeezed his arm in reassurance. Before the moment could grow awkward, their names were called for their table.

This time, when Connor placed his hand on her back, she didn't flinch. Not even a little.

THOUGH HARPER HAD been prepared to choose the dishes they would order, she found herself more than content when Connor took charge of their dinner. He selected a variety and focused on the crab and seafood dishes, which would likely be featured heavily in the competition. As he spoke to the server, Harper tried to observe him secretly, pretending to sip from her water glass as she studied him.

He was dressed for the evening in a simple white T-shirt with a black blazer and jeans. The outfit was relaxed, but he looked rather dashing in it. Had he been trying to impress her? As much as she'd told herself she'd choon the teal dress because it had been the first thing she'd found among the nicer outfits she'd brought to town, she also knew it was one of the garments that fit her best and was bound to make an impression. She had to concede she'd taken care when she'd dressed for her dinner with Connor, even when she knew she probably shouldn't. She shifted restlessly in her seat as she realized how much she hoped he found her attractive.

"Harper?"

She shook her head as she realized Connor had been speaking to her as she daydreamed.

"Sorry, what?"

"I asked if you'd like a glass of wine."

"Sure."

The server recommended a vintage, and Connor ordered them each a glass. As the server walked away, Connor turned his full attention on her, and she tingled all over, as if she'd already tasted the wine, and it had gone straight to her head.

"So tell me more about your sisters," he said, initiating the conversation once more.

She made a face, and he eyed her intently.

"Sorry. Did I say something wrong there?"

"Not really. It just brought back memories of high school. Usually, when a guy started talking about my sisters, it was because he wanted to date one of them. Typically my older sister, Paige." She busied herself with unrolling her silverware from the linen napkin.

"You said she lives in DC? What's she like?"

Harper laid her utensils aside and carefully smoothed the napkin across her lap. "Well, Paige is pretty much...perfect."

He arched an eyebrow. "I find that unlikely."

She made a face. "That's because you don't know her. Trust me on this. She works for my dad, as a risk management analyst for his investment firm. She graduated *magna cum laude* from college, and she married a lawyer. She's probably the only woman in history to have actually looked attractive during labor when she gave birth to my niece last year."

"You sound jealous."

"Jealous?" The word startled her. "Oh, I'm not jealous of Paige. She's just a lot to measure up to. That's all. She succeeds at everything she attempts. It's absolutely exasperating."

"She sounds like a proper nuisance."

Harper blinked. "Exactly. I mean, when we were kids, and we'd go outside to play, somehow Paige always came back in looking even *neater* than when we'd left. I could never figure out how she did it. And my mom would scold me for getting dirt all over my new tights, and Paige wouldn't have even a single hair out of place."

She took a breath and lowered her voice.

"Once, when I was a little older than Molly, I convinced Paige to let me give her a make-over. We set everything up in our bedroom, and I even snuck some lipstick and stuff from my mom's makeup bag. I told Paige to close her eyes, and then I swapped out the real makeup for permanent marker and told her I was filling in her eyebrows and then outlining her lips."

Connor was already starting to chuckle.

"Her face looked like a Kabuki mask by the time I was finished. When Paige looked in the mirror, her eyes got really wide, and then she started crying. I think that was the worst part, for me anyway. For Paige, it was probably waiting for the marker to wear off."

Connor shook his head. "That sounds exactly like something Molly would do, if she had siblings. She did something just as bad to a friend a while ago."

He filled her in on the incident with Piper Evans as Harper covered her mouth to contain her laughter.

"She also shaved her playmate's dog using an electric razor. And I once caught her cracking a dozen eggs onto her hair because she heard eggs make your hair shiny."

He shook his head as Harper held her sides, laughing too hard to speak.

"I knew she was a handful, but I had no idea," she gasped when some of her laughter subsided.

"She keeps me on my toes," he agreed. "Her granddad would be proud of her for that. He doted on her."

The server reappeared with their appetizers, and they fell silent for a few minutes as they shared and tasted the dishes.

"The crab Rangoon is delicious," he noted, sounding rather disappointed. Harper shared his regret. Her crab-stuffed mushrooms were nicely seasoned and cooked to perfection. They nibbled on each other's appetizers as they talked.

"Tessa seems nice," Connor offered.

Harper nodded her agreement. "She's the baby of the family and by far the sweetest of us all. Everyone likes Tessa. You can't help it. She's just lovable. She was the first person I wanted to see after I lost my job because I knew she'd help me put things in perspective.

I felt better the minute she opened the cottage door to me."

"It's good to have family like that, someone you can rely on." He lowered his voice. "That's how my dad was for me. After my first restaurant failed, his support inspired me to try again. He never voiced a single disappointment. Sometimes I think he believed in me too much."

"In what way?"

"He had this unshakable belief that I was meant to be a chef with my own restaurant. But maybe I'd have been better off doing something else with my life. I can't say I've made him proud since he's been gone."

"But he entrusted the Anchor to you."

"And I've driven it right into the ground." He ran a hand through his hair, mussing it so that Harper longed to reach out and run her fingers through it. "The truth is, I don't know what I'm doing half the time. My dad had such faith in me. Sometimes, I think he worked so hard on my behalf that it killed him."

"Connor. That's a horrible thing to think. You're not responsible for your dad's death."

His eyes were filled with sadness as he looked at her. "He mortgaged the restaurant so he could pay for my culinary school training. He invested in my first restaurant and lost a lot of money. And he still left his own restaurant to me in his will."

The server came and then departed with their empty appetizer plates.

"Was the restaurant already losing customers before he died?"

Connor shook his head. "The Anchor used to have a regular clientele made up of locals. It was a lot more laid-back when Dad was in charge. The menu was filled with local favorites, the sort of home cooking people grew up with. I changed all that after he passed, and a lot of people didn't like the haute cuisine I started serving. They said they could get that at any of the newer restaurants in town. I think a lot of them felt I'd betrayed my dad, in a way. So they quit frequenting the restaurant, and things went downhill from there."

"But why did you change the menu? If the Anchor was doing well…why not leave things as they were?"

He tapped a finger distractedly on the tabletop. "Because my dad asked me to before he died. He paid for culinary school because he believed I could do better, turn the Anchor into something exceptional. He invested so much in me over the years. I felt like I owed it to him to try to fulfill his vision of turning the place into a fine-dining restaurant. But I'm failing him in the same way I failed with my first restaurant."

Harper didn't know what to say.

"Well, anyway." He seemed to shake off his melancholy. "What about you?"

"What about me?"

"How is it that you ended up as a restaurant critic?"

"Oh." She looked down at the tabletop. "That's a long story."

"I have time, if you'd like to share it." The warmth in his voice compelled her to raise her head so she could see his face. He was looking at her with an expression of both care and interest, as if she was the only thing that mattered right now. She swallowed at the sight and lowered her eyes once more.

"I'm just curious, Harper. If you don't want to talk about it—"

"I'm afraid you'll laugh." She looked back up. "And I wouldn't blame you if you did."

His features softened even more. "I won't laugh. I promise." He laid a hand over his heart, as though to confirm this statement, and she knew he told the truth.

"Okay, so I used to want to...to be a...chef."

His eyebrows rose for the second time that evening. But to his credit, he didn't laugh. Not even so much as a smirk crossed his lips. "You? A chef? How did you make the leap from that to critic?"

"Because I couldn't afford culinary school on my own, and my dad didn't believe it would provide a solid education. He wanted me to follow Paige's lead and come work for him. My parents paid for me to attend an academic college, but in the end, I didn't want to work for my dad. It had been tough enough, growing up and trying to earn his approval. I didn't want to spend my adult life like that, constantly being compared to Paige. So I started out interning for a newspaper and worked my way up from there." She swallowed. "My mom was proud when I became a restaurant critic. She enjoyed showing my critiques to her friends. But my dad... I don't think he ever quite forgave me for going my own way instead of the one he had planned for me."

Connor was silent for a long time. The server appeared with their entrées, asked if they needed anything else, and when Connor didn't respond, she looked to Harper, who shook her head. Once the served walked away, Harper stared down at her plate of food.

"Are you thinking I'd have been better off working for my dad instead of becoming a restaurant critic?" She forced herself to look up and meet his eyes.

He appeared surprised by this question. "Not at all. I was thinking that it took courage to follow your own path instead of doing what your dad expected of you."

"Oh." She picked up her fork. "Thanks for that.

He reached for his own utensils. "So what do you think you'd like to do next then? I don't suppose you plan to remain a server forever."

"No," she admitted, feeling a swell of uneasiness at the direction of the conversation. But perhaps this was her opportunity to broach the subject of the restaurant with Connor. "I've been thinking that I'd like to own my own restaurant someday."

She waited to see his reaction. Her stomach was so twisted into knots that she barely looked at the steaming entrée before her.

He scoffed. "Are you sure about that? It's not an easy road, that's for sure."

"I know that," she said, feeling slightly defensive. "But to have a restaurant of my own, a place where people can come together and connect, to make memories and celebrate special occasions…it's something I've wanted since I was a little girl, playing at pretend restaurant like Molly."

After a long pause, he nodded. "I can understand that. It's the same for me. I grew up around the Anchor so becoming a chef was something I'd dreamed of since childhood. I always knew I'd take it over someday, but as I grew older and expressed my interest, my dad refused to let me settle for simply following in his footsteps. He wanted so much more for me. And having my own place, even with all its difficulties…" He looked sober. "It's what I've always wanted. Giving up the Anchor will be…" He searched for the words. "It will be the hardest thing I'll ever have to do, if it comes to it. Seeing it pass into someone else's hands will be like burying my father all over again."

Harper wrapped her fingers around her wineglass. She couldn't quite meet Connor's eyes.

He picked up his own wineglass and tilted it in her direction.

"Well, here's to following your dreams, no matter where they might lead."

Harper raised her glass to his and tapped it lightly.

"Sláinte," he said.

"Sláinte," she repeated.

There was no way she was going to share her plans of taking over the Anchor with Connor now.

CONNOR DIDN'T WANT his evening with Harper to end.

They'd lingered much longer than necessary at the restaurant, using the excuse that they needed to try dessert, even if it wouldn't be part of the competition. And then they'd drawn out the hour by sipping at their coffee. Connor had shared tales of his childhood in Ireland, and Harper had told him her favorite memories of Findlay Roads from summers with her grandmother. They'd chatted about working in restaurants when they were younger. Then they'd moved on to schooling, and while Connor had talked about training at the Institute of Culinary Distinction, Harper related her experiences writing a food column and a few self-help articles for her college newspaper. Next were stories about relationships and anecdotes concerning first dates, and the next thing either one of them knew, the restaurant was preparing to close for the evening.

They both felt terrible for having held the

table all night and tipped their server gener-
ously for the inconvenience. Connor wasn't
quite ready to head home, but he didn't know
how Harper felt. When she said it was a lovely
night for a walk, they headed the few blocks
toward the promenade and strolled along it by
the glow of the moon and the lamps illuminat-
ing the path. Connor told her what it had been
like when his father died, making changes to
the restaurant and trying to keep both his and
his dad's dream alive.

"Connor," she said, after he'd confided in
her about some of the mistakes he felt he'd
made when he took over the Anchor, "why
do you keep resisting my suggestion to cook
something Irish for the competition?"

He stopped walking and leaned against the
railing of the boardwalk. "Because it feels like
I'm going against what my dad wanted," he
admitted.

She came to stand beside him, her hair shining like burnished gold in the moonlight. "I
think there's no better way to help your dad's
legacy live on," she countered. "If you cook
those Irish recipes of your dad's, you're hon-
oring his memory as well as using the skills
he wanted you to learn. I didn't know him,

but from what you've said, if he were here, I think he'd tell you the same thing."

He looked out over the water, at the way the moon's light lay in twisting ripples upon the waves. Maybe Harper was right. His dad had been proud to be Irish. He'd instilled that sense of Irish pride in his own children—that America was their homeland, but Ireland was the country of their birth...of their history. He was a man who'd been proud of both countries. What better way for Connor to honor that than to embrace where he'd come from?

"You might be right," he admitted.

Harper relaxed. "Of course I'm right," she teased.

"Don't go getting cocky on me now, girl."

She beamed all the brighter at this, and he couldn't resist reaching out and tucking a loose strand of hair behind ear. She moved closer to him, and he shivered, but in the heat of the summer twilight, he didn't think it had anything to do with being cold. He pulled her to him.

"We'll do it your way," he said. "I'll put together some Irish recipes for the competition, using local ingredients. And we'll pray that a few of them are winners."

"They will be," she stated, her voice full of conviction as she stared up at him, eyes bright.

He placed his palms against her neck and felt the rapid pace of her heartbeat.

"Harper," he murmured, "I want to thank you."

Her eyes were wide at the feel of his touch, and she'd wrapped her arms around his waist as if it were nothing out of the ordinary.

"Thank you for fighting to help me keep the Anchor and for pushing me to enter this competition. Whether I win this thing or lose it, I won't forget that you were there for me."

He felt her stiffen in his arms, but he held her fast so she couldn't pull away.

"Don't give me so much credit, Connor," she said, turning her face from his. But he moved his hand from her neck to grip her chin and force her to look at him again.

"I mean it, Harper. You have more than made up for that review."

"I didn't do it because of the review," she murmured.

"I know," he answered.

And then he lowered his mouth to hers. Her lips were every bit as soft and tender as he remembered them. She tasted of plums, from the wine they'd had earlier in the evening, and when she melted against him, he wrapped his arms possessively around her. His kisses fell not just on her lips but along her cheeks and then her eyelids. He'd never wanted anything in the complicated way that he wanted her—she challenged him at the same time she brought him unbelievable joy. She had been an unexpected highlight during one of the lowest points of his life.

And he poured every one of these thoughts into the kisses he dropped across the plane of her face and her soft lips. When they finally pulled apart for air, she gasped breathlessly.

"You have to know that I…" He was afraid to speak the words aloud and at the same time, afraid to hold them in. "I care about you."

"Of course, I care about you, too—"

He shook his head with a sharp jerk, cutting her off. "No, I mean I *really* care about you. I think… I think I might be falling in love with you."

Her voice trembled as she said his name, "C-Connor…"

"You don't need to say anything back," he said, not wanting to pressure her into something she wasn't ready for just yet.

She swallowed but said nothing. Though he might have felt a faint disappointment that she didn't contest his words, he was mostly thrilled that she hadn't denied she had feelings for him, too.

"I know it would be difficult, with the restaurant and Molly. I'm not in much of a position to be thinking about a relationship." His eyes slid closed. "I don't want to repeat the mistakes I made with Chloe.

"But I'm not Chloe."

These softly spoken words caused him to open his eyes. Harper was looking at him with a mix of regret and longing.

"No," he agreed. "No, you're not. So, maybe after things are settled with this competition and the Anchor, maybe you and I could…talk. You know, see where things might lead?"

She hesitated, as though holding something back.

"What do you say, Harper?"

She seemed to struggle briefly with herself before nodding.

"Okay," she breathed.

Her agreement caused him to smile, and he pulled her tightly to him to kiss her once more.

CHAPTER ELEVEN

A WEEK AND a half after his evening with Harper, Connor entered the ballroom of Baltimore's Harris Inn and Convention Center. Beside him, Harper tucked her hand into his in a quiet gesture of support.

He swallowed and tried not to let his nerves show. The large ballroom had been converted to an arena with eight different sections to accommodate the competing chefs. Each competitor's name was emblazoned in bold letters across the front of their workstation. Connor's eyes were too busy taking in the various cameras and officials to bother locating his own name.

This was far grander than what he'd expected. There were bold-colored banners highlighting the sponsors. Each kitchen area was outfitted with state-of-the-art equipment from oven ranges to blenders. There were stacks of pans and utensils being delivered to each spot. The stainless-steel fridges would hold the ingredients each chef had requested in order to create their dishes.

Surrounding these mini kitchens were staff and technicians who scurried to get everything set up before the competition got under way. In the corner were reporters and celebrities from the food industry, including several notable hosts Connor easily recognized from the EATS Channel. It seemed the chefs were being directed off to the side until the event began. They wouldn't be allowed in their sections until shortly before the competition was about to start. He had already registered before being sent into the ballroom so now all he had to do was wait. He noticed a few of the entrants being interviewed by a local reporter, but he shied away from that group for the time being.

Harper's hand squeezed his. "You ready for this?"

He forced a laugh, ashamed of how shaky it sounded. "Yeah. Of course. Piece of cake, as they say."

Her face showed her concern. He pulled her closer to his side.

"I'll be fine. Don't you worry about me."

"You will be fine, I know it," she replied

and then looked over the busy ballroom, "but that won't stop me from worrying."

He felt a swell of happiness cut through his agitation. In the past week, he and Harper had maintained a respectable distance from each other, but the promise of things to come hovered between them. After this was over, he planned to ask her out on a proper date. The idea left him nearly as nervous as the competition did.

They'd continued to work together in the cottage kitchen, starting from scratch with brand-new dishes that reflected his Irish heritage. Harper had been ruthless as a taste tester, arguing for changes where she thought they were needed. He found he didn't mind so much. He knew she was only doing it for his own good, wanting to see him win this as much as, or possibly more than, he did. He was still a bit skeptical of the direction they'd gone— his recipes were good, but they were also simple. He could only hope the flavors would outshine the entries' lack of complexity.

"Why don't we get something to drink?" Harper suggested and gently tugged him toward the refreshment table set up on the other side of the room. They each grabbed a bottle

of water, but before Connor could even un-
screw the top, one of the officials approached.

"Hi, you're…" She consulted a clipboard
and then looked at the name tag he'd been
given to wear. "Connor Callahan. I'm Missy
Donahue. I'm the chef liaison. If you have a
few minutes, I'd like to go over some of the
details of the event."

He swallowed, feeling a fresh swell of
nerves. "Sure."

"Great." She took his arm and began to
lead him away. He looked over his shoulder
at Harper, and Missy noted his distraction.
"Oh, spouses can wait over there in the section for family and friends." She pointed to
a spot a few feet away where several rows of
chairs were set up. He felt an odd thrill that
Missy had assumed Harper was his wife. If
the flush on Harper's face was any indication,
she hadn't missed that little detail, either.

"I'll be over there," she reassured. "Come
and find me when you're finished."

He held her eyes until Missy dragged him
away, and he was forced to turn his back on
Harper.

HARPER WATCHED CONNOR until the chef liaison
sat him in a chair and began pointing to items

on the clipboard. Then she headed in the direction of the family seating, carrying her water bottle and bag with her. She knew Connor was nervous about the competition. She felt the same flutter of anticipation concerning his participation. But on top of that was another layer of nerves that had nothing to do with the Best of the Bay. Her business proposal was tucked in her purse. She'd brought it with her because, whether Connor won or not, she planned to show him her concept. If he won the prize money, she'd give him the prospectus as a suggestion to leverage the Anchor into something more lucrative. And if he lost, she was going to ask if he'd be her business partner. Her father had called her the week before to confirm Paige's approval of her proposal. The words had left her giddy as she'd realized she had both Paige and her father's support. Her dad had followed up with an email, listing her potential investors and highlighting the ones he'd already spoken with who had confirmed their interest. He mentioned he was planning to set up a meeting in the near future so she could meet the investors and present her plans.

With things set to move forward, Harper had determined today was the day she told

Connor the truth about her plans. Because in the past week and a half she'd realized that while she wanted the Anchor, she wanted Connor more. She couldn't keep this from him any longer. She'd only convinced herself to remain silent over the past week because she didn't want to add to his burdens. He'd been driving himself relentlessly, narrowing down recipes, revising them and then practicing the dishes until they reached perfection. He hadn't needed any distractions, so she'd kept her confession to herself. But each day, the knowledge of it increased her uneasiness. She could only hope that when she told him the truth, he'd still believe she was on his side.

She took a long drink from her water bottle and then placed it on the floor as her eyes swept the room. She recognized quite a few industry professionals and hoped she wouldn't have to make small talk with too many of them. Near the ballroom entrance, she noticed Daniel Roth, owner and executive chef of Celadon, alongside his celebrity wife. They were being interviewed by several reporters, and she wished she were closer so she could eavesdrop on the conversation. Maybe she could find out what Roth planned to prepare for the competition. Of course, the knowledge would do little good at this point, but she was curious.

"Harper Worth. What a pleasure to see you again."

Her attention jerked from Roth and his cluster of interviewers to the tall man who had addressed her. She stood as she recognized Nathan Pratt, owner of the Pratt Restaurant Group. Nathan was an iconic figure in the food world, and he'd always enjoyed her biting restaurant reviews. Perhaps because she'd never targeted any of his establishments.

"Hello, Nathan." She moved to extend a hand, but he leaned forward and placed a kiss on her cheek instead.

"I hear you've been hiding yourself away in some bay town along the coast."

She gave a short nod. "Findlay Roads. I have family there."

"And soon, a new business, if the buzz is to be believed."

She shifted her weight and looked over her shoulder. Connor was still in discussion with Missy Donahue.

"The food world is always rife with rumor, Nathan, you know that."

He shook a finger at her. "Don't be coy with me, Harper. I have it on good authority that you're planning to open a restaurant. Richard Hart is a good friend of mine."

Richard Hart was one of the principal partners looking to invest with her. She had to keep Nathan quiet about what he knew.

"I'm trying to keep things under wraps for the time being."

Nathan nodded. "I understand. But I've heard promising things about your plans. I was worried about you after I heard you lost your column and decamped from the city. I'm pleased to know you've got some grand ambitions."

She dipped her head in acknowledgment but didn't say anything. The sooner they moved on from this topic, the better. She feared Connor might finish up at any minute and come to find her.

"Well, you have my number. Should you ever need anything, don't hesitate to reach out."

"Thank you, Nathan. I appreciate that."

Harper didn't relax until he'd moved some distance away and started up a conversation with one of the officials. She finally released a breath, only to suck it back in sharply as Connor appeared at her side.

"You're jumpy," he remarked with a grin as

she turned to him. "And I thought I was the only one on edge today."

Perhaps it was partly her relief that he hadn't overheard her conversation with Nathan, but she suddenly wanted nothing more than to wrap her arms around him and kiss away his nervousness. She settled for taking his hand instead.

"There's no need for jitters. You're going to be amazing. I know it."

"As long as I'm a winner," he added, and she saw the uncertainty in his eyes.

She squeezed his fingers in hers. "You don't need to win the grand prize to know that's true."

He relaxed a little at this and leaned his forehead closer to hers. "Maybe I've already won something better," he whispered.

Her breath caught at these words as well as the look he rested on her just then. It was an expression loaded with promise and adoration. Never, in her entire life, had anyone looked at her the way Connor was right now.

"I think you might be my good luck charm," he murmured, his breath fanning over her lips.

"Oh." She felt a tingle of happiness at this sentiment. "That reminds me." She leaned down and searched through her bag until she found the sheet of stickers she'd brought.

"Molly said to give you one of these." She peeled one of the shamrock stickers off and affixed it to his chef's jacket, right beneath his name tag.

He looked down at it.

"She said it's for good luck."

He ran his finger over the glossy green and then raised his eyes to Harper. "Between you and Molly, I have all the luck I need."

Then he dropped a kiss on the tip of her nose just as one of the officials stepped up to the podium in the center of the room.

The competition was about to begin.

EACH CHEF HAD two hours to construct three dishes—a soup, an appetizer and an entrée. The time would be displayed on a large digital counter on the wall opposite the chef stations. News crews and camera operators all huddled beneath that counter to get a good view of the competitors as they worked.

After a final wish of good luck from Harper, Connor took his place at the section marked with his name and began prepping his area. At first, his nerves still churned with anxiety, especially when he happened to look up and see the row of cameras facing him. But then his eyes shifted to the seats for family and friends and he caught sight of Harper. She gave him a thumbs-up and a brilliant smile, and he relaxed.

After that, he was able to focus better. He blocked out the presence of the cameras and even his fellow chefs on either side. He narrowed his vision to the tasks at hand, checking the items in the refrigerator, testing the oven range and mentally inventorying the ingredients stocked on the rolling shelves. Once he was satisfied with his stock and the equipment, he began assembling the pots, pans and utensils he'd need and storing away the ones he didn't in the bins beneath his workstation. Finally, convinced that he was as prepared as he could possibly be, he positioned himself behind his stainless-steel countertop and waited for the countdown to begin.

He looked down at the shamrock sticker Harper had placed on his jacket. He was grateful to his daughter, and to Harper, for that added touch. It allowed him to keep his focus, to remember what he was competing for. But, more important, it served as a reminder that whether he won this prize or lost it, whether the Anchor remained his or not, he was still blessed with people he loved…and who loved him.

He was absorbing this knowledge when the tap of the microphone cut through his musings and their host announced it was time to begin.

As soon as the timer sounded, Connor jumped into action. He immediately began measuring ingredients for his Irish soda bread into the bowl of an electric mixer. He and Harper had timed this portion over and over again. Baking the bread took the longest of any of his dishes' components, so it had to be started first, and it could not fail because he wouldn't have enough time to begin again. Once he had the bread in the oven, he turned on the stove burners and began melting several tablespoons of butter.

He immersed himself in the tasks at hand. He was only barely aware of the announcer occasionally speaking and giving updates on the time as the clock ticked down. For him, it was all about these three dishes. Each ingredient invoked a memory, and even as he worked, he could hear his dad's voice sharing his memories of growing up in Ireland, of meeting Connor and Rory's mom, of the difficulties that had followed when she grew ill and passed on and of taking his children with

him to start a new life in the States. Connor
remembered things he'd thought long forgotten—cooking with his father, making dishes
such as these for holidays and celebrations. A
way to honor where they'd come from while
still valuing their new identity as American
citizens.

For the length of those two hours, Connor almost felt as though his dad were beside
him, encouraging him. Maybe even reminding
him that this was what mattered, these dishes
that spoke so deeply of home and family. And
somewhere in the midst of it all, Connor realized in a distant part of his brain that this was
what he should have been doing all along. His
father wouldn't have disapproved of him returning to his Irish heritage. On the contrary,
he likely would have applauded it.

The Anchor had been his dad's way of laying down roots in his new country. But perhaps Connor's path was to merge the old with
the new—the past with the present.

As he put the finishing touches on his
dishes, dimly aware of the timer counting
down the last few minutes of the competition,
he realized he'd somehow overlooked the obvious. He could still honor his father's memory
while doing things his own way. By entrust-

ing the Anchor to his care, hadn't that been what Patrick Callahan was trying to tell him? That his greatest legacy was his children— not Connor's ability to elevate the Anchor, but simply his wish to keep his father's memory alive. His dad had invested the same sense of appreciation in Rory, by encouraging her love of Irish folk music. That was how Patrick Callahan lived on—in the passions he had helped instill in his son and daughter.

As the timer sounded, Connor could only pray that knowledge hadn't come too late, and that he still had a shot at saving his restaurant.

ONCE THE TIMER SOUNDED, Harper felt some of her tension drain away. Connor had managed to finish on time and stood behind the counter that displayed all three of his carefully constructed dishes. She breathed a sigh of relief at the sight. Then her breath caught as Connor's eyes went directly to hers. She smiled and gave a tiny wave and was rewarded with his broad grin in return. He felt confident about the dishes then. That was a good sign. Now she could only hope the judges enjoyed them.

The host was introducing them now. There was a panel of five judges, each with a lofty culinary background. One was the editor of an international food magazine who had worked as a food critic at the *New York Times* for years. Two others were renowned for their multiple awards and lifetime contributions to classical cuisine, both in America and abroad. The fourth was closer to home—the owner of a string of restaurants throughout the Chesapeake Bay region and the recipient of not one but two James Beard Awards. And the fifth judge was a celebrity chef with his own cooking and reality show. It was a daunting panel, even to Harper, who was generally unintimidated by the upper echelon of the food world.

First would be the presentation scoring. Connor and Harper had worked out a relatively uncomplicated way to showcase his dishes. They'd decided on dinnerware that had a bit of a rustic feel, fired clay pottery that echoed the setting of an Irish fishing village.

Harper had given the presentations her stamp of approval, but now she nervously tapped her foot, wondering if she should have encouraged Connor to do something bolder.

She frowned as her eyes moved to Celadon's display. Roth had presented his soup in a gorgeous seashell bowl, resting on a bed of presumably faux seaweed. His crab cake appetizer and the entrée were similarly plated on smooth platters of driftwood with carefully placed parsley and lemon wedge garnishes. She felt a stab of uneasiness as she looked back to Connor's simple display. His dishes were presented so that the food itself was the main attraction, but she could see how Celadon's elaborate display might appeal to the judges. She could only trust that they knew better than to be caught up too much in fancy plating.

The panel moved from each section, making marks on their clipboards and privately consulting among themselves. When they finally finished their presentation scoring, they turned their papers in to the host and prepared for the tasting. Harper wished she could break away from her seat and go stand with Connor, but it wasn't allowed at this point in the event.

The judges reconvened at their table while the chefs were given permission to deconstruct their presentations and portion out the food for serving. Harper tapped her foot nervously as she waited through the plating of the food, and the chefs who presented their dishes before Connor. At last his name was called, and she watched as two of the assistants on hand helped carry his plates to the judges' table.

First, they tasted the soup course. Connor

and Harper had supposed that most of the entrants would be serving their take on Maryland or cream of crab soup, as the standard fare of the region. So Connor had decided to risk going in a different direction, taking an old recipe for Irish seafood chowder and changing it up to make Maryland blue crab the star ingredient. It was Harper's favorite of all three dishes Connor was competing with. The blue crab would be succulent and sweet, pairing well with the sweet corn, carrots and potatoes that filled the rest of the bowl. But she couldn't read the judges' expressions well enough to know what they thought of the flavors.

Next was the appetizer. It had been Connor's idea to take traditional Irish soda bread and use it as the base for a seafood bruschetta. The rustic bread was grilled for crispness and topped with Maryland oysters and a mix of wild mushrooms, green onions and crumbled bacon, all dressed in a simple vinaigrette. Harper thought that for all its simplicity, it was a rather brilliant dish and showcased both the bay oysters and Connor's Irish heritage perfectly.

His entrée was the result of both their labors. Grilled rockfish, seasoned with Connor's own spice blend instead of the cream sauce he'd originally paired with it, served alongside Irish colcannon—a mash of potatoes and cabbage. A bright drizzle of thyme-infused olive oil added a golden-green touch.

Harper couldn't see the judges' faces as they tasted and scored. One said something to Connor, though she couldn't catch the words. But Connor smiled and nodded, his posture relaxing, so she breathed a little easier.

After the tasting was finished, Missy Donahue stepped forward to escort Connor across the room to where each chef was being interviewed on how they thought the competition had gone. Harper's eyes never left Connor as he spoke with a couple of interviewers, cameras rolling to catch his responses, and then posed for several photos.

It strained the limits of her patience to be sidelined and waiting through the rest of the tastings. After Connor's time in the limelight was concluded, Missy directed him back to his station. He stood in front and waited along with the other chefs as the judging continued.

At last the final chef presented his dishes and then went through the interview round. The judges sorted through their scoring with the help of one of the competition officials.

Harper felt her blood pressure ratcheting up as they compared notes and determined the winner. Did they know they held a man's future in their hands? She wanted him to win so desperately. Perhaps it was counterproductive to her own goals, but she didn't care anymore. She just wanted Connor to keep the Anchor.

After what felt like hours of deliberating, the official nodded and gathered the scoring sheets for the final tabulating. She grew restless with the long wait but every time her eyes went to Connor's and found him looking in her direction, she experienced a wave of calm. She wanted to be down there with him, to hold his hand and wait this out at his side. She longed for a future with him, and with Molly. He'd said he thought he was falling in love with her. Though she'd tried to dodge the idea for some time, she knew that she was already in love with him. He was a good man who had shouldered so much on his own. She wanted to help share that load with him, to be there for him through every high and every low. Because she knew that he, in turn, would never leave her side. He was loyal and loving, and he celebrated the little things in each day: a kiss, or a touch, enjoying a good meal and laughing with friends. He was the very thing she'd always wanted and never quite hoped to find.

The microphone thudded as the host took it from its stand. Harper jumped at the sound, her gaze jerking away from Connor.

It was time to announce the winner.

CONNOR COULD BARELY take his eyes off Harper. Just knowing she was there, silently cheering him on had made getting through this competition possible. But now, as the host took the stand, he forced himself to look away. This was the moment he learned if it all had been for nothing.

The host began with the usual preliminaries—extending their thanks to the entrants as well as the sponsors, naming each one and reminding everyone of their generosity in providing not only the prize money but the equipment and ingredients. Connor certainly appreciated the people who had made this event possible, but he just wished the host would get on with it.

He went on to discuss the Chesapeake Bay area and what it meant to be named the Best of the Bay winner for the year. There was the prize money as well as a feature on the EATS television channel. There would also be high-

lights in several local magazines and news-
papers.

Connor tried to keep from fidgeting impatiently.

Get on with it, mate...

"And now the time has come to announce
the winner of the 12th Annual Best of the Bay
competition."

Connor straightened as they finally came to
the point. The host shuffled through the notes
he held and then cleared his throat.

"In third place, we have Baltimore's own
executive chef of the Oyster and Pearl, Jennifer Houghton."

There was a round of applause as Jennifer
bowed and stepped up to accept her plaque,
the paltry prize for being a runner-up. Jennifer
shook hands with the host and then returned
to her station at the end of the line. Connor
tried to slow his pulse.

"I have to say," the host went on, "that in
all the years of the Best of the Bay, this is the
first time we've come so close to a tie. There
was only a difference of three points separating the first place winner from the second,
and it just goes to show what amazing talent
we have represented here today."

Connor ground his teeth together, willing

the host to announce the winning chef. What did three points matter? It was still the difference of first and second place, and that's all that counted.

"In second place, we have a newcomer to the event. Though born in Ireland, he moved to this region when he was a boy and received his chef's training at the Institute of Culinary Distinction. His dishes today evoked both the charm of his native country and the flavor of his adopted homeland. Second place goes to Connor Callahan."

Connor couldn't move. Second place. Only second. Three points from first but still second.

"Congratulations, Connor, on placing so close to first," the host said. "Please join me here at the podium to receive your prize."

He forced himself to move, one foot in front of the other, so that he could step up and receive his plaque. He pasted a smile on his face, though it felt false. He shook hands with the host, though his fingers were numb. He expressed his gratitude, posed for a photo with his prize but all the while he kept hearing the words *three points separating* drumming inside his head.

Three points had just cost him his restaurant. Three points had just put an end to his battle to hold on to the Anchor. Why even bother to announce this fact? Three points might as well have been three hundred. He'd lost. That was the heart of it.

He returned to his place in the line and waited for the winner to be announced. He didn't even hear who the host named, but when Daniel Roth stepped forward to accept his award and pose for photos, he had his answer.

As the final thanks were given, and the chefs were encouraged to mingle, Connor looked immediately for Harper. She was pushing her way through crowd in an effort to get to him. And suddenly, everything felt all right again. Harper was here. He had her. Wasn't that better than any amount of money or prestige?

She fought her way through the people surrounding Daniel Roth and finally closed the distance between them. He swept her up in his arms, and before she could utter a word, he lowered his mouth to hers. He kissed her fiercely, having had enough of waiting. He was going to make Harper his. That would be the real prize to come from this day. She kissed him back, matching his force so that he knew how much she cared for him, too. They didn't pull apart for some time, and when they did, she looked up at him with flushed cheeks.

"Second place is still pretty impressive in a competition like this," she declared.

He shrugged. "It doesn't matter. It was all about saving the Anchor, and if I can't have that... I can still have something better."

She sounded breathless as she asked, "What's that?"

"You," he whispered.

Her face glowed with joy. She tilted her face up for another kiss, and he obliged her.

"Mr. Callahan."

Reluctantly, he released Harper to see who had addressed him. A stocky but tall and muscled man in an expensive suit held out his hand. Harper straightened beside him.

"Congratulations on second place, son. Those were some impressive dishes from you, so different from the usual fare we see at these events. I'm sorry you didn't win first. It isn't as if Roth needs another trophy. It would have been better off going to someone with a unique vision."

"Um, thanks, Mr...."

"Just call me Nathan," the man insisted. "I know Harper from way back." He nodded in her direction. Connor looked briefly at Harper. Her smile appeared tight.

"I'm the owner of the Pratt Restaurant Group," he explained.

"Oh, Nathan Pratt." Connor placed him by name, if not by his face. He'd heard of the well-connected business mogul.

"Harper, you didn't tell me you were here with one of the competitors."

Harper was acting strange. She was incredibly rigid, he could feel her tension all through the arm he had wrapped around her.

"Harper and I have been working together for the past couple of months," Connor explained when she didn't speak up. "She's the reason I entered this competition in the first place."

"Is that so?" Nathan mused with interest. "Harper's a sharp girl, as I'm sure you know. Takes after her old man that way. Allan Worth has made millions by speculating on the right investments."

Connor hadn't really considered that Harper's dad might be worth millions. The thought unbalanced him for a moment.

"...her new restaurant?"

Connor had been distracted and missed the first part of what Nathan had said. He realized it must have been notable in some way, however, because Harper jerked, breaking contact with him. Nathan was smiling placidly, though, so Connor couldn't quite reconcile their two different reactions in that moment.

"What was that?" Connor asked, hoping to find out what it was he'd missed.

Nathan placed a hand on his shoulder, and Connor resisted the urge to shake it off.

"I know you have a restaurant of your own, but I asked if Harper here is planning to have you consult with her on her new restaurant? You'd be able to offer some great suggestions, I'd imagine."

Nothing was making sense. Harper didn't own a restaurant. In another few weeks, neither would he.

He felt an uneasy ripple go up his spine, something his subconscious recognized before his brain brought it to his attention.

"I could see great things coming from the two of you."

"Thanks, Nathan." Harper had wrapped her arm through Connor's and was forcefully steering him away. "But we better move on now. There are many more people to see."

"Of course, of course. But remember what

I said, Harper, if you need anything, you give me a call."

She waved him off and practically pushed Connor out of the man's presence. Connor was still trying to make sense of the conversation as Harper led them to group of food bloggers and writers. They immediately pounced, offering congratulations and raving over his choices of dishes. One woman asked if he was really Irish. He assured her he was and explained how he'd lived in Ireland for much of his childhood. He didn't have time to process the meaning behind Nathan's words, and he couldn't understand Harper's reaction to them. The man had been confused, that was what Connor assumed. And he didn't have a chance to think otherwise as he was introduced to various attendees and asked for another post-competition interview.

By the time everything wrapped up, he was too exhausted to consider the strange conversation with Nathan Pratt. He and Harper gathered their things and headed to her car. They followed I-95 back to Findlay Roads in silence. He assumed Harper was as drained as he was, but she kept her attention focused solely on the road. Eventually, he slipped into a doze, coming awake every so often as the car rolled along. In this state of only partial sleep, his mind replayed the day's events, reliving the competition and wondering what he might have done differently to close that three-point gap. It had likely been the scoring concerning the complexity of the dishes, he decided. That must have been what set him behind.

He came awake to realize they'd exited I-95 and were on the road toward home. After a few seconds, he closed his eyes again, letting his mind drift. He found himself replaying the conversation with Nathan Pratt, trying to make sense of it.

"…consult with her on her new restaurant…"

Harper's new restaurant.

And then he recalled something she'd said. "I've been thinking that I'd like to open my own restaurant someday."

He felt the car brake to a stop and heard Harper shift into Park. He was wide-awake, but his eyes remained closed. Something about the conversation prodded him, as though he had missed the major part of the meaning behind it. He opened his eyes and saw they had pulled up to the Moontide Inn. He'd have to head inside and tell Molly about losing the contest…about giving up the Anchor.

The two thoughts collided in his head—Harper's strange reaction and the realization he'd be giving up his restaurant.

"Harper." He looked at her. "What did Nathan Pratt mean when he said you were opening a restaurant?"

Her breathing quickened. The sun had set on their way back from Baltimore, but there was enough light from the moon through the windows that he could read the uneasiness on her features.

"It's something I've been meaning to talk to you about."

He waited, a faint sense of foreboding creeping over him.

"When the Anchor goes into foreclosure, I… I'd like to buy it."

He blinked. "What?"

She reached behind her into the backseat and pulled something out of her bag. "And I want you to be my partner." She handed him a thick folder, and he took it automatically. She continued talking as he flipped it open and began to look through the pages.

Sketches. There were detailed sketches of what he recognized as the Anchor, from the position of the bar and the layout of the entry and back. But this wasn't his Anchor. It was being transformed into something else.

"... Irish pub," Harper was saying. "We can rethink the menu, incorporate more Irish flavors. There's nothing like it in Findlay Roads at this point and given the town's history, its Irish heritage, it's perfect. It could bring in locals and tourists alike. I have a marketing plan..." She reached over and pulled out another paper, laying it on top of the drawings. It was a detailed outline of advertising and other opportunities to bring in business.

Harper's enthusiasm for the project was evident in the way she rushed ahead without pausing to see his reaction. Or perhaps that was nerves because she certainly seemed a little agitated, as well. He let her talk as he continued flipping through the business proposal. When he reached one of the papers in the back, he paused. There was a list of investors and notes from a meeting. Along with the date it had taken place.

He slammed the folder shut and raised his head. Harper stopped talking.

"How long have you been planning this?"

She didn't answer him right away. He zeroed in on her.

"How long, Harper?"

She swallowed, "A while."

He held up the meeting notes and pointed to the date. "Almost from the beginning, was it? It had to have taken time to come up with a proposal like this. And more time to bring on investors. So tell me, were you really looking for a job when you first turned up at the Anchor? Or were you just looking for a restaurant?"

"No," she said. "No, the reasons I came to the Anchor were the ones I gave. I lost my column. I needed a job. I was desperate."

"Then how long was it before you realized you wanted my restaurant?"

She winced, and the sight of it, almost an admission of guilt, caused him to curse. He reached for the door handle and let himself out of the car. Harper followed his move and came around to stop him before he could step up onto the Moontide's porch.

"Connor, listen to me. You don't understand."

He turned on her. "What's not to understand? It's all in that folder, in black and white. You want to take my restaurant from me."

"That is *not* what I want," she protested. "I only thought that if the worst happened, and you lost the Anchor, that I could be the one to purchase it from the bank."

He narrowed his eyes. "You knew," he breathed. "You knew about the foreclosure, before I ever brought it up."

She swallowed and didn't deny it. The sting of betrayal pierced him.

"You've been playing me all along," he rasped.

"No. No, I found out about the foreclosure by accident, but I never intended to use it against you."

"Then, what? You thought you'd *help* me? Is that why you suggested I enter the Best of the Bay competition?" he demanded. "Or was that part of your plan to sabotage me?"

"Sabotage you?"

He nodded. "You let me enter that contest and convinced me to cook simple, rustic dishes even though I knew they wouldn't be complex enough to win. And then, when I lost, you'd say you did everything you could to help me keep the Anchor. But maybe you were planning this all along, knowing I'd never win."

She was shaking her head, her eyes wide. "Connor, stop it. Listen to yourself—that's ridiculous. You were three points away from being the best chef there. You have all the skills you need to win a competition like that. And I never wanted for you to lose the Anchor. In fact, that's why I want you to join me, when I buy it from the bank. I want you on board—"

"I'll not be part of this to assuage your guilt, Harper."

"It's not about that!"

He paced the yard in front of the inn, trying to lower his voice to keep from rousing the curiosity of those inside the house.

"I thought I'd misjudged you. I didn't believe you were the harpy I'd assumed you to be. Was I wrong, Harper?"

The weight of what she'd done suddenly settled on his shoulders, draining the anger from him and replacing it with sadness. He'd fallen in love with this woman. He'd wanted to share a life with her.

"Was all of that a lie?" he asked, hating the vulnerability he heard in his tone. He should never have let his guard down. He should never have hired Harper on at all.

"It wasn't a lie." She tried to move toward him, but he took a step back. He simply didn't trust her. If she touched him, he would break. He'd sweep her into his arms and forget this treachery. He couldn't let her near him.

"But the thing is, I don't believe you," he

said. "Because even if it's true that your motives weren't entirely selfish…you should have told me about this. You shouldn't have kept these plans from me."

"I didn't want to," she said. "But, Connor, what would you have done if I'd told you? You'd have pushed me away. Maybe even fired me. I didn't want that. Because I love you."

He took another step back, stunned to hear these words from her. He'd known she had feelings for him, but she had never said… Never admitted that she loved him.

"I love you, Connor," she repeated. "I don't want to see you hurt, and I don't want you to lose the Anchor, either. But more than anything, I don't want to lose *you*."

He had a choice, he knew. He could accept Harper's claims and choose to believe she spoke the truth—that she hadn't told him because of the reasons she'd named. But there was the niggling doubt in his head that she had known perfectly well what she was doing all along. Just how devious was she? He'd once thought her capable of anything, but then he'd gotten to know her and changed his mind. But what if he didn't know her at all? Could he really risk letting her into his life, into Molly's life, after she'd kept her plans from him all this time?

He shook his head, and he watched her expression fall.

"You should have told me," he repeated. "Go ahead with your plans for the Anchor. But leave me and my daughter out of it."

He turned his back on her then and moved up the steps of the inn, leaving her standing alone in the moonlight.

CHAPTER TWELVE

HARPER HAD NO intention of getting out of bed. She'd prefer to just bury herself beneath the covers and forget the past twenty-four hours. If she could just stay wrapped in the shelter of her coverlet, perhaps she could pretend that yesterday had never happened. No competition. No encounter with Nathan. There would still be the possibility of Connor winning the grand prize, and there would certainly, under no circumstances, be an argument like the one they'd had the night before.

Every time reality intruded, she dug deeper into the blankets, willing it away. She couldn't bear to face the day without the possibility of seeing Connor. So she simply wouldn't face it. That was her philosophy.

Until Tessa knocked on her door and then entered without Harper's permission, seating herself on the edge of the mattress and tugging the covers free.

"It's nearly noon," Tessa observed even as

Harper tried to pull the covers back up over her head. "What happened?" her sister asked in that knowing way that only sisters have.

Harper released her grip on the blankets and met Tessa's eyes.

"He hates me," she whispered, and then she promptly burst into the tears she'd been holding back since last night's fight.

Tessa didn't ask questions, at least not immediately. Instead, she handed Harper tissue after tissue until her eyes were so swollen, she could only see through tiny slits. Only then did the tears stop.

"Get up and wash your face," Tessa urged, "and I'll go make us some coffee."

By the time Harper entered the kitchen, face washed and dressed for the day, Tessa had laid out coffee as well as a plate of cinnamon rolls.

"Let's take them out on the back porch," Tessa suggested, "and you can tell me everything."

Harper didn't protest but dutifully followed Tessa outside and curled up on the swing with a warm cup of coffee in hand. The cinnamon rolls looked delicious, but she didn't have much of an appetite. Tessa took one, though, and nibbled at it as she waited for Harper to speak.

"I take it Connor didn't win the competition," she prompted after several long minutes of silence.

Harper swallowed at the memory. "No," she managed to get out. "But he was so close. Three points away from the win. It was the nearest to a tie they've ever had in twelve years."

"Poor Connor."

Harper nodded and tried to tamp back the tears she felt rising to the surface.

"I assume that's not what all the crying is about, though," Tessa prodded.

Harper bit the inside of her cheek. Once she had herself under control, she shook her head. "No. He found out—or I told him about—my plans to buy the Anchor."

"Oh."

"He thought I'd been planning it all along, that everything I did was a means to my own ends."

Tessa reached out and took the coffee mug from Harper's hands as the tears threatened to spill once more. She set the beverage aside.

"I'm in love with him, Tessa," she admitted, "and I can't bear the thought of letting him go."

Tessa's words were gentle as she said, "But you wanted his restaurant for yourself."

"Well…yes. But not like this."

"Oh, Harper. How did you think he was going to take the news? This restaurant has been in his family for years."

"I hoped he'd be happy to see someone who knows its history buy the place?" She could hear the doubt in her own voice.

"But, Harper, it would be so much easier if a stranger bought it, someone who maybe didn't know how much it meant to him."

Harper ran her fingers over the smooth wood of the swing. "It wasn't going to be like that, though. I was going to offer him a job, a partnership. I wanted us to work together."

"But you never *asked* him," Tessa reminded her. "You moved ahead without broaching the subject first. He probably felt blindsided when he found out."

Tessa had a point. Harper hadn't handled this well at all.

"I got carried away," she admitted, "in the idea of owning my own restaurant. And…" She didn't want to speak the words out loud.

"And maybe proving something to Dad in the process?"

The words pierced Harper, going straight

to her heart. She looked away. Had that been her motive? To finally prove to her father that her dreams had merit, that she was every bit as worthy of his approval as Paige?

"I'm not trying to prove anything," she argued. "I just don't want to work for Dad. I have different dreams. I'm not Paige," Harper pointed out.

"Why do you always make that sound like such a bad thing?" Tessa asked.

"Because… Paige is the perfect daughter, the perfect businesswoman, the perfect wife, mom, everything. It's no wonder Dad always compares me to her."

Tessa shook her head. "Harper, Dad isn't comparing you to Paige. You're just so busy comparing yourself to her that you think everyone else is, too." Her sister leaned forward. "It's okay if you're not Paige. I love her, but I wouldn't want to have two sisters just like her. Paige may be the one I turned to when I had questions about my studies or schooling, or even when I moved to town and into the cottage. But she's not the sister I called when Justin Rankin stood me up on prom night. And when I locked myself out of the house *twice* during senior year because I kept sneaking out with friends, which of my sisters drove an hour each way just to help me get back inside without waking up Mom and Dad?"

Harper's lips twitched at the memory. "You'd have been grounded straight through to graduation."

"Of course I would have. But Paige would have told Mom and Dad everything, thinking she was doing the right thing. And when I was in college, and I couldn't decide on a major or what I wanted to do with my life, which sister spent hours on the phone with me, asking questions about what made me happy until I realized I wanted to work with children?"

Harper swallowed. She had never thought about it that way. In all the times she'd compared herself to Paige, she had never once considered that their differences didn't make her less...they were her strengths.

"So you're not Paige. So what? I, for onc, wouldn't want you to be. Because I'd miss who you are way too much."

Harper managed a watery smile. "Thanks for that."

"I mean it." Tessa reached for her hand and squeezed it. "I don't want you to give up on your dreams, Harper. I just want you to be sure what those dreams are. Do you still want the restaurant?"

Harper thought about this for several minutes. "I do," she admitted, "but it doesn't mean nearly as much if Connor isn't with me. Everything about that place reminds me of him. I had all these plans—to convert it into an Irish pub so he could showcase his best dishes and preserve his father's memory. Dad loved the idea. It has so much potential in a town like this. But without Connor…it seems a little silly."

"Why?" Tessa pushed. "If you believe in the idea, why not try to make it work? Connor may have been the inspiration behind it, but it's still your dream, Harper."

This much was true. She'd already embraced the changes she'd had in mind for the Anchor. As much as she wanted Connor to be a part of them, did losing him also mean giving up on her dream?

As difficult as the idea of running the Anchor without him seemed, she couldn't bear to lose the restaurant and Connor, too.

"All right," she agreed. "I won't give up on the Anchor."

"Good." Tessa released her hand. "But, Harper, don't give up on Connor, either. Not just yet."

Though Tessa might have had a point,

Harper also knew Connor better than Tessa did. And knowing Connor, she didn't think he'd forgive her anytime soon.

CONNOR HAD BEEN dreading this conversation with Molly, but he had put it off long enough. So he took her to the ice cream shop and then they headed down to the boardwalk to stroll the promenade together. She was on her best behavior. In fact, he'd noticed that in the past month, her manners and mischievousness had improved dramatically. It seemed to have started after Harper had taken the little girl under her wing, spending time with her on the pretend restaurant and lavishing her with attention. In turn, he suspected Molly was doing her best to mimic Harper in a lot of ways, which may have translated to the change he'd noticed. Was that what Molly had been missing all this time? A mother figure, someone to look up to? There were several women in her life…but none who had taken as much time with her as Harper had. Rory tried, of course, during her rare visits home. And since her return she'd been trying to make up for lost time. But still, there was something about Harper and the way she cared for his daughter…

He clamped down on the thought. It had

likely all been part of Harper's endgame, cozying up to his little girl.

But really, what could that possibly have gained her in this situation? Perhaps she'd liked Molly simply for herself. She'd said as much on different occasions. Maybe, just maybe, she'd been genuine where Molly was concerned.

The thought was a balm, but it didn't manage to salve the deeper wound of Harper's duplicity.

Molly had been skipping ahead on the boardwalk, chasing a pair of squirrels until they dived off the promenade and onto the grass. Her quarry lost, she headed back to him and stuck her hand in his. She was obviously enjoying this father-daughter outing. She hummed one of Rory's Irish tunes under her breath, and Connor loathed destroying her happiness with the news he had to share.

They walked for a little while longer, passing the occasional jogger or couple out for a stroll. The weather was perfect with late-summer sun and a temperate breeze off the water. A few white clouds crowded together in the blue sky, but they didn't block the sun as it cast a net of glittering diamonds on the waves of the bay.

Connor finally stopped walking as they came to one of the benches positioned at intervals along the promenade. He held on to Molly's hand as he led them to the seat. Molly plopped down beside him, dangling her legs over the bench and kicking them back and forth.

"Molly, love. There's something I have to talk to you about."

She must have recognized the seriousness in his tone because her legs suddenly stilled. She looked up at him in concern, her tiny eyebrows lowering.

"What is it, Daddy?"

He drew a breath and then exhaled it. He wished he knew how to soften this blow. He'd have gladly spared her this, if he could have. The Anchor was the only home she knew. "I'm afraid I'm going to have to give up the restaurant." He waited to see her reaction to this news.

Her frown deepened. "You mean…we're not going to live there anymore?"

He brushed a strand of hair behind her ear. The wind immediately caught it and tugged it free again.

"No," he said. "We're not going to live there anymore, and I won't own it. So I'll have to find another job. And another place for us to live."

Her lower lip quivered slightly. "Can't we just live at the Moontide?" she suggested. She'd come to enjoy the attention she received at the B and B, from Lenora and Erin and from having Rory in town. Plus, she liked helping take care of Kitt. He wondered if a newfound sense of responsibility in addition to all the female companionship had contributed to his daughter's improved behavior.

"For a while," he agreed, "but not forever." Lenora had assured him he could stay as long as he needed, but he didn't want to take advantage of her hospitality longer than necessary.

"Then…where are we going to live?"

This was the most difficult part. "I don't know yet. But there's a chance we may need to leave Findlay Roads."

She looked stunned at this, and he reached out to draw her a little closer. She resisted. "But we can't leave."

"We might not have to. It will all depend on where I can find a job. But the truth is, Molly, that there will be more chances of that elsewhere."

"But *Harper's here.*"

His hand dropped back to the bench. He

couldn't tell her that Harper would be the new owner of the Anchor. He was at a loss as to how he'd explain that one. "Harper has her own life to live. We won't be seeing her anymore."

Molly stared at him. "But you love her."

He felt a shiver run over him at his daughter's perceptiveness. "Molly...it's a lot more complicated than that."

She shook her head. "No, it's not. You need to be wherever she is, no matter what happens."

"Molly, you have to understand."

But she was having none of it. She worked her way off the bench and stood before him.

"We can't leave," she insisted.

He leaned forward, resting his elbows on his knees so he could be at her eye level. He hesitated and then decided he might as well share the full truth with her. Her recent attitude shift made him think she was probably growing up enough that he could be a bit more open. "I know this is hard to understand, but... Harper is going to buy the restaurant. She's the new owner of the Anchor."

"So?"

He knew she was just a child, but didn't she understand what this meant?

"Then we don't have to leave," she reasoned. "We can all be together."

"No, Molly. That's not going to happen."

Her face was set into the defiant lines he knew so well. She folded her arms across her chest. "I'm not leaving. I'll live with Harper."

"No, you won't."

She stomped her foot in frustration. "We can't leave! It's our home!"

"We can create a new home—"

"But *Grandpa is buried here*. We can't leave him." She burst into tears, and he saw where at least some of her distress stemmed from. He gathered her into his arms, and this time she didn't resist.

"Shh," he soothed. "Oh, my love. Don't you worry about such a thing. Your granddad lives in your heart. He'll be with us wherever we are."

She hiccuped into his shoulder, and he stroked her hair.

"Even if we have to leave, we'll come back to visit, yeah? We'll see Erin and Kitt, Rafael and Leah."

"And Harper?"

He felt a stab of pain. For all his talk, leaving Harper would be the hardest of all. Despite what she'd done, he couldn't forget her so easily. And he didn't want to distress Molly further, so he nodded.

She relaxed slightly and sagged against him.

"And Findlay Roads will always be home, won't it, Daddy?"

He swallowed back the lump that rose in his throat at these words. "Aye, love. It will always be home."

ON THE WAY back to the Moontide, Connor decided to swing by the Anchor and pick up the mail. The kitchen renovation was still under way, which was why he, Molly and Rory were still staying at the inn. But he'd made a point to stop by every few days to collect his mail and see how things were progressing. He didn't linger today, however. What was the point in checking up on things when the property would only be his for another two weeks at most? So he made a quick stop, gathered the mail and returned to the pickup before heading back to the bed-and-breakfast.

By the time Connor pulled up at the inn, Molly seemed in better spirits. They entered the B and B's foyer only to have Lenora amble in with a smile.

"You're just in time, young lady. I have an

entire batch of oatmeal raisin cookies that need tasting."

Perhaps Connor should have protested, given the ice cream Molly had just consumed, but he didn't have it in him to disappoint her yet again so he said nothing as she scampered off toward the kitchen. Lenora began to shuffle after her.

"Don't let her eat too many cookies and ruin her dinner, Lenora," he called as the woman departed.

He caught a brief glimpse of her waving a dismissal at this concern. He couldn't help a smile at the way Lenora doted on his daughter. He remembered the mail he'd left in the cab of the truck so he headed back out the front door to retrieve it. He flipped through a few inconsequential notices and then prioritized any bills and insurance paperwork by placing them at the front of the pile. There was a large manila envelope that he saved for last, surprised when he pulled it forth and noted a company name and return address he recognized as Harper's father's investment firm.

He placed the rest of the mail inside the truck's cab and carried the larger envelope with him back to the front steps of the inn. He took a seat on the porch and opened the packet, pulling out what appeared to be the same proposal he'd looked at in Harper's car the other night.

He wasn't sure how it had ended up being mailed to him. Had Harper asked for it to be sent? He checked the postmark and noted it had been sent the day before the competition. He wasn't sure when it had arrived since he'd avoided going to pick up his mail for the past week and a half. But if Harper had chosen to send this to him, it had obviously been before they'd experienced their falling-out.

The sight of the proposed plans irritated him slightly, but he was still unable to resist taking another look at them. He'd only scanned them that night in Harper's car, not bothering to note her proposed changes. But now he reviewed the sketches as well as her business and marketing plans.

She had some good ideas, he grudgingly admitted. He almost wished he'd come up with some of them. Her plans included a light remodel to convert the look and feel of the Anchor into an Irish pub. Her marketing included such avenues as the historical society, given the town's Irish beginnings, and advertising with the local sightseeing groups to place the restaurant on their walking tours of the town. The proposal went on to cover a variety of other advertising and promotional opportunities. He continued flipping through the pages until he reached the section on the menu. He opened it to find his name listed as prospective executive chef at the top along with a suggested menu that included, as the house specialty, Patrick's Shepherd's Pie. He swallowed at the sight and felt the first hint of doubt.

Could it have been that Harper really hadn't planned to take over his restaurant but rather rebuild it...*with* him? He turned a few more pages, looking at the business plan with new eyes. Every word she'd voiced to him about his abilities was evident in her prospectus. She'd even written up a bio about him that he found on the page following the menu.

Irish-born chef Connor Callahan trained at the Institute of Culinary Distinction, one of the most prestigious culinary schools in the world. Having grown up around the restaurant his father established following his family's emigration from Ireland, he is trained in classical techniques with the instincts of a natural-born cook. One of his many talents lies in his ability to take the most humble dish and elevate it to a meal worthy of being served in any four-star restaurant.

He reread this paragraph three times, unable to believe that Harper had written such a thing about him. This was not inflated praise for the sake of her proposal…this was belief. Belief in him and in what he could do.

He flipped through several more pages and encountered more sketches of the exterior. He liked her vision. It echoed the feel of old-world European pubs but still retained modern lines and style.

How had he not seen this the other night? His pride and anger had blinded him to the obvious.

He turned another page and then stopped, staring at the image there. If he had ever doubted Harper's intentions, this proved that no matter how the idea had begun, she'd proceeded with Connor and his father's legacy in mind. If she had told him she'd planned to change the name of the restaurant, he'd have probably been angry. But seeing it like this only served to show him just how wrong he'd been.

She'd kept the symbol of the anchor, including it on the base of the sign beneath the restaurant's new name. And there, in bold, brilliant letters was the proof that he had never been far from Harper's planning.

The new name of the Rusty Anchor was Callahan's.

HARPER APPROACHED THE front of the Rusty Anchor and tried to quell the nerves churning in her stomach. When Connor had asked her to meet him here, she'd assumed it was to discuss the future of the restaurant. Did he plan to fight the foreclosure? But how? As far as she knew, he still didn't have the ten thousand he needed to forestall the bank. Perhaps he had changed his mind about partnering with her?

But she pushed this thought aside for the wishful thinking it was. He'd sounded distant on the phone, coolly professional. It was unlikely anything had changed. This meeting would have nothing to do with the two of them. It would be all about the restaurant. She felt a well of sadness at the thought. She still wanted the Anchor, but much of her enthusiasm had ebbed over the past week. Things were set to move forward, though. The investors were in place, and everything was ready for that next step.

The next step being that Connor would have to relinquish the restaurant. Imagining how that must make him feel left her faintly nauseous. She drew a deep breath. There was no point in delaying the inevitable. She braced herself to enter the restaurant and see Connor, dreading the look of aversion she expected to see on his face.

She tried the front door and found it unlocked so she stepped inside, noting the "Closed for Repairs" sign that kept the general public out during the kitchen renovation. She took a moment to savor the feeling of walking through these doors. Everything had changed since the first time she'd crossed this threshold. She'd gained—and lost—so much since then. She closed her eyes and breathed deeply, wanting to remember the Anchor as it was at this moment, before things changed. Then she opened her eyes and closed the door behind her, calling out a greeting, "Hello? Connor, are you here?"

She stepped past the hostess podium and into the dining area, her heartbeat ratcheting up as she saw Connor seated at one of the empty tables in the center of the room. Was it only the days spent apart or had he grown handsomer since she'd seen him last?

He wore a charcoal-gray button-down shirt with the sleeves rolled up. The gray suited his dark coloring. His black hair was styled neatly, but the day's worth of stubble she'd come to love still dusted his jaw.

His green eyes were fastened on her, never moving an inch. She felt another ripple of nerves run through her at the intensity of his gaze. She forced herself to move farther into the room, one foot in front of the other, willing herself not to hesitate under his unwavering stare.

"You said you wanted to talk," she continued, since he had yet to say a word. She came closer to the table and tried to avoid running her damp palms over the cargo pants she wore. She felt suddenly warm in her pale pink jacket and removed it for the simplicity of the scoop-necked ivory top beneath.

Connor stood as she drew near, and she halted in her tracks. But he only moved around the table and pulled out a chair for her in a gentlemanly fashion. He took her jacket and draped it across the back before she slid into the seat. His chivalry only made things more difficult. If he would yell at her or show some sign of irritation, then maybe she could manage to get through this. But any further display of kindness might just break her.

She took the seat he offered.

"Would you like something to drink?"

It was a polite enough question, but for Harper, the formality only served to drive her pain deeper.

"No, thank you."

He didn't say anything else. He just watched her with that aggravatingly intense stare. She fidgeted beneath it.

"You wanted to talk?" she prompted a second time.

He gave a nod and then lifted a stack of papers from an empty chair beside him, placing them on the table. She glanced at the top sheet and recognized a copy of her business proposal for the Anchor.

"How…how did you get that?" she asked.

He shrugged. "It arrived in the mail from your father's investment firm. I assumed you sent it."

She shook her head. "Oh, no. Connor, it wasn't me. It must have been an accident. My father's secretary must have mistakenly sent it to you. Your name and address was on a lot of paperwork because I had hoped—" She stopped. She dared not voice aloud the things she'd hoped. "I would never purposely throw this in your face after our…" She tried to phrase things delicately by saying, "…our discussion regarding the restaurant. I am so sorry."

"I'm not."

It took her a second to register his words. When she did, her eyes darted to his. The concentration remained in his gaze, but there was something else there, too.

"You're…not?"

He took the proposal off the table and flicked through several pages before laying it back down. She stared at the sketch she'd created of the Anchor's exterior with the new sign she'd planned in the center.

Callahan's.

"I didn't believe you."

His voice had softened, like melting chocolate. It was velvety, nearly a caress. She looked up at him.

"I'm the one who owes you an apology."

She tingled from head to toe at these words.

"I was daft," he said, "letting my pride get in the way. The truth is that if the Anchor couldn't be mine, I'd want it to go to you. I was just too blind and hurt to realize it."

"No, I was wrong. I should have told you

what I was planning rather than letting you find out the way you did. It was ridiculous of me to think you'd embrace the idea when you didn't know a thing about it."

A corner of his lips turned upward. "Well, maybe we both could have handled things a bit differently."

"Yes," she agreed, "definitely."

He drew a breath. "So I was wondering…" He cleared his throat. "If that position for an executive chef was still open?"

The way he looked at her nearly made her curl her toes in her sandals.

"Oh, well…there's a problem."

He looked startled. "A problem?"

"Yes, see, I'm not just looking for an executive chef. I need a business partner."

His features relaxed, and he broke into a grin.

"A business partner, is it?"

She nodded. "It's a lot of responsibility. And I can't have just anyone in the role. It has to be someone I'm comfortable with, who doesn't mind sharing the load and the long hours."

"Hmm. Well, I might consider it." His eyes had taken on a teasing glint. "But I have a daughter to raise, and I'll need to have time for her."

"Of course. That's why I'll be working as the full-time manager. It will leave you free to focus on your chef duties. And with Erin as sous chef, provided she wants the job, we should be able to manage better hours for you."

He nodded, looking introspective as though he were thinking through the offer. "There's one more thing." He looked so serious that she felt a flutter of doubt. "I want more than just a business partner. I want someone to walk with me through this life, to challenge me and to be honest when it looks as though I'm getting it wrong. I want someone to stand beside me when things get rough, and I want to be able to hold her up and care for her in return. My dad used to talk about a woman who keeps a man on his toes. I've met her. And I don't want to lose her now."

He reached down again, this time into his pocket, and pulled out something small and silver. He placed it on the table between them. It was a Celtic Claddagh ring, the two hands reaching across the circumference of the band to hold a heart between them.

"It was my mom's," he murmured as Harper felt tears filling her eyes. He stood from his seat and came around the table to kneel before her. "And now, if you'll do me the honor,

Harper Worth… I want it to be yours, and for you to be mine."

At first, she couldn't speak around the lump of emotion in her throat. She kept him waiting so long that he sighed.

"Don't keep a man on pins and needles, love. Say something."

She nodded then and kept on nodding until she could find the words. "Yes. Yes. Yes."

He broke into a grin and took the ring from the table to slide it onto her finger. It was a perfect fit.

She ran a hand through his hair and let her palm come to rest against his jaw. The Claddagh ring winked in the dining room light.

"Ah, what's this?" He reached out and touched a finger to her cheek. When he pulled it back for her inspection, she saw an eyelash resting on the surface of his skin.

"Make a wish, Harper."

She leaned her forehead against his.

"I don't have to. All my wishes are already coming true."

EPILOGUE

Seven months later

HARPER KNEW SHE should get back inside. The early-spring air was chilly, and the light was fading fast. She wrapped her arms around herself in an attempt to keep warm, the glow from the windows beckoning to her. It was hard to believe that less than a year ago, she'd stood in this same spot, looking up at the Rusty Anchor's sign and wondering what her future held. Such a short time for so much to change. She unwrapped her arms and held out her hand to marvel, as she sometimes did, at the Claddagh ring on her finger. Connor had offered to get her another ring, a more traditional diamond, at Christmas, but she had refused. She would never trade the silver band for something fancier. It was part of Connor and his family, and so it was a part of her. The ring that had once been his mother's felt right.

These days, everything felt right. The restaurant's grand reopening was a great success. Even from outside its doors, she could hear the laughter within. The place was packed with members of the community, curious at its unveiling. The new menu, a blend of traditional Irish dishes with Connor's contemporary twists had the reservation book filling up fast, and the summer season was still several months out. It looked as if the Rusty Anchor, now known as Callahan's, was going to have a comeback.

Harper's attention was drawn from the anchor on the sign to the sound of the restaurant's front door as it opened. Her eyes dropped and saw Connor emerging, holding her sweater in his hands. Her heart jumped with happiness at the sight of him, and she nearly sighed aloud at the handsome figure he made in his new black chef's jacket. As he approached, he leaned down for a kiss, and she ran her fingers along his jaw.

"What are you doing out here?" he asked her as he slipped the sweater around her shoulders.

She smiled and leaned into him. "Just taking a moment to be grateful."

"Hmm." It was a sound of agreement, and

he wrapped his arms around her as they both looked to the glowing windows.

"It's perfect, isn't it?"

"The perfect blend of you and me," he agreed. "Rory and Erin are already making plans to hold our wedding reception here. But I told them I'm not sure it's a large enough venue."

"It will have to be. This place is practically like a member of the family. I want it here. We'll just have to keep the reception small."

"Unlikely." He snorted. "Half the town is expecting an invitation."

"Then we'll spread out on the deck."

She shivered happily as Connor warmed her by dropping a kiss onto her neck.

"I'm glad Rory decided to stay and help us run things," she remarked.

"Me, too," he agreed. "It's been grand having her around more. And not just for babysitting Molly so we can have the occasional date night." He nuzzled her neck, and she shivered all over again.

After another moment, he pulled back with a regretful sigh. "We'd best get back inside. Your dad is in there telling stories about you to anyone who will listen."

Her eyes narrowed in suspicion. "What kind of stories?"

He grinned. "How you've always been independent, doing things your own way. And look where it's gotten you—a brand-new restaurant, a handsome Irish fiancé and a doting daughter in the package."

"He did not say all of that."

"Well, I may have elaborated about the handsome Irishman part."

She shifted in his arms, staying close but brushing off the shoulders of his chef's jacket.

"It's not that much of an exaggeration." She blinked innocently up at him. "You are an Irishman, at least."

He threw back his head and laughed, a sound she had become accustomed to in the past few months. She hoped she never stopped hearing Connor laugh. His head lowered to look at her, his green eyes locking with hers. They still twinkled with mirth as his expression became serious.

"I couldn't have done this without you, you know."

She rested her palm along his face. "And I wouldn't have wanted to do it without you."

"Daaaaad! Harper!"

They turned at the same time to see Molly

in the restaurant's doorway, beckoning them impatiently.

"Aunt Rory said I can't have any more cake until you come back inside! So hurry up!"

Connor looked back into her eyes. "Now there's a girl who knows how to keep a man on his toes."

"You poor bloke," she mimicked his accent. "And now you have two of us on your hands."

He tenderly ran the back of his hand along her cheek.

"I wouldn't have it any other way."

He dropped another kiss on her forehead and then took her hand as they headed back inside to the family and friends who made Findlay Roads home.

* * * * *

LARGER-PRINT BOOKS!

GET 2 FREE LARGER-PRINT NOVELS PLUS 2 FREE MYSTERY GIFTS

Love Inspired®

SUSPENSE
RIVETING INSPIRATIONAL ROMANCE

Larger-print novels are now available...

YES! Please send me **The Montana Mavericks Collection** in Larger Print.

This collection begins with 3 FREE books and 2 FREE gifts (gifts valued at approx. $20.00 retail) in the first shipment, along with the other first 4 books from the collection! If I do not cancel, I will receive 8 monthly shipments until I have the entire 51-book Montana Mavericks collection. I will receive 2 or 3 FREE books in each shipment and I will pay just $4.99 US/ $5.89 CDN for each of the other four books in each shipment, plus $2.99 for shipping and handling per shipment.*If I decide to keep the entire collection, I'll have paid for only 32 books, because 19 books are FREE! I understand that accepting the 3 free books and gifts places me under no obligation to buy anything. I can always return a shipment and cancel at any time. My free books and gifts are mine to keep no matter what I decide.

263 HCN 2404   463 HCN 2404

Name	(PLEASE PRINT)	
Address		Apt. #
City	State/Prov.	Zip/Postal Code

Signature (if under 18, a parent or guardian must sign)

Mail to the **Reader Service:**

IN U.S.A.: P.O. Box 1867, Buffalo, NY 14240-1867
IN CANADA: P.O. Box 609, Fort Erie, Ontario L2A 5X3

MMLPBPA15

READERSERVICE.COM

Manage your account online!

- Review your order history
- Manage your payments
- Update your address

We've designed the Reader Service website just for you.

Enjoy all the features!

- Discover new series available to you, and read excerpts from any series.
- Respond to mailings and special monthly offers.
- Connect with favorite authors at the blog.
- Browse the Bonus Bucks catalog and online-only exculsives.
- Share your feedback.

Visit us at:
ReaderService.com